Reckless Dare

Reckless Billionaires Series

Maxine Henri

"All we have to decide is what to do with the time that is given us."

The Fellowship of the Ring, J.R.R. Tolkein

Chapter 1

London

"So what's your next adventure?" My brother alternates between swiping and typing on his phone, not even looking at me.

I sigh. Since we're at his upscale gentlemen's club and he's paying, I should just endure his antisocial behavior, but sometimes I wonder why I even bother.

"Northern lights."

He looks up for the briefest second and then returns to his screen. "You're escaping New York's winter by going to the Artic Circle?"

"Oh, how you always find a way to criticize me," I quip. "I'm going to find my own personal Loki and fuck his brains out." It's not unlikely, but I say it more to provoke him.

"Yell it louder, so you get escorted out and they

revoke my membership." He shakes his head while typing again. "I thought women were into Thor."

And there it is—a tiny, almost invisible grin on his face. That's why I like Gio. He's annoying as hell, but deep down, he cares.

"Why thank you for your suggestion. The jury is out until I return from my adventure."

My adventure. Most people believe I leave every winter to escape the dreadful weather, or to blow off steam after my biggest event of the year. There is some truth to that, but my motivation has its roots elsewhere.

I started traveling in memory of someone who can't experience it anymore. But it's become my church. It makes me alive. The crazy adrenaline sports, reckless parties, and nameless hookups where I can let go completely are acts of rebirth for me.

Moments in time to find peace despite the wildness of the actions. The thrill of it grounds me and liberates me at the same time.

"Are you going anywhere this winter?" I ask, but keeping this conversation alive is a genuine struggle.

Okay, it's not like we need to catch up on anything, but it would be nice to talk while we wait for our food. After we placed our order, I tried to spark his interest in a new project I want to finance. After that failed, I moved onto a recent political scandal, the price of gold and a mining crisis in Brazil. I even tried discussing our siblings' sex lives. Not that I know much, but I certainly know more than him.

Gio stares at his phone. We must look like a couple who has lunch out of obligation and has maxed out their daily quota for discussing life's logistics. He works, and I try not to be bored.

Nothing. I get nothing. If I don't count hums, nods and a few other acknowledgments. Though I suspect his *animated* reactions relate to the issue at *his* hand. Or on the screen, in this case. Finally, he glances up for a millisecond.

"You know I only travel in summer."

The lack of patience in his voice would irritate me, but I have too many other grievances in my life.

"Sorry to break it to you, bro, but spending a month at your house at Lake Como while still working is not a vacation. It's another level of workaholism."

"We all enjoy different things." He holds my gaze for a moment and it's unnerving. Perhaps it's better when he stares into his phone.

I look around and spot Finn van den Linden, the billionaire playboy, entering the restaurant. Satisfaction washes over me. It won't be a wasted lunch after all.

The hostess walks him to his table, practically tripping over her own feet in an effort to draw his attention. He acts with the detached politeness of people with his pedigree and takes a seat.

He's alone. Perfect. I snatch the white linen napkin from my lap and place it on the table. There will only be a brief window before someone joins him.

"I'll be right back," I tell Gio, though he probably doesn't hear me. He never looks up.

For some outlandish reason, I wonder if that's the case even during sex. Yuck. I shiver at the idea of my brother having sex. Gross. He's my stepbrother and we're not related by blood, but still... ugh.

A few eyes follow me as I head to Finn's table. Good thing I chose the curve-hugging dress this morning.

I care little for things, but I dress for success. My clothing ensures I look the part I'm playing. It's all just wrapping, but it helps me get what I care about, and that's what matters.

The Madison Club is quiet at lunchtime. Hushed conversations full of pretense hum through the air. I've never understood why men feel the need to socialize in members only clubs. At least this one allows women as guests. Not that many of them use that benefit. It's a boys' club.

While the rules here are a century old, the decor isn't the stereotypical, stuffy mahogany darkness with marble undertones. The floor-to-ceiling windows bring a lot of light into the beige and birch wood restaurant. It's a large space where members enjoy high-end cuisine, and the only room where guests are allowed.

"Finn, it's been a while." I turn on my biggest smile, fake but ample. It might dislocate my jaw, but my work smile garners attention all the time.

He looks up and frowns, his shoulders stiffening. Is he going to pretend we don't know each other?

"It looks like you haven't bought a table at the fundraiser yet," I chirp. "Perhaps an oversight?" I bat my lashes at him. Van den Lindens have never missed the event.

"London," he sighs. "Of course." He stands up, smoothing his yellow tie. "My assistant must have forgotten. My family has always proudly supported the cause."

"Great. There are many research projects benefiting from your generosity." I might fake my smiles, but the words are honest. The efforts to find a cure for leukemia need all the money I can find.

"Sure, of course. More causes need a—" he pauses a moment, "dedicated ambassador like you."

"I appreciate your support." *And I believe you should do more.* But I learned a long time ago that shaming people into donating only works short-term. "But if you have time later this week, I'd like to tell you a bit more about a project I'm currently sourcing funds for."

He scratches his neck, making me brace for an excuse. I've worked on many members here already, and very few get truly excited about leukemia research. It's not a sexy topic, but I don't give up.

Finn clears his throat. "Why don't you call my people and let's have coffee later this week." He bows his head and sits down, dismissing me, but at least he agreed to buy a table at the biggest annual event my foundation hosts and didn't reject a future conversation. Yet.

Fucking van den Linden. He could sponsor a research lab for decades without even noticing the dent in his finances, but people like him diversify their donations.

Frustration coils around my stomach, but I maintain my smile. "Thank you, Finn. It was nice to see you again."

"And you." He doesn't look at me anymore, completely over with the exchange.

I return to my table and watch Gio work until our meals arrive.

Unsurprisingly, he digs into his meal while swiping over the screen. He ordered pasta, probably due to his unwillingness to put his phone down, and eats with one hand. Lunches with him are tedious, but I gain access to the members here, so I endure them.

I don't want to eat in silence though. "What do you think is behind Bianca and Dad's sudden summons for regular family meals?" I take a sip of my sparkling water.

My sisters and I are meeting in a few days to discuss it. The unexpected insistence on spending time together smells sinister to me. I'm worried either my dad or his wife, Bianca, who is Gio's mother, is sick or something.

They served us the life-is-short speech as an appetizer, and I can't shake the odd feeling about the whole situation.

"Hmm." Gio nods his approval to *my question.* Screw it. Is access to this dining room really worth being ignored for a whole meal?

Despite his abhorrent manners though, he has supported my projects in the past and helped me wisely invest my trust fund. It's allowed me to donate my salary to the charitable arm of the Kyle West Foundation, an institution I founded and have been managing for almost ten years now.

Gio shows up when I need him, and while he constantly questions how I spend my money, he does help me all the time.

"You have blood on your shirt," I say, just to mess with him.

His eyes snap down to his chest and he reaches for his collar, as if he could find the stain by touch. When our eyes meet, I'm pleased his irritation mirrors mine.

"So you do listen," I mock him. "Good to know." I give him a smile. Not the one I use when chatting with people like van den Linden. I don't pretend with Gio. We grew up together, so he gets my glaring smile.

"For fuck's sake, London, let's not pretend this is a pleasant family affair. You don't do that. I don't do that. You schedule these *lovely* occasions to get access to the other members. To pump them for money or to hook up. I'm just the asshole who has to sit through a meal with you."

"I don't come here to hook up." Indignation spreads through my veins. How dare he? I'm no prude and I love sex, but I'm not stupid enough to mix work with pleasure. "I'm sorry these lunches are such a waste of time for you. Why do you even indulge me?"

He drops his phone and takes another bite before he pierces me with his gaze. He chews in silence, perhaps contemplating his response.

"This pasta is actually fantastic."

I halt my fork halfway to my mouth. "Asshole," I snarl, and Gio laughs. Like throwing his head back, full-on laughter.

"I'm just teasing you, London." He shakes his head at me. "I've been preoccupied with a merger in Europe, so my head is elsewhere, but I *indulge* your company here because I think your work is valuable and important. Because while I don't understand your way of life and how your remarkable altruism goes hand-in-hand with that bubbling anger and hatred you harbor under your well-put-together appearance, I believe you're doing an important job, a service really. And people like me and my peers here need to be reminded to distribute our wealth beyond investments that multiply our return. Into something that matters."

His words stir a fuzzy feeling inside me. I don't know when something—or someone—last rendered me speechless. Outside validation of my mission isn't normally important to me, but hearing the praise from my brother means more than I would have suspected.

"Thank you." My voice comes out hoarser than usual.

Gio nods and picks up his phone, so I jump in quickly. "Perhaps I can tell you about a project—"

"Don't push it, London," he growls.

Got it.

We finish our meal in silence, but this time I don't mind it. While he works, I make a mental list of things to finish today. The gala is in a few weeks, so the list is long. I have two wonderful assistants, but this is still the busiest season for me.

Before we wrap up, I identify one more target. Gilbert Sutton is the heir to a global food conglomerate, and we've never been introduced. I consider my options while Gio signs the bill.

"Let me introduce you to Sutton," Gio says when we stand up.

"How did you—"

"Seriously, Lo, I might be distracted, but I'm not completely absent-minded." He gives me a disapproving look, like he hasn't just spent an hour staring into his phone.

I bite my tongue. The Suttons have never come to my fundraiser and if I can do anything well, it's keeping my eyes on the prize.

By the time I leave the club, I have commitments for two more tables, which makes me cautiously optimistic. I call my assistant, Ashley, to ensure she follows up and closes those ticket sales.

One goes for ten thousand dollars and provides enough funds to support several long-term research efforts and my staff. Not enough, though. It's never enough.

Two months ago, the lead researcher on a project at Stanford University presented an encouraging theory. If the drug works, it would revolutionize the treatment of leukemia. It would take years to prove the concept and run all the testing before the clinical trials on people can start, but it would be the first significant improvement in decades.

Unfortunately, they ran out of state funding and private partnerships are hard to come by, unless you want to be married to the pharmaceutical industry. Instead of steady progress, they have encountered hurdle after hurdle. I've only managed to drum up moderate support commitments over the past eight weeks.

The walk to my building gives me too much time to think, and the high from selling the gala seats evaporates by the time I reach the front entrance.

The familiar helplessness hugs me tightly again. It doesn't matter how much I try—I don't seem to make any progress. There is always more money needed, more people desperate for help.

I'm failing you, Kyle.

The elevator door slides open on my floor and frustration bursts in my chest.

If I thought I had maxed out my daily dose of irritation during my lunch with Gio, I was wrong. Oddly, it pleases me, because having someone to blame for all my issues is the best medicine.

A very temporary one, but still.

There are only two condos on this level. The

hallway between them has been lined with boxes for two weeks now. I haven't met my new neighbors yet, but I'm confronted with their fucking boxes on a daily basis.

I march to their door and knock. No, I bang, my palm curled into a fist. Nothing. They must be at work. I decide to bang one more time, just to release some of my frustration, not really caring that it's not directly related to my neighbor.

My hand connects with the wood. And then it doesn't.

Losing my balance, I tumble into a wall of muscles.

Two strong hands steady me and I look up. I'm not short, but I have to crane my neck to meet this man's eyes.

My center clenches involuntarily and I regret—briefly—my rule not to hook up with people I might run into afterward. My new neighbor is a descendant of Greek gods.

His black T-shirt stretches across broad shoulders and a chiseled chest, exposing arms with defined muscles. He's wearing black sweatpants that hang low enough to draw my attention, and I briefly fantasize about the bulge suggested in between his thighs.

"May I help you? Other than keeping you upright?" His voice is laced with annoyance and something I can't identify. It could be sarcasm, or amusement. The emotion aside, his baritone is like a decadent caress.

I jerk back as if his touch burned. And it did. A little. Or a lot.

His eyes are mesmerizing, those dark irises too seductive. And so is the stupid sly grin on his face. And the lazily tousled dark blond hair falling into his eyes. I don't even like facial hair, and yet here I am, oddly attracted to whatever is happening on his face. It's not even a sexy three-day stubble. He is sporting a full-on hipster beard.

I take one more step back and hit a stack of boxes. The impact snaps me out of my temporary brain fart and reminds me why I'm here.

"The boxes," I bark. "It's been two weeks. Get rid of them."

He cocks his head. "Who are you?"

"I live next door." I gesture to my door on the other side of the hallway.

"Oh, my neighbor." He smiles, an X-rated kind of a smile. "Finally, we meet. Dominic Cressard." He offers me his hand.

I raise my eyebrow and put my hands on my hips.

He leans against his doorway casually, unaffected by my animosity. "I would invite you inside, but I'm afraid I have nothing to offer you. In fact, I don't have any chairs yet."

"You have no furniture?"

"Practically none," he drawls.

I smile. "Wonderful. These fucking boxes must fit inside, then. Take care of it."

I turn on my heel and march to my door. And though I can't see him behind me, his gaze still burns holes in my back. Shit. This interaction was far from the intended outlet for my frustration. And why can't I find my keys, damn it?

"It was nice meeting you, *neighbor*."

For some—not very mature—reason, I'm proud I haven't introduced myself. I finally unlock my door, and before I can close it behind me, I glance back. Dominic, the picture of nonchalance, smiles at me.

I flip him off.

Chapter 2

Dominic

Maybe I should unpack some boxes. One, at least.

I've been stuck in this apartment for two weeks now, living out of my suitcase. But wasn't that the point? To enjoy life without things? I've managed two weeks with minimum *stuff*. Achievement.

A depressing one, but still. I wouldn't say I've been enjoying it but, well, I haven't enjoyed much of anything for months now, so at least now I have a change of scenery.

Really fucking ambitious.

I've been busy. Sitting on the couch and staring out my windows. They are floor-to-ceiling glass with views of Central Park, so not too dull. Not that the view is sparking anything in me.

If I don't stare into space, I spy on my neighbor. Okay, one thing has provoked something beyond dull emptiness.

She is an angry thing, but my cock stirred when she fell into my arms the other day. Two days ago? Five? Whenever it was, my physical reaction was an event by itself.

My laptop rings with an incoming video call. I grin and answer.

"Fuck me. What's on your face?" my best friend, Rocco, asks.

"Language," his wife, Vanessa, says somewhere in the background.

"Nice to see you too," I deadpan. "You can't swear now? This marriage thing is more interesting by the minute." I slouch deeper into my sofa.

"Apparently it's frowned upon to swear in front of babies." Rocco shrugs and takes a sip from a mug. "Like that would stop them from cussing later in life."

He sits by the window in his large apartment in Madrid and the city bustles below. Despite being six hours away, the night is still young over there.

Rocco has lived there for five years now. The secret move was the only way to get out of his line of work and be with Vanessa. With a new lease on life, he settled in Europe.

Vanessa comes into view, heavily pregnant. She bounces their six-month-old in her arms. Poor bastards will soon have two infants to keep them up at night.

They tried and failed for their own child for a while, so they adopted a baby from a Russian orphanage, and as soon as the adoption went through, Vanessa found out she was pregnant. The universe has a fucked-up sense of humor.

"Dominic, you look like shit. I thought you moved to feel better." Vanessa places her hand on Rocco's shoulder and he turns to kiss it lightly.

"Yeah, lovebirds, I've only been here for two weeks, so no results yet." Feel better? At this point I would take any feeling. Something that isn't the hollow abyss swallowing me now.

"I still don't understand how moving from Chicago to New York is supposed to reinvent you. Isn't it a different shade of the same color, asshole?" Rocco says, patting Vanessa's ass as he talks. With his last word, she rolls her eyes and saunters away.

"The idea was to focus on myself. I wouldn't be able to do that in Chicago." I crack my knuckles. I've never realized how often I fidget like that. Or perhaps it might be a new habit.

"But since you are clearly going for the lumberjack look, why didn't you just rent a cabin in the woods? I thought you were stressed out. New York is not a city to find your zen." He walks over to his sofa, props his phone against something and lies down.

A huge cat immediately jumps up and nestles into the crook of his armpit. I can't believe how domesticated my friend has become since he met Vanessa. And he doesn't mind it either.

"The objective is to find new inspiration, to spark desire. I'm not ready to abandon civilization. New York is far enough from Chicago not to tempt me with its familiarity, and routine but urban enough not to drive me crazy."

"Spark desire? Have you been banned from all the strip clubs?" Rocco strokes his damn cat.

"Fuck you, asshole. Things are not all right with..." I don't want to admit it out loud, but Rocco draws his own conclusion and starts laughing.

"Let me get this straight—you had an episode resembling a heart attack and now you can't get your dick up." He laughs, the bastard. "I'm sorry, man."

I let out a long sigh. "Yeah, you look and sound sorry."

"Wouldn't Viagra solve that problem? I mean, you're still fairly young, but..." The asshole is laughing his head off.

I crack my knuckles again and consider closing the

laptop. Why have I even tried explaining something? He knows I collapsed in the middle of the courtroom. He is well-aware the media had a field day with that. But I didn't share more details with him.

I don't tell him how, despite spending time with beautiful women, I can't find a release. How everything I used to enjoy isn't cutting it anymore. The thought is too depressing. I won't verbalize it.

"Any particular reason you called?" I growl.

Rocco stops laughing. He sits up, resting his elbows on his knees. "All right, man, talk to me."

And while he is a dickhead, Rocco da Bonno is the only person in the world I trust with my life, so maybe I can relate some of my shit.

"I haven't been able to find joy in anything. Work had been dull and tedious, so I took on more. More cases, more challenges, more wins, but the emptiness inside only grew. And the workload sent me to the hospital. I got a new Ferrari. I had the most beautiful women. I even bought a fucking yacht. I played golf, tennis, you name it. There was nothing missing from my life. Yet it's been empty.

"My therapist thinks I filled my life with so many things and achievements for so long that I've lost the ability to desire. Apparently, I'm so attuned to instant gratification that I'm unable to find satisfaction in anything. It's like a drug—I get my high but immediately hit a low. Only the lows started stretching and seeping into all areas. So laugh all you can, but yeah, even Viagra only helps with the technical issue. Who am I without my libido, man?"

"Shit."

What else can he say? I partied, spent money, and fucked myself into depression.

"Okay," Rocco says. "Let's face it, our lifestyle wasn't something we could have sustained anyway—"

"Hugh Hefner seemed to go strong."

"Yeah, if you trust the media. Is that your goal, to stay a playboy for the rest of your life? Because let me tell you, I get little sleep lately, but I have never been happier. Ever since I—quote unquote—crossed to the other side and settled, I've found a new purpose in life. I've never thought that being with the same woman for five years would only get better every day."

"Are you suggesting I find myself a wife?" I shake my head.

He laughs. "Dude, no woman would consider everafter with you. Unless she knows you're rich."

"Screw you." Not that I want to get married, but his lack of confidence in my inability to achieve that pisses me off. And pissed is better than the flat nothing I've been mired in.

"Don't be so sensitive. Get some rest, hit the gym,

figure out what you want to do with your life, and then perhaps attempt a relationship."

I frown.

"Yeah, dickhead," Rocco continues. "Not a hook up, not casual sex, not a one-night stand. Dating."

It's my turn to laugh. "You think holding hands and walking in the park after a movie would breathe new life into... well, into my life?"

"Wow, you're so fucking eloquent, but yeah. I think a relationship is the opposite of instant gratification. It's hard work, constant compromise, and the most difficult thing I've ever succeeded at. And the success is something you need to maintain with daily attention. And yet, my friend, the reward is beyond anything you can imagine. The reward is constant, ever-changing and overwhelming."

"Don't get sappy on me, Rocco." His description is intriguing but, shit, not for me.

"Look, you're not ready, anyway. You left everything behind, so what's the endgame here?"

"I take six to twelve months off, trying to rediscover simple things and find what brings me joy. Whatever that means. I'm just following my shrink's suggestion."

"Oh, and by the enthusiasm in your voice, you're so into it." Rocco chuckles and picks his cat up from the floor to pet it.

"Anyway... that's why I left most of my things back

in Chicago. I took a sabbatical and moved here with only some essentials."

And about thirty boxes of non-essential things that I consider important. They should have gone to a storage unit back home, but when a last-minute bout of anxiety gripped me, I decided to have them delivered here.

It's pathetic, but having my things closer, even if I won't be using them, provides a bit of comfort. It's like gradually weaning myself off of material possessions.

Shit, it hasn't even been a month yet and I'm already failing. I think. Two years ago, a woman from my office suffered major burnout and took a leave of absence. She spent it in a monastery in Nepal, in silence.

Compared to that, my attempt looks like a half-assed pretense. On the other hand, I'm reasonably sure I can find my groove here. It's not like Nepal's monastery won't be there in a few months if my urban reinvention fails.

"Good. Take it slowly. I don't want you calling me from the hospital again." Rocco sighs.

As much as I hate to admit it, he might be the only person in the world who was genuinely concerned after my collapse. My parents have never approved of the clients I work for. Defending well-known criminals and winning their cases wasn't a point of pride for my family, so we're not very close.

There were a few women who came to cry by my sick bed, but their motivations were as selfish as my life has been. I don't hold it against them, but Rocco's words make me realize how isolated I've been.

Surrounded by clients, coworkers, ass-kissers, women, and I-don't-know-who in the whole fucking entourage of my life. Never alone, yet always lonely.

"Thanks, man." I'm touched. Another positive of the day. Not my favorite feeling, but a feeling nonetheless.

"Start with shaving." Rocco, sporting his own stubble, gives me a disgusted look.

"I really hope both your kids scream all night." I flip him off and scratch my beard. It's kind of long and scruffy under my fingertips. He might have a point.

We continue talking shit about Rocco's business in Europe, sports, and some other inconsequential stuff, but my mind lingers on Rocco's suggestion that I'm not capable of having a relationship. The challenge of it is igniting something inside me.

Would a steady partner help me with my problems? After fucking many women in my life, can I find the one who sparks my interest again? One who wouldn't bore me after a while? Is that something I even believe in?

My life has been uprooted so dramatically and nonsensically I'm almost tempted to admit that trying something as ridiculous as dating might be at least a partial solution for me. Rocco seems to thrive in his shackles. How bad could it be?

After we hang up, I stay on the sofa for a moment. Or an hour. The light outside shifts, so it might be longer than that. I've done a lot of that lately. Just sitting and staring, my thoughts freely floating around, without coming to any conclusion or inspiration.

This time, they are all coming back to the silky black hair I want to wrap around my fist. And the fight burning in my neighbor's eyes. They were kind of green, but almost brown, shaped like almonds.

But it was the way she pinned me down with bubbling anger. I can't imagine she was truly that pissed about my boxes. Something set her off, and I was just the outlet.

For some outlandish reason, the idea pleases me. Then it hits me. I experienced an array of emotions due to my brief interaction with her. Perhaps moving to Manhattan was a step in the right direction. Even if it's an annoying neighbor situation that would snap me out of my lethargy.

I indulge in a few more fantasies, wondering how she would feel if I dug my fingers into those slender hips while she rode me. How her sultry full lips would curl when screaming my name. How her breasts would fit into my hands.

I try to imagine the feel of her against me, building on the brief closeness when she stumbled in, letting the imagery free-dive through my body and mind.

The snapshots of my imagination run like B-roll in my head, finding a comfortable residence and accompanying me for the rest of the afternoon as I try and fail to meditate, burn my dinner, wait for takeout, shower, and sit without purpose.

The entire time, my neighbor—or by now a completely new, improved and fictional version of her—occupies my mind.

As the night rolls in and I, yet again, don't know what to do with myself, another emotion seeps through. Frustration and anger. I don't want to be obsessed with my fucking neighbor. She's not even that attractive, not really my type. And clearly full of drama. And what's with that voice? She sounds like an old carburetor.

Have I really gotten so desperate that I latch onto the idea of a woman who came to yell at me? And my reaction pisses me off even further. I wish I had my punching bag here.

Okay, damn it, let's channel the newly acquired anger into something productive. I sit down at the high stool at the breakfast bar in my kitchen and make a plan for the following week. It includes three items: shave, join a gym, and move the boxes into storage.

Writing the list fills me with a sense of accomplishment and I briefly consider completing the first task. But there are seven days in the week, and I only have three concrete tasks so far. No need to push it.

Goddammit. I feel like a loser, despite the minuscule progress. I have done nothing for a month. While my therapist suggested a mild antidepressant, I chose to move halfway across the country instead.

Voices in the hallway pull me to the door. I don't care about my new neighbor. I don't want to see her again. As I raise these objections in my mind, my hand reaches for the handle and I open the door. Whoever kidnapped my head needs to give it back. Fast.

My neighbor smiles at me. There is another woman with her. They share similar features, perhaps sisters. I don't have time to contemplate that because I'm still stunned by the smile. I actually liked her more when she glared or faked her grins.

This smile is too cheerful, and I can't imagine what prompted her to shine like that. It's disconcerting. And then, she steps forward and extends her hand.

"Hi, have you just moved in? I'm—"

"What the fuck?" I growl and leave her standing there, slamming my door.

Is she completely deranged? Her sweetness

confirms the other day was a reaction to something else, but why would she pretend we haven't met?

Fuck it. I take two pills and get into my bed, hoping darkness claims me quickly. Before my roaming thoughts lead me back to the crazy woman next door.

Chapter 3

London

The words on the page blur in front of my eyes, but I push through, blinking away the tears. This is the only place I allow myself to cry in public. Not that anyone sees it or cares because despair and sadness are part of the decor here, along with comfortable beds, peaceful paintings and kind staff.

Madeleine's head nestles small in the middle of the large pillow, her fine silver hair framing her pale face like patches of dandelions. One blow of a draft and she might float away. So fragile. So spent.

In the two months since she's been admitted she seems to have shrunk, but at least she looks serene, courtesy of the drip flowing into the tiny vein in her arm.

People come here to die and there is nothing I can

do about it. Or very little, so I ignore my tears and read. Because if there is one thing I can offer, it's my company. And money to run this place. So that's what I do.

I finish the chapter and close the book. I want to say something, but what is there to say? That's why I read, because I need to borrow words when I'm here. Madeleine doesn't require conversation anymore.

I put the book on her nightstand, pat her hand and stand up. I lean in, pressing my forehead against the window's cold glass. Outside, the unseasonably strong sunshine kisses the busy streets.

Large windows with a lot of natural light were one of the conditions when I was looking for the building. I found this one and we have been offering free care for three years now. Not enough. Never enough. Only a drop in the ocean.

This building—aside from my condo—is the only thing I own. This cause is the only reason I'd even contemplate such a binding purchase. But here we are, and I'm glad I took the leap.

Madeleine can enjoy a lot of natural light in her last days. Not all dying people have the same possibility. Frustration seeps deep into my bones, making room for the simmering anger. That's more like it. That's the emotion I can rely on to cope with life. And with death. It's the source of my energy.

As soon as I'm fired up enough, I look at Madeleine.

"I'll see you this weekend. You better wait here for me." I sigh and march out of her room.

I peek into a few other rooms on my way out. At the end of the hallway, Ralph looks my way from his bed.

"Why so grim, London?" He barely pushes the words out, but he never fails to tease or entertain. God, I admire his strength. Sometimes I want to yell at him. *Don't you know you're dying? Why are you so cheerful?*

I don't respond, I glare at him. Everyone and everything pisses me off, because no matter how much I try, it's never enough.

"Listen, sunshine—" A bout of coughing eats his words. I rush to his side and hand him a cup of water. With my palm on his shoulder, I watch as he struggles to catch his breath. Helpless. I'm always so utterly helpless.

"I'll tell you a secret. Death is sad only for those who are left behind." He winks at me like an utter flirt.

"I know, but it doesn't make it any easier on any of us." I squeeze his hand, then point at him. "You better be here this weekend."

"I came here to die, woman. Let me succeed for God's sake." Another coughing attack cuts his laughter short.

Fucking Ralph. I wish I had an ounce of his dignity and perspective.

"May I have a word, London?" Zelda, the manager, asks as she stops me in the hallway.

I check my watch. My meeting with van den Linden is in an hour. "Okay, what's up?"

"We received a letter last week." She moves behind the reception desk and opens a drawer. Zelda is one of those people who is always cheerful.

Where I retort with anger, she normally fights the gloomy emotions of this place with a smile. Today, her warm brown face is ridden with lines of concern.

She hands me an envelope and I yank the paper out of it, almost ripping it in two. As I scan the words, my stomach and the muscles of my neck tighten. If I grind my teeth any tighter, I might lose all my enamel. Goddammit.

"What are we going to do?" It's Zelda who speaks, but I'm aware of several sets of eyes on me. In the moment it took me to read the letter, half of the staff have gathered around.

"I don't know. I'll have to talk to my lawyer. I doubt we can stop them, but we'll try."

"The construction could go on for months, a year even. We can't operate under such noise and disturbance. We strive for dignity and peace here—"

"I know that," I snarl. "I'll see what I can do."

I shove the letter into my purse and march out of there, leaving them standing behind.

Goddammit.

When I bought the building this neighborhood was underprivileged, but I knew it wouldn't stay like that for too long. Three years later, here we are. A developer has bought several properties around us and plans to tear them down to build condos and a shopping center.

I should have known Felicia Warren, the developer, didn't buy two tables at my gala solely out of the goodness of her heart. I've never minded that people use the foundation's biggest annual charity event to network and conduct business, but in this case I have not one, not two, but a fucking myriad of objections.

On instinct, I almost call Felicia to tell her we're sold out, but while I operate in the nonprofit area, I apply my business acumen and I know that such a move would achieve nothing. Keep your enemies closer and all that.

My phone vibrates as I climb into my car. The car with a driver is a luxury I allow myself in order to get work done while in transit. I don't use it often anyway and I pay for it from my money, never from the foundation's budget.

"What is it, Ashley?"

"Where are you? Mr. van den Linden called to

cancel. He said he'd be in touch to reschedule." The keyboard clicks in the background and I can picture Ashley typing away with the phone on the speaker.

Fucking Finn. He didn't even have the guts to call me directly. "Okay, I'm coming to the office. Can you schedule time with one of the volunteer lawyers for me as soon as possible? We have an issue."

Irritation bubbled deeper inside me over the next hour as we fought traffic heading toward Midtown. My dad didn't answer his phone, nor did Bianca, Finn, or my sisters, so I was left to stew in the back seat. I tried to review a few documents, but my mind has been running a mile a minute in many directions.

I need to slow down and find some time to unwind. Between the upcoming gala, lack of support for the new research project, concerns over my parents' health and the construction around the hospice, I might just explode.

I march into my office, ready to rule, but Ashley's face nearly stops me in my tracks.

"What happened?" I bark.

Eddie, my second assistant, and two interns jump and scatter away while Ashley faces me. And not with her usual determined, unperturbed countenance. Despite her five feet four frame, she generally commands a room with confidence.

With her German father and Japanese mother, she

grew up with discipline, loyalty and respect, but she is no push-over. Her salary is way above market, and she is worth every single cent.

She's been with me for five years and we understand each other without words. Which means whatever she is about to share is going to make my shitty day thus far look like a vacation.

"Larissa called…"

Larissa is the event planner in charge of the gala. There are always last-minute screw-ups with an event of this size and reputation. I relax, knowing we have contingencies in place.

"She is in the hospital…" Ashley's words fall like boulders on me, and I grab a table for balance. "… for the foreseeable future."

I drop my purse and rush into a small boardroom for privacy. Then I lean against the door and scream. It might not be the most mature or effective reaction, but it's the only thing I have right now. I yell until my throat hurts, leaving me exhausted and only marginally composed.

When I come out, Eddie hands me a cup of tea. It's not hot. A warm jasmine tea, the way I like it. The first sip burns my raw vocal cords, but it soothes me at the same time.

"Is she okay?" I ask. "What happened?"

"It's not clear. She fainted and they're running

tests. In any case, she's been put on bed rest for the time being," Ashley explains.

"Okay." As much as I want to be pissed at Larissa, I can't. "I suppose we don't have a contingency plan for losing our event planner."

Ashley bites her bottom lip and Eddie shakes his head. I pull out my phone and send a quick note to Larissa to wish her well and reassure her we'll be fine. Let's hope the universe gets the message.

"Is there anyone we can bring on board?" I move toward my office, but the silence stops me.

The grim faces almost make me laugh. We stand there in silence for what feels like a lifetime. In the middle of the beige and dark blue office I love so much. An office that might not be the CEO's corner suite I used to dream about, but it's so much more.

"Let me flip through my contacts. In the meantime, is there a lawyer I can talk to?" As a nonprofit, we have several young students and recent graduates on call, pro bono.

"I can't get anyone to come down right now, but I'll keep calling," Ashley says.

"Let's leave that for tomorrow and start calling whoever we can to save the event."

But a couple of hours' work gets us nowhere. A lack of availability, or a fee above our budget, pushes us further and further from solving the issue. Those who are available and reasonably priced are not crazy enough to take over two weeks before the event.

My frustration grows into rage, so I decide to leave the office. I can make calls from home. "Let me know if you get someone. I'll keep calling my contacts."

The wretched heels I put on this morning are not meant for walking, but I can't be confined in a car right now. My building is ten blocks from my office. Plenty of time on my aching feet to work through all the frustration that's built up today.

Halfway home, my phone rings. Hopefully it's Ashley with good news. But no.

I accept the call. "Dr. Carlson, how are you?"

One of the key opinion leaders in leukemia treatment is always too busy, and we coordinate our occasional work calls weeks in advance.

Given the day I've been having, my heart hammers against my ribcage as I wait for him to speak. A second that stretches into an excruciating moment.

"London, I couldn't get in touch with your father... is this a good time?" He can probably hear the street noise around me.

What? How does he know Dad? "I'm outside, but sure. What's going on?"

"My office left him several messages. Could you please have him get in touch with me?"

His words swell in my head, drowning me. I try to

draw a breath, but my whole body feels submerged under water. The world around me moves in slow motion as the sounds drone on dully. My heartbeat echoes in my ears, deafening me.

"London?"

His voice snaps me back to the conversation. "What's going on, Dr. Carlson?" He can't tell me, but I ask anyway.

"London, you know—"

"Of course, of course, thank you for taking the time to call. I'll make sure Dad calls you back."

I drop my phone and someone leans down and hands it to me. I blink a few times, trying to focus on my surroundings. A blurry line of cars floats along as I try to avoid people who seem to jump into my path.

Even without any details, Dad being treated by Dr. Carlson paints a gloomy picture.

I barely make it to my building. The doorman greets me and I summon all that's left to nod. In the elevator, I realize I might feel better if I take off my shoes.

But once they're clutched to my chest, I don't feel better. Paris and Sydney don't know, so I can't talk to my sisters. Not yet. I have to talk to my dad first and confirm what's going on.

The elevator opens up, and I attack the first outlet for my anger and helplessness I find. As my bare foot connects with the pile of boxes, no relief comes. I might have broken my toe, but the stupid stack hasn't budged.

I drop my bag and my shoes and push against one of the columns. The boxes tumble down, but I don't stop, kicking and shoving. Giving each move all I have, needing the distraction. Getting the poison out, so I can breathe.

Instead, with every desperate, compulsive move, I access a new level of despair. The burning defeat doesn't stop me. The unhinged energy doesn't recede, it multiplies.

By the time a pair of hands grabs me, most of the boxes are strewn around the hallway like blocks of Lego. I whip around to kick whoever's halting my destructive mission, and my eyes lock with my neighbor's.

He holds me at arm's length, his gaze heated, and something unexpected happens. I sag in his hold and start sobbing. A brief jolt of shock passes through his face and then he pulls me close.

His gesture should piss me off, but instead I bawl even louder. Soaking his T-shirt with tears, saliva and mucus, I ugly-cry while he stands there like a supportive pillar, not really hugging me, more like holding me steady. Sobbing provides slightly more catharsis than the thrashing.

Eventually, my wails turn into hiccups and my

body gains awareness of the solid muscles surrounding me. Of the faint scent of citrus and something very masculine. Of the warmth that seeps into my bones, caressing my wounded soul.

I absorb all the pleasant sensations his closeness stirs and pounce without thought.

He is taller than me, but I hook my hands around his neck and crash my lips against his. He hesitates for an instant, but then welcomes my attack. I channel all my frustration into devouring his mouth, desperately seeking relief.

Release.

Respite.

Or simply oblivion.

We stumble and he hits the wall, tripping over one of the boxes. My body collapses against his as he pulls me toward him, never disconnecting the frantic kiss. I attack with all the selfish need I harbor, but he doesn't seem to mind.

He grabs my ass and my leg swings up to his hip. I fist his hair, desperately hoping he can give me what I need.

You don't sleep with your neighbors, a little devil snarls from my shoulder. I jerk away to find confusion in his eyes. We glare at each other, our chests heaving.

What the hell is wrong with me? Part of me actually wants to drag him to my bedroom and let him make me forget, let him improve my day, but somehow that seems too intimate. Too visceral.

He reaches for my hand and the touch burns me. Not in a bad way, which scares the shit out of me. I jump away like he hurt me for real. I look at my door, and before I can make this day even worse, I grab my purse and rush inside.

Chapter 4

Dominic

"**F**uuuuuuck!" I kick the stone pillar outside the courthouse and curse again because it's a fucking stone pillar. Great way to break a tiny bone.

I look up. My faith goes as far as occasionally attending church with my family when I was a boy. Not often. Not voluntarily. And definitely not since I've been on my own. And even if God does exist, He's been a real asshole lately.

A mother shields her child and an elderly gentleman takes a wide berth around me. Yeah, that's who I've become. A menace to society. Not that I was an upstanding citizen before. But still. I rein in my temper and hop down the stone stairs.

My therapist suggested I try to sit in the courtroom. In the audience. I need to replace the dickhead. All that achieved was a sweaty T-shirt and humiliating myself when I ran out of the building.

Mission failed. Therapy failed. Self-esteem boost failed.

Wanting to avoid my empty apartment, I enter a coffee shop to grab some java while I decide what I want to do next.

"Dominic?" A male voice surprises me.

"Ben, hey." What are the odds? Putting Ben in charge of Rocco's clubs was the last legal task I did for my friend.

Ben has done well, with the clubs, for himself, and for the other owner who wouldn't take any other result kindly. Five years later, Ben is still alive and thriving.

"What are you doing here?" His eyes run me up and down, assessing my attire. I guess this is the first time he's seen me in anything but a suit.

"Just visiting." He doesn't need to know that I'm hiding… I mean, *rediscovering* myself.

"You should come to Roxie's in Chelsea. It's still the best nightclub in Manhattan. The girls would love to see you."

"Sure, I'll come by when I get a chance." Probably not. He's already judging me, probably wondering how many shades of crazy I've gone.

With his eyes narrowed, like squinting at someone has ever uncovered anything, he shakes my hand.

"Great. I'll put you on the guest list. It was nice running into you. I like the new look." He gestures around his chin, clearly hating the beard as much as Rocco. Or me, for that matter. "Take care, man," he adds, concern lacing his tone.

His appearance screams money, prestige and composure. His expression paints a picture I don't want to see. There may as well be a flashing sign across his forehead: Fuck, man, you've sunk low.

He is not wrong. I turn to leave before remembering I didn't order. Walking away would only confirm Ben's assessment, but it's not like staying here will improve it. Fuck it. I'm not staying here to endure his glares.

The fresh air does nothing to regulate my breathing. The idea of returning to my building squeezes my lungs even more. I should take care of the boxes at least. They are still scattered around the hallway.

The memory of that kiss is spicy-sweet. It was an angry kiss. I definitely want to know why she cried. What happened to her? She jumped me because she needed to release tension. But I enjoyed her lips on mine. Eager, almost aggressive, taking. Full and soft, her lips tasted like sin and promise.

The best part was that even my dick showed interest in finding out how the rage sex would be after that angry kiss. Shame she cut it short. Too short.

Leaving the boxes could provoke her again. What a little pissed off princess she is. God, she'd be angry if she knew I referred to her like that.

Her hot and cold treatment confuses me though. Why did she pretend not to know me last week? Or smile and wave when I saw her in the lobby the other day?

I don't get the wigs either, but maybe she likes changing her hair all the time. She should stick with the black. Not that she'd care about my opinion.

"Good morning, Cesare, how is it going?" I greet the doorman at my building with a grin. Oddly, a courtesy of my angry neighbor. Or the memory of her.

"I'm fine. How are you, Mr. Cressard? You seem in a good mood."

Why I am in a good mood after the morning debacle at the court, or the less than pleasant run in with Ben, I will never know, but I'm going to run the wave.

"I guess I am today."

"Mr. Cressard, I don't want to overstep, but I took the liberty to inquire about a storage facility."

I frown.

"For your boxes, sir," he adds, fidgeting with the cufflinks on his uniform's jacket.

"Oh, thank you. I was actually going to take care of that. That's helpful, Cesare. Give me the address."

"I can have someone pick them up today and have them moved. Unless you want—"

"Perfect. Thank you, Cesare."

I guess that's it. I'm moving on to the next stage. As I should. Those boxes don't hold anything that I need.

My pulse quickens though, and I crack my knuckles as the elevator rises. There goes my cheerful mood.

My attachment to those boxes is pathetic.

Cesare texts me to confirm the movers will arrive in two hours. It's probably someone he knows because there is no way he found movers on such short notice, but that's fine. If I can help his family or friends, why not?

It turns out it's his brother, Alonso, and a nephew who comes for the boxes. Alonso has been laid off. He tells me the story as they are piling the boxes into the service elevator.

"But that's a wrongful dismissal, man." I hand him a box. They protested my help, but I'm so desperate for company and something to do that I insisted. They probably assume I'm a control freak, or that I'm expecting them to steal from me.

"Yeah, and what am I going to do about it? I went to a legal clinic, but they are so overworked that by the time they get to my case I'll be retiring." He wipes his forehead.

"I'll help you." The words surprise us both. Have I just offered legal representation to this man? At least I'm licensed in New York.

"What are you, a lawyer?" He chuckles.

"Yeah, I am." This would be an out of court settlement, so I don't need to worry. And maybe a good way to ease back into things. "Load the truck, then come back up and explain everything to me."

"I can't afford a fancy lawyer who lives in a building like this one." He shakes his head, like my offer is the most preposterous idea he's ever heard.

"You can after I win, and I always win." Something splashes through me, a current, making my heart race and my fingertips tingle. I grab two boxes with ease. The sensation is thrill. "But you wouldn't need to. I'm taking your case pro bono, Alonso."

"I can't—"

"Yes, you can, and you will, or I'm not paying you for the move today." I've never shied away from threats. I earned my first three million working for criminals. Not that pressuring this poor bastard is in any way similar, but here we are. I guess it's like riding a bicycle. A habit I can't shake.

"Mr. Cressard..." He rubs his hand on the back of his neck, but then chuckles. "Okay. We load the truck and then I'll tell you everything. You're really something."

I grin. "If you knew the half of it…"

We finish the last load, and as the two of them take the boxes downstairs I walk back to my apartment and make a pot of coffee. The hallway looks much bigger—the boxes really cluttered it up. I snicker, thinking of my neighbor.

A white envelope shines in the middle of the dark floor. I pick it up and quickly realize it's not mine. Why is there an envelope addressed to a hospice in Harlem in the middle of an upscale building on the Upper East Side?

I shove it into the back pocket of my jeans. Alonso appears half an hour later, still shaking his head about my charitable offer, but he gives me all the details and we discuss his case over coffee.

As soon as he leaves, I sit with my laptop and get to work. I don't know how long I'm at it, but the energy thrumming through me makes me want to jump out of my skin. Maybe it's too much coffee. I grab a bottle of water from the fridge, and when I close the door, the three items I scribbled a few days ago glare at me.

With a sense of unhealthy satisfaction—my achievements have become laughable—I cross off one task. Boxes are gone. Perhaps I should shave and then go work off some energy in the gym. Get rid of this stupid to-do list.

When I sit down at my computer again, the envelope in my back pocket crinkles. Huh—forgot it was in there. Curiosity gets the better of me, so I pull the paper out and read it.

It takes me a few searches to learn how the envelope ended up on our floor. She must have dropped it when she trashed my things. London Lowe. She owns the hospice's building and is the chair of the hospice's board.

She also runs the Kyle West Foundation. It looks like Kyle was a young boy who succumbed to leukemia at nineteen. His parents must have started the foundation in his honor.

There are more charitable activities on the record, and they all lead to my neighbor. Photos online highlight her enticing greenish gray eyes, and the lips I could kiss some more. This persona is so far removed from the woman I've met that it piques my interest.

This construction notice must be creating havoc for the hospice. I quickly check zoning codes in that part of the city, then on an impulse, call my researcher in Chicago.

"Dominic, how are you?" Theodora asks with surprise. Shit. I forgot I shouldn't be calling.

"Listen, T, I need help looking into Felicia Warren." This looks like I'm working, but I'm not. I'm just curious.

"Why?" Her question is so loaded with layers I

could peel them off and chew on them. It's not just why I need info on Warren. It's also why do I need anything? Why am I calling? How am I doing? Am I still on the verge of collapse?

But T doesn't specify. She lets me decide which of the whys I want to answer. I choose my close coworkers well.

"Just someone I came across. Can you do it? Today?"

"Are you asking me to get you a file on a woman because she is a woman?" Mockery replaces her carefulness.

"Shut up, T. It's not like that. When have I ever asked you to screen a woman for me? She's a developer and I need to know how dirty she is."

"Why do you think she's dirty?"

"She's a developer." Why did I call for help? I need to tame my impulses.

"Fair point. What should I bill it against?" T sighs.

"Pro bono," I say without thinking, but then I realize it might trigger interest from my partners. "Or could you do it off the books? I'll pay you."

"What the hell, Dom. Who is she? Where are you, anyway?"

"T, just fucking do it, okay?" I hang up. If there is something I can count on, it's T's discretion and reliability.

I fully intend to shave, but as I dig deeper into the zoning laws there's more that I question, and I end up drafting a request for an injunction. Then an email from T pops into my inbox.

Dom, this is just a list of red flags. I can't investigate more right now. Definitely don't date her.

I laugh and open the attachment. By the looks of it, Felicia Warren is as corrupt as they come. Mostly allegations, but if necessary, we can find proof easily. Officials and the public wouldn't find anything, but I've built an empire on finding shit people want to hide.

I re-read the request, cross-check it against the local regulations and pump my fist in the air. Let's see how Warren barks. Or does she bite?

Energy pulses through my veins, untamed as I go in search of my gym clothes. I glimpse myself in the mirror. Fuck the beard, I'll shave it later. I copy the documents to a flash drive then head downstairs.

"Cesare, sorry to bother you, but could you please have this printed for me? But be careful, it's confidential." I hand him the drive and add buying a printer to my list.

"Of course, Mr. Cressard. Thank you very much for helping my brother. Is this for his case?" He practically bows in gratitude.

I pat his shoulder. "I'm glad I can help, but no, this is another case."

What? What the fuck am I doing? This is not my case.

"I'm going to work out and I'll pick it up on my way back." I practically run for the exit. Next time I know I'll be promising to pay off his mortgage, because clearly there is something wrong with me.

For all I know, London doesn't even need my help. She might not care about the construction around her property. Or more likely she has a team of lawyers already shredding Warren into pieces. But is her legal team as good as me?

What the hell is wrong with me?

I step outside, and speak of the devil...

London is getting out of a black BMW. After practically cyber-stalking her the entire afternoon it's best to avoid her, and I set to cross the street quickly.

Don't look back. Don't look back.

I turn. King of willpower, that's me.

A man stumbles from the car and London wraps her arm around his waist to steady him. Their eyes meet and she smiles at him, her expression full of kindness. Who knew she could be this soft?

He leans in and kisses her forehead. It's a tender moment I shouldn't be spying on. Also, it shouldn't bother me. She is all cozy with a man who is older than her and clearly inebriated.

She says something and they laugh as they

approach the building, him relying on her heavily. She rubs his back as she helps him take the three steps to the main entrance. Drunk in the middle of the afternoon with a woman half his age. Good for you, asshole.

I jog away, adrenaline rushing through me. It's not the positive rush of the last few hours when I dove into work. This energy is laced with annoyance. Why the fuck do I care London has a silver fox making her all sappy-looking?

The Hunter Club is only a block from my building, and I join on the spot and hit the boxing ring. The owner, Hunter—not the creative type clearly—is there and we spar for half an hour. Not enough to get a good workout, but long enough to release some of my pent-up irritation.

Hitting Roxie's tonight could be a good idea after all. Maybe Ben crossed my path this morning to remind me of life's joys. Hooking up would be a pleasant end to a reasonably successful day.

After I shave, I will have accomplished all my tasks. I also picked up pro bono work for a good cause by helping Alonso. And I might have potentially helped my neighbor. If London wants my help. Maybe her sugar daddy is a lawyer.

My emotions are running in all different directions. By the time I reach my building, common sense and rationale win and I acknowledge that hooking up with a stranger tonight would be akin to falling back to the same old patterns.

As much as I would like proof that the arousal London sparked is something to stay, regardless of who the woman is, I don't think I should take that route. Not yet, anyway.

I grab the printed documents from the front desk, and in the afterglow of my first workout in over a month I start up the stairs. By the time I reach the fifteenth floor I'm panting like a loser. Shit, gym twice a day from now on. How have I let myself go like this?

After I yank the stairwell door open, the lights come on and I stop in my tracks. A body is on the floor, propped against the wall.

"What the hell?" My heart jumps into my throat. Enough fucking adrenaline for one day.

The body—or rather my *lovely* neighbor—scrambles to stand up, wiping her cheeks and... I think she stifles a sob.

Something akin to anger and a strong sense of protectiveness winds its way to my stomach. Jesus, for someone who was numb for weeks, today has been a damn roller coaster.

"Has he hurt you?" I grab her shoulders, inspecting her for cuts or bruises. My pulse drums in my temples, not leaving any room for reason. Why I'm so vehemently involved in her situation is beyond me.

"What?"

"Has he hurt you? What's wrong, London?" Anger continues to creep up my spine.

Satisfied she is unharmed, I finally snap my eyes to hers. A web of red lines veils her watery eyes.

We stare at each other. My hands slide down her arms, but I don't let go of her, holding her wrists. Her pulse beats as frantically as mine, like a miniature drum against my fingertips.

Our chests heave. Her eyes burn me. My mouth goes dry. Energy zaps around us, probably short-circuiting the grid on this block. We stay completely still. Every encounter we've had in this hallway has been fucked up.

I rake my gaze over her silky hair, barely stopping myself from fisting it. With my thumb, I wipe a tear from her cheek. Her protruding cheekbones feel delicate under my touch. But she isn't delicate.

I don't know her, but I've seen her unleash the dragon within twice already. She is not delicate, and that's why the sorrow is more concerning.

I trail my thumb over her bottom lip and her breath hitches with a gasp or another swallowed sob. I'm about to lean in when she jerks away.

"I'm fine," she rasps.

Sure you are. I'm confident she is pissed at herself

for momentarily allowing me to see her vulnerable. Yet again. She wanted a kiss.

"Okay, you're fine. Were you just waiting for me? No need to cry, sweetheart, I'm here," I drawl.

She looks for a moment like someone made her eat garbage, and I fear she is going to puke. Then she shakes her head and rolls her eyes. "You're such an asshole."

"Yet you kissed me the other day." I allow my smile to stretch languidly.

She puffs out an exasperated breath. "It was a momentary lack of self-control."

"You can't control yourself around me?"

She closes her eyes briefly and growls. "I don't have time for this." She turns to leave.

"Wait." I dropped the documents on the floor in my haste when I opened the door from the stairway. I pick them up and try to give them to her.

She looks at them as if I'm handing her a plate piled with shit. I'm ready to flip her off. This woman is infuriating.

Finally, she snatches the documents. "Fuck you." She leaves.

So much for helping her. Fuck her with her rage problems and abusive partner. She is not my problem.

Time to shave, shower and head to Chelsea. Hooking up is just what I need.

Chapter 5

London

The stylist fusses with my hair, but I keep my eyes closed. Chitchat is the last thing I need. Tonight is the event of the year, and I can't imagine how to get through it without lashing out. Or worse. Crying.

Dad finally told everyone about his illness. He starts radiation therapy next week and asked me to accompany him. He didn't ask Bianca, Syd or Paris. He asked me.

Why am I his choice to handle the situation? Am I the toughest? Or does he want someone by his side who knows the system best? Or is it his attempt to compensate me for the similar opportunity I *didn't* get all those years ago?

I'm not even sure why I try to dissect his motivation. It's not like him choosing me is the point here. My father is about to embark on a journey that will be grueling for him, and all of us.

He might not get out of it on the other side. I don't care what the statistics say about his chances for full remission. Because I know very well that when it comes down to a real person, not a number in a spreadsheet, the chances are binary. He either lives or...

I wince.

"Did I pull too hard?" The stylist apologizes, but I wave her concerns away, so she shuts up. Thank God for that.

Shit. I need to focus on tonight. Thank God, my brother's social media manager, Mila, was able to take on the coordination of the event. She dove in at the last minute with expertise and enthusiasm, relieving me of the biggest headache.

She is a bit too cheerful for my taste, and I think she's not faking it, which is weird. Gina, my brother's wife, advocated for her a bit too eagerly, and I suspect Mila's motivation is purely financial. The woman needs any job she can get. But she delivers, so who cares?

"Do you have any vision regarding your makeup?" the stylist asks. I should probably remember her name, but I don't.

I make it a point every year to hire someone new.

These people are too chatty and nosy, so I don't want a regular.

"Let's go natural."

"Is that your gown on the bed?"

I nod.

"It's beautiful. Who is it?"

Here we go. "It's rented, but I think it's Stella McCartney."

My lips curl up at her expression. "Rented?"

"Yes. I don't like to spend money on unnecessary things."

If I'd just grown three heads, she wouldn't be this stunned. Frozen, she stares at me in the bathroom mirror. She probably doesn't get to meet clients who don't trip over themselves to wear a designer, tailored-made outfit to big social events.

It's not that I don't like fashion or that I can't afford to buy a dress. But intimately knowing so many areas where the money is truly needed, I can't spend it on something so useless as a dress I would wear once.

"Could we move on?"

Red-faced, she turns back to finish my makeup.

Half an hour later, I walk the woman to the door, and she peeks at the dress again. Seriously, I'm as vain as any other woman, but by the looks of it, she would accept the situation easier if she thought I had stolen the gown.

As I open the door to shove her out finally, my eyes meet the smoldering gaze across the hallway. My neighbor leans against his doorway, saying goodbye to a young woman who is smiling at him from the elevator bank.

"Good afternoon, neighbor." Dominic's voice, like honey and poison, floats through the air.

I respond with a glare—my ability to act mature around that man is seriously concerning—and I shut the door.

I tap my foot. The encounter stirred me the wrong way. Not because he was seeing out his date—in the afternoon—or because it's the same hussy who left his place the morning after our last encounter in the hallway. I'm just generally irritated by his presence.

Seriously, why is he always around when I have a breakdown? Goddammit. My previous neighbor was a bitch, a nosy old lady, but this is worse. And that girl, Jesus, she is too young for him.

Why do I care?

Though I must admit that the legal—unsolicited—advice he provided for the hospice came at the right time and was helpful. Which reminds me of two things. I need to thank him. Ugh. And I'll have to face Felicia Warren tonight.

By the time I get to the venue, annoyance has flourished into irritation. Not for one particular reason. Just all of them together, including the tingling feel in my stomach I usually feel in anticipation of the silent auction.

The evening starts off without a hitch, and as I mingle, I realize a natural smile lingers on my face. I'm actually having a good night, the ire lingering in the background only.

"Enjoying yourself? I love your dress." I join my sister Sydney at the bar. She came with her boyfriend, who bought two ten-thousand-dollar tickets for them. Of course, Syd attends every year, but since she can't afford the ticket, she comes as a volunteer. This year is different.

Her eyes linger on her boyfriend, Hunter, as he laughs at something with our brother, Massi. Gio is there too, with his phone, of course.

"It's from Hunter." She runs her hands down the silky fabric of her maxi skirt, blushing. "They seem to have hit it off."

We look at the laughing men, and something catches my attention. I follow Gio's gaze—not on his phone—across the room and land on Mila. She stands by the silent auction table, oblivious to his covert attention. Interesting.

I'm about to walk over and tease him, but my steps falter as I spot a man standing at the bar behind my brothers.

Not standing, owning the bar.

Owning the room.

My lungs suffer a sudden loss of oxygen, because it's all sucked out by the ego of Dominic Cressard. Why else would I be breathless?

His hair is styled carelessly and he's shaved. Without the ridiculous lumberjack mask, the sharp edges of his jaw protrude, begging to be touched. It's unfair how, in a room full of tuxedos, it's his sexy confidence that snags my attention. Fucking James Bond.

I walk over, the tiny hairs on my neck prickling with a mixture of emotions, mostly negative ones.

"What are you doing here?" I say through my teeth, while smiling. There are too many people around to cause a scene. A scene? I'm not a scene-causing person. Usually.

He frowns and cocks his head, assessing me, perhaps waiting for a punchline. I'm not telling a joke here, mister.

"What do you mean? *You* invited me." He rolls his lips.

If he only didn't ooze pure masculinity, my heartbeat would go back to healthy levels. Or not. Because as good as he looks, irritation bubbles through every fiber of my being every time he is around.

"Wow, so now I have memory loss in your presence. I never invited you. Are you here to claim a better spot in purgatory?" How have I not seen his name on the guest list? He must have bought his ticket last minute.

"Oh, but then I'd find myself right beside you, which is already where I live." His tone is mocking, but his voice washes over me with an unexpected thrill.

"Don't tell me you actually know anything about this cause." My glare is at odds with the rest of my body that is drawn to this man.

I'm attracted to him. I can't change that, but that doesn't mean I'll melt into a puddle around him. I don't like the man, despite my body's vehement disagreement.

He takes a sip of his clear drink, probably vodka or gin. I'd have pegged him as a whiskey drinker.

"Of course I don't, but I hear fancy fundraisers are the place to pick up classy ladies. Apparently I was misinformed." He scans me up and down with a cocky, languid gaze.

I want to wipe that look off his face. And wrap my legs around his waist and ride him to oblivion.

"You came." Paris joins us before I get a chance to insult him back. But I don't need to because the shock on his face gives me immense satisfaction.

"I see you've met my sister, Paris." I bite the inside of my mouth to stop myself from laughing.

People have mistaken me for my twin sister countless times, and the ensuing surprise has grown less entertaining over the years. Seeing Dominic Cressard off-balance, even for a brief moment, gives me an unreasonable jolt of triumph.

Recognition seems to sink in slowly for him. "Now that explains the hot and cold treatment. I see I live next to the evil sister."

Asshole.

Paris chuckles. "Behave," she scolds him. She turns to me. "He growled at me in your hallway—"

"Shocked you're being nice to me after *you*—" his gaze pierces through me, "yelled at me for my boxes a few times."

"And then we took the elevator together when I came by last week," Paris chirps.

The smirk returns to his confident face. "That's when she told me about this event. I'm glad I could contribute. So, twins..." He shakes his head, clearly entertained, but then his face falls serious as he notices someone behind us. "Forgive me, ladies, I need to take care of something."

He pushes between us before I can say anything. Rude. Despite myself, my gaze follows him. The way he owns the room with that assured saunter is very appealing. I wish he wasn't my neighbor. I wish he didn't annoy me so much. I wish...

Jesus, London, snap out of it.

And I do, immediately, when I see Dominic pulling Felicia Warren to one side. What the actual fuck?

Paris sighs beside me. "He is so hot, funny and—"

"Don't be ridiculous." I pat her arm and excuse myself.

Speaking to a guest or two, I have a problem focusing. I scan the room, trying to find Dominic. I can't see him or Felicia, which I hate to admit disappoints me. I don't get disappointed because of a man. But it's not just about him. Out of all people, he goes after Felicia. Perhaps he likes older women.

No, the hussy that frequents his apartment proves he doesn't. Or perhaps age is not a consideration. Could it be a business conversation he needed to have so urgently?

I had Ashley Google him to ensure he's a lawyer, since his document proved helpful and I didn't want to make a fool of myself when filing it with the city. Now I wonder if he's not working with the enemy.

"Lo, here is the preliminary number." Mila approaches me with a folded piece of paper. "Do you want to announce it now or wait?"

She's pale and her signature smile is missing. "What's wrong?"

She looks at me, startled, and then a mega-watt smile spreads across her face. "Nothing."

So, the cheerfulness isn't all that genuine.

I glance at the number she wrote down. We're at eighty percent of last year's funds raised from the silent auction. This should thrill me because it's not even midnight, but I was really hoping I could beat the goal by at least fifty percent.

I'm still stuck without the capital for the research project. Gio doesn't want to hear about it and van den Linden has been avoiding me. This was my chance to at least get the bare minimum. Or a small portion of it.

"I'll make the announcement now."

Mila nods and walks to the audio station. I make my way to the podium, and after she nods, I lean into the mic.

"Ladies and gentlemen, I hope you're having a great night. I won't bore you with statistics, no worries. You've heard enough to paint a gloomy picture of the state of treatment and care for people with leukemia and related illnesses at the beginning of the night."

Hundreds of pairs of eyes are on me as I scan the room to command their attention. "I see the bar is busy and the dance floor is teeming, so why don't we add to the excitement with a challenge?"

My dad smiles at me from his seat next to my stepmom, Bianca.

"We're at almost five million in the silent auction, but that only means we're about to reach last year's level. The research and support for what this cause needs might be a marathon, but tonight can be a race. Who will join us in doubling the donations?"

A few people hoot and several walk to the silent auction table where Mila makes sure our volunteers assist them.

I could have told them more about the research project, more about the struggles people go through while on treatment, or any other detail to appeal on an emotional level. But years of experience have taught me that their sense of competition and the validation of their social status are the biggest drivers. So that's the emotion I stir, and by the look of it, the race is on.

Two hours later we're at a hundred and fifty percent of last year's contributions, and I allow myself the first drink of the night.

"May I have this dance?" The husky voice tickles me like a siren's song. I should resist, but I can't.

I nod, hoping that if we don't talk I can enjoy his masculine presence. A girl can fantasize, after all. He leads me to the dance floor with his hand on the small of my back.

Warm. Electrifying. Shiver-inducing.

He takes my hand and pulls me close to him. Too close.

His citrus scent wafts toward me and wraps me in a blanket of summer. He holds me confidently like a professional dancer, though we're not dancing. We're swaying in one spot, but somehow it feels like intricate choreography. I feel good in his arms. Too good. The realization awakens my default state of annoyance.

"Thank you for taking the time to prepare the case for the hospice. I was short of legal help and your assistance came at the right moment. Next time maybe ask before you take the initiative, though. How did you even know?"

In my six inches heels, I still have to crane my neck to look into his eyes. The amber spots in his irises glimmer. His usual cocky grin is replaced with a confident smile.

"You dropped the notice while you were trashing my valuable possessions." He twirls me around, so suddenly that I lose balance and collide with him. His body, so hard and... *Don't go there, London!*

I clear my throat. "Oh, yes, you finally moved in properly. Including a girlfriend. Where is she, by the way?"

He wiggles his eyebrows. "Jealous much?"

I laugh. "Were two tickets too expensive for you?"

Now he laughs and shakes his head. "I think you *are* jealous."

I roll my eyes. He's so full of himself. "More curious about how you keep up. What is she, like, twenty years younger?"

"If you're wondering about my sexual prowess, I recommend personal experience. I'm happy to satisfy your curiosity."

He spreads his fingers and subtly glides his hand up and down my back. It's daring and I want to step back to maintain distance. Well, my head wants to. But my head is losing every vote tonight. Damn it.

I wet my lips, and when his gaze drops to them I shudder involuntarily. I don't like the command he has over my body. I don't like that at all.

"Let's get back to the injunction. I hope it will give me a breather for a few months at least."

"It should, although I'm pretty sure Felicia Warren is a worthy opponent who probably has enough people at city hall in her pockets. I'm helping her to find an alternative."

I frown. "What do you mean?"

"Let's just say I know people who know people, and in the end Mrs. Warren might find a different property to develop."

"Why?"

His confidence is overbearing most of the time, but right now it adds to his attraction. I like it even less than the sexual tension between us. I've already embarrassed myself around this man twice. What am I doing seeking more trouble?

"To keep certain information about herself out of the public domain."

"I meant why are you helping me? What do I owe you?" Half of me wants to tell him to leave the case alone, and the other half really wants his input.

Not for his expertise. Gio has lined up someone from his firm already, but... No, no, no, I don't want to like or enjoy anything around this man. I don't do relationships. And never hook-ups with people I know. No. Period.

"A date." His answer causes me to stumble. I never stumble. I want my cool back. Goddammit.

"That's not happening." I shake my head a bit too enthusiastically. Apparently not even in refusal can I muster indifference.

He curls his lips up, languidly, with the utmost enjoyment. "I insist."

Chapter 6

Dominic

I don't know why I asked her on a date. Maybe just to prove I can. To wipe the smirk off Rocco's face when I tell him I had a normal date. He talked about a relationship, but just because he is all pussy whipped, it doesn't mean that's for me.

I have been with many women, but I haven't dated. I took them to dinner or events as my plus one, but it was always understood the evening was part of the foreplay. An obligation, so to speak.

Why do I want a date with London Lowe then? The challenge. Yes, that's why. Just to rile her up.

Cesare calls to alert me that my food has arrived. I check myself in the mirror as I wait for the delivery by the door. A black T-shirt and a pair of jeans. Too casual. I miss my suits. But then, I don't expect London to dress up. And I would look like an asshole in a suit for a casual date.

She refused the invitation several times while we danced last night, but that only makes the challenge sweeter. I get the food, tip the delivery person, and walk across the hallway.

I knock and wait. Nothing. I knock again. I tap my fingers on my thigh in a rhythm suspiciously similar to nervousness. I don't get nervous! Okay, aside from the past two months of emotional roller coasting.

But ever since I started working—okay, taking a few... *one* pro bono case—and exercising, I'm back to normal. No anxiety or all that other bullshit.

I'm about to turn when I hear footsteps on the other side. London opens with an eye roll.

"Is this what you're wearing on our date?" I scan her naked shoulders, feeling an irrational need to touch them. With my tongue. She is wearing a black tank top and pink pajama pants with yellow... pineapples?

But it's not the fruit that catches my attention. A delicate chain hangs from her neck with a locket nestled deep in her cleavage, teasing me. Not likely that she wears it for that intent, but the effect is there nonetheless.

"Eyes up here, asshole." She leans against the half-opened door and points her fingers to her face. What woman doesn't like a man's lingering gaze? "I told you I'm not going on a date with you."

I take advantage of her relaxed posture and push through, dangling the takeout bag in front of her face. I can almost pinpoint the moment she starts salivating as the aroma of Indian food tickles her nose and she licks her lips.

I crack my knuckles to distract myself from images of that mouth and tongue doing things other than craving dinner.

She might try to hide her excitement, but her stomach growls. The sound is followed shortly by her own growling before she shuts the door.

"Did you move in recently?" I take in the room.

The layout of this place is like mine. While my walls are white, London's are some brownish pastel tone. The color choice and a set of frames covering the wall in front of me to my right seem the only designer touches made to this place.

Thank God for the view of Central Park, because those drawings are ugly. The woman has an interesting taste in art. Or none.

A large sofa is nestled right in the middle of the open space. A narrow wall—really a rectangle-shaped pillar—that separates the living room from the kitchen is empty. Mine has a TV and a fireplace. Hers seems to be waiting for a decorator.

"What?" She frowns at me and shuffles to the kitchen. "I've been living here for five years now."

I follow her. "Were you robbed?"

"Look, I'm tired." Her stomach growls again. "And hungry, which is the only reason you're here. Stop asking nonsensical questions."

"Nonsensical? I'm wondering why you don't have furniture."

By the looks of it, I might have woken her up. After last night's gala, she must be exhausted.

She pulls out two plates and cutlery and drops them on the table against this side of the bare partition wall. "I have a table." She points to it as I'm placing the bag on it. "I have a sofa and I have other essential pieces."

I sit down, pulling the containers out. "Are you a minimalist?"

She sighs. "What did you order?"

"Indian. I hear it's your favorite." I open one box and a tantalizing scent of coriander, cardamon and cinnamon fills the space.

"I'm going to kill Paris. Why don't you dine with her? She is the nicer sister, after all." She throws back my comment from last night, and somehow that hoarse croak of her voice sounds like sweet harmony.

"She's *too* nice for me. Come on, London, we can't

deny we're attracted to each other." I enjoy her snarling and scowling way too much.

"Oh, yeah, we can. I'm denying it. Eat your dinner. And for the record, this is not a date. I let you in only because I'm hungry and you brought food. Take out in pajamas is not a date." She sits down and serves herself a bit from each box. I follow.

"So you want me to dress up and take you on an actual date?" I straighten my tie. Fuck. I don't have a tie, but I realized a few days ago I keep playing with it. Some crappy subconscious bullshit.

London apparently notices as well. "Not so much for a casual weekend, are you? What are you doing in New York, anyway? Don't you have assholes to defend in Chicago?"

I take a bite, a smile stretching across my face. "You Googled me."

"After the number of accidental encounters in the hallway, I needed to make sure you're not a serial killer." She attacks her plate with the appetite of an athlete in training. I like that about her. She seems to be a woman who attacks life with ferocity.

"Oh, sweetheart, that information isn't readily available online." I take another bite. I don't particularly like Indian. I got it because, as London deduced, Paris told me it was her favorite. I'm not delving into the fact I cared to find out. For the good of our neighborly relationship, of course.

"Okay, don't answer the question. I'm happy to eat without talking to you," she deadpans.

"I turned forty last year." An odd part of me wants to tell her the real reason.

The words are on the tip of my tongue, but instead of becoming a voiced sentence, they seep through my body, eliciting a dry mouth, sweat beading down my spine and a sudden lack of air. I blame that on the Indian spice.

"I didn't know there was a rule about moving once such a milestone is reached." London is not looking at me, thank God.

She stretches her legs, moves her chair sideways and eats out of a container, abandoning the plate. Her attention is on the food.

I swallow and try to come up with an answer. Preferably one that buries this conversation. "Are you pleased with the amount you raised last night?"

London whips her head to face me and studies me for a beat. I'm a well-practiced lawyer and an experienced liar. Tonight my verbal skills have taken a day off.

"It's never enough." She sighs and returns to her food. The weight of the world is in that sigh.

"How did you get involved with the cause?" I really want to know. I care to know more about this woman. The piqued interest rubs me the wrong way. I shouldn't have come here. I don't even know what I was expecting.

"I'm not ready to talk about it." She stands up and leaves.

Great. She is not willing to talk about her lack of furniture. I'm not ready to talk about my breakdown. She is not ready to talk about her work. I have no work to talk about. That leaves us with a severe lack of topics. And a whole lot of attraction.

I'm not sure where she went, but I continue eating. Would I find her in her bedroom if I went after her? My mind wanders to her cleavage. Those bare shoulders. I clearly need to fuck someone soon, because my cold shoulder neighbor is more trouble than I care for, and yet... I care. Or not care per se—

London returns, wearing a hoodie. Interesting.

She pulls out two wine glasses and saunters away again. I hear a swoosh and she comes back with a bottle of wine. "Red or white?"

"Thank you, I'm fine."

She cocks her head, narrowing her eyes. "I don't have gin. Or vodka."

What? I frown.

"That's what you drank last night." She gets an

opener from the drawer and knocks it closed with her hip.

It's a simple movement. And yet, it stirs something in me. Something that alerts my dick. If I watched a model coming out of a pool, tossing her hair in slow-mo, I wouldn't be as aroused as I am now.

Jesus. She closed a stupid drawer. I stand up and snatch the opener and the bottle from her. I channel my frustration into the fucking cork while London watches me, amusement playing on her face. *Now* the angry ice queen is amused?

"I drank sparkling water last night and I'm fine with tap tonight." I grab the wine glass, pour from the bottle and hand it to her. I fill mine with tap water and sit down. Pissed. Not even entirely sure why.

"Where is your girlfriend?" London sits and takes a sip.

"You mean Patagonia?" Right now, I wish she was my girlfriend. Or at least my lover. I wouldn't be all tense and upset here.

"Oh God, is that her name?" London tries, and fails, to stifle a laugh.

I don't blame her, it's not a name to be grateful for. More like one you give your child because you want them to be bullied. "Everyone calls her Patty, so I call her Nia."

"Of course you do." London snorts. "I guess when

you don't excel at anything, you try to be unique in every possible way, don't you, Dominic?"

Sassy. If I wasn't currently annoyed—not even understanding why—I would like her smart mouth. And, of course, I immediately imagine that mouth around my cock.

I close my eyes and shake my head. It does nothing to the image now permanently engraved in my mind.

"Anyway, what does Nia think about you having *a date?*"

At this point, I'm not sure if she is curious about the young woman she keeps running into or just trying to salvage the resemblance of a conversation. Pull yourself together, asshole.

"I don't think she cares where I am. She's with her boyfriend."

London's eyebrows shoot up. "I didn't take you for a man who shares."

She smiles, as if this was the most intriguing thing I've said all night. It might be, given my complete failure at my typical greatness. I thought the recent influx of energy got me back into my groove. Idiot.

"She is my research assistant."

"Sure she is." London shakes her head. "Patagonia the researcher."

"You *are* jealous," I drawl, regaining some control.

"Actually..." She takes a sip before she continues,

weighing her words. "I hold a great amount of sympathy for her."

I smirk, expecting more sass. "I'm going to regret this, but… do elaborate."

She perks up. "Well, for starters, she's spending time with you. But also… since my parents felt inspired by geography when naming us, I feel a strange connection."

I chuckle. "That's right, London and Paris."

She rolls her eyes. "And you haven't met Sydney or Brooklyn yet."

"Wait a minute, I met Sydney last night. But is Brooklyn adopted?" I pick up my fork again.

London laughs. Not full laughter, more like an extended chuckle, but it's so genuine. Probably without realizing, she let go of the control and allowed herself to express emotion. It's a brief sound too, but God I enjoyed it.

"She would love you for pointing that out." She bends her leg to her chest, her heel on the chair, and rests her chin on her knee.

Again, it's a simple move, like the drawer closing with the sway of her hip, but what it does to me…

"Brooklyn decided that since our parents didn't bother to name her after an international metropolis, she would fill the role of black sheep of the family."

"What about your brothers?" I met one or two at the event last night.

"The Cassinettis are my stepbrothers. No geography in their names, if you don't count the Italian heritage: Massimo, Giovanni, Andrea and Baldassare. Four boys on their side and four girls on ours. One large, mostly happy family. Do you have siblings?"

"I have a sister, but she doesn't speak to me. Do you get along with all your siblings?" I want to dodge her questions, mostly because I'm disturbed by how much I want to share with her.

Nothing good would come out of it. Judgment? Yes. Understanding? Hardly.

"Eight kids thrown together in the aftermath of trauma after losing a parent? Considering all of that, we get along just fine. I'm closer to Syd and Gio. And Paris, of course. Massi had recently rediscovered his happily ever after and before that he was in a dark place, hating the world. Andrea doesn't talk to me. And Baldo and Brooklyn, well, none of us have seen much of them in the last few years. Why doesn't your sister talk to you?"

So much for avoiding the topic. "My family doesn't approve of my work."

"Defending criminals?" She snickers. "I don't see why?"

"You don't approve either." I sigh. Not that I care.

Who am I kidding? A tiny part of me wants her to validate my existence. An insignificant part.

"Why did you choose that path?" She looks at me, genuinely intrigued. Jesus.

"I didn't choose it per se. My best friend was the son of a... He grew up in a family involved in the Mafia. At that point, I only cared about making money, becoming someone important, showing my father how capable I was." I lean back and stretch my legs. "We were young, and ego was the only part of us that mattered. So we lived. Like fucking *lived*. Selfishly. Fully. No regrets."

"Still no regrets?" She tilts her head, resting her cheek on her perched-up knee. It might be the lighting or the silk of her skin without the makeup, but she looks so young and innocent. I should leave her alone. Not taint her with my life choices.

"I don't know. Regrets won't change much. I loved that life. Money, cars, parties, women, travel. Anything and everything one can desire. Until I didn't. Until all of it meant nothing."

I don't particularly want to open up to her, but once I started every word seems like a release. Much-needed release I've been seeking for months now.

"Nothing mattered anymore," I continue. "The more people I saw, met, got with, the lonelier I felt. I kept making money and spending it, but the void in my life grew bigger. So I buried myself in more work. Until I collapsed in the middle of the fucking courtroom."

"Is that why you left Chicago? To hide from the embarrassment?" There is no judgment in her tone, just interest. She wants to understand. Or perhaps has some morbid need to know the entire story.

"Not embarrassment. More like survival. I needed a change of scenery. An opportunity to leave everything behind. Theoretically, that should uncover what I miss the most. The thing I should lean into once I return to my life."

"You want to return to work for the Mafia?" Again, it's an interest, not judgment I detect in her voice and body language as she leans forward, studying me.

"Don't believe everything you read. I don't work for the Mafia. I wouldn't be on a sabbatical if I did. You can't just take time off from such employment. Yes, they hire me as a defense attorney, and yes, I used to manage the legitimate business of the Da Bonno family. Someone has to defend the criminals. It's part of our legal system. I won't apologize for doing that or for being damn good at it. And ninety-five percent legit about it." Shit, was there fucking truth serum in that food?

"What about the other five percent?"

I study her for a moment. It was a good call to put the hoodie on. I still imagine her lips on different parts of my body, but at least I can maintain some kind of cool.

"Enough about me. Why don't you tell me about your charitable work?"

She licks her lips, drawing my attention to them. I came to New York to seek my lost desire. I didn't expect it to come in the form of this angry dragon with the body of a mermaid, but God help me, do I want to sink my teeth into her throat.

"Unlike you..." There is venom in her tone now, but I've come to believe it's a mask. Why is she hiding, and who is the real London is the question? It intrigues me as much as her body.

She swallows hard. "I use my money to help people. There is so much that can be done if the wealth was better distributed, and the irony is the rich wouldn't even feel the difference. I run the foundation, as you know from last night, and make sure that much-needed funds flow into research and service for people with deadly blood disorders."

"Unlike me, hmm? What are *you* trying to atone for, London?" I use last night's words against her, because for some bizarre reason I want to know why she is so angry, why she doesn't own more furniture, why she isn't the socialite her status calls for but rather this good girl. Good girls don't harbor as much boiling emotions as she does.

She winces and straightens her legs. No, she snaps into a rigid position, practically building a wall around herself. "So you took a sabbatical and what? You're just going to work from home here? To stay away from the temptations of your usual life, but other than the scenery you won't change much else?"

"Whoa, your ability to segue is non-existent." I laugh. "I'm not staying away from temptations. I changed the scenery and cut a few—a bunch of people —from my life to learn to recognize what's real. I lost track of that. So no, London, I'm not just in a different apartment doing the same thing."

"But you have been working. You have a research assistant. Have you done all the work for the hospice just to get a date out of me? I don't think you're that desperate." She raises her eyebrow, taunting me.

"I found the notice and felt the urge to solve a problem. I guess that's something that excites me. I also took a pro bono case, and frankly the satisfaction is akin to the feelings I used to have after winning a case. It's just this little thing for Cesare's brother, but it's fun."

"Who is Cesare?" She frowns.

"The doorman." I put the empty containers into the bag.

"What doorman?" She stands up and starts helping me, clearing the table and placing the dishes into the sink.

"What do you mean?" I snort. "Our doorman."

"Oh, I don't know his name." She shrugs.

What the fuck? "He said he's been working here for ten years."

"So?"

"Let me get it straight. You care about all the anonymous people. Yes, they are sick, but not really in your life, you throw fancy parties to raise money for them, but you don't give a shit about someone you meet every day? That's rich."

She whips around from the sink, her breathing shallow. "So you spend your whole life getting criminals back on the street and then take one pro bono case, and suddenly you're on higher moral ground? Judging me?"

Okay, she took this way out of proportion. "I'm just surprised you care so much in one area of your life and don't give a shit in the other. I know the names of the people who are regulars in my life. Is this caring, charitable London just a pose?"

"Maybe I'm not a people person," she snaps. "I think you should go now."

She's riled me up. Again. I grab her arm and pull her closer. It takes her by surprise and she collides against me. I don't quite understand how and why our conversation escalated this quickly, but God the feel of her is maddening. And talking to her is no less taxing.

We glare at each other. Our chests heaving. The silence between us fills with pent-up frustration and borderline anger. Why?

What the hell am I doing? Forget the attraction. We could engage in a casual hate-fuck, but we're both so headstrong we would probably kill each other in the process.

I let go so suddenly that London collapses against the counter. She gasps and I storm out of there.

Chapter 7

London

"Dad, we need to talk to Bianca about this. You can't just leave without discussing it with her." The scent of steaming coffee reaches my nose as I fill my cup.

Dad sits at the bench by the window, his hands trembling. Fragile, his face is pale, and it's breaking my heart, but I promised myself to be strong for him. I'll be his person. Just like I used to think I was Kyle's person. Until I wasn't.

"Darling, it's not like she won't find out, but this is one of those situations where I prefer asking for forgiveness rather than permission." He pats the spot beside him and I sit down.

He drapes his arm over my shoulder and I lean in, relishing the comfort of his warmth. I should be the one comforting him, but right now I need to take as much as I can give.

Despair swims at the edges of my mind and I'm pushing it away, but it's leaking through, darkening my already pain-tainted soul.

I don't want to treat him like a sick person. He deserves to go through his treatment with as much dignity and comfort as I can provide. And more.

"I know commuting after your therapy is not a good idea, but you can't just leave your wife."

"I'm not leaving her. I just don't want her to fuss. I don't want to get into discussions about the best possible solution. If you'll have me, I want to be here, at least for the time being. You know the other option is inpatient treatment, and I would rather spend my last days close to my daughters."

"Don't talk like that." I straighten up and frown at him.

He chuckles. "Okay, if we want to pretend I'm invincible, we can." He kisses my forehead.

His phone buzzes and he braces himself to stand up, but I leap forward and grab it from the table. With a shaky hand, he declines the call.

"Who was it?"

"Bianca." He looks away and fidgets with his phone before pushing to a standing position. He shuffles to the sink. Opening the cupboard, he retrieves a glass and turns on the faucet to fill it.

It's a simple task, but it feels like the clock moved at least a quarter of an hour forward by the time his lips touch the edge of the glass.

It takes all my willpower not to help him. I stay seated until the glass shatters on the floor.

"It's okay. Don't move, Dad. Let me clean it up first. Do you need to sit down?"

Resigned, he supports himself on the counter while I collect all the shards.

"I'm sorry, darling, I'm just feeling weak after yesterday's radiation. I promise I won't be so clumsy all the time."

Jesus. He's apologizing for being sick. "Dad..." I don't even try to hide my exasperation. "If you want to stay here with me, you're going to let me take care of you. I will work from home as much as possible, I will get Syd and Paris to help. And I will get a nurse, but you have to be a good patient and let us help you."

I can see the war in his eyes. He might be reduced to a shell of the man he used to be, but he is not ready to surrender. His self-assured poise, a trait I've always admired, is taking a hit.

I hate this situation. I hate seeing him like this. I hate that we have to even deal with any of this. Hate. Hate. Hate.

He doesn't answer, and out of respect I don't press for his commitment to let us in. He's been struggling enough. We'll figure it out. Even if all my glasses are destroyed by the end.

"Why didn't you answer Bianca's call?" I ask after he's settled back in my guest room, propped on the bed with his book.

"She doesn't know I came to the city for the treatment. She's already suspicious about me wanting to spend the night here, and the woman has an overdeveloped sixth sense. She would know over the phone this wasn't a casual visit."

"Dad, I thought she knew about your illness." Seriously, taking care of a parent might be as challenging as taking care of a child. Not that I would know.

Dread washes over me. How am I going to deal with this? I couldn't even keep a hamster alive when I was a child.

This apartment is so small. Where will I cope with all these overflowing emotions? I don't want to treat him with pity, but the only emotion left after that is frustration. Shit.

And the last time I used the hallway, hiding my breakdown from Dad... I can't use it anymore, because the hotshot next door seems to be there every time I need to vent.

Hotshot? Jesus. I need a day at the spa to find my groove.

It doesn't help that I haven't slept well since he left my kitchen three nights ago. His closeness was robbing me of my composure. I don't get into situations where I lose control. In my neighbor's presence, I'm already questioning my sanity.

I've been ignoring the disappointment that crept in after he shut the door behind him. How dare he judge me? I have good reasons not to get attached to people. I help where I can, but I don't get personal with... with anyone.

People come and go. I don't need to be affected in the process. Yet it pisses me off that Dominic called me on it. He latched onto the topic with his mockery and fucking disbelief. I know the doorman just fine. I won't apologize for giving all my attention to people in the hospice. That's all the loss I can cope with.

Still, I keep thinking about our conversation and arguing with Dominic in my head. There, unspoken and in private, I win every argument. With every imaginary win, my desire to wipe his face clean of that self-assured grin multiplies.

If I don't get over this frustration soon, I may attack him again in the hallway. This time there would be nothing sexual about it, though.

I should never have kissed him. That one moment of weakness gave him ideas. Not going to happen.

"She knows. Some of it." My father snaps me back into our conversation, and I forget the dark eyes and the confident half-smile.

Dad avoids me, looking down, fidgeting with his book.

"Some of it? What the hell, Dad?" Did he seriously think Bianca could handle being blindsided like this? "I'm calling her right now."

I'd never admit it out loud, but as much as I love my stepmother, I would think twice before crossing her.

"Don't." Dad stretches out his arm, his look bewildered like he is stopping me from pulling a trigger on an innocent victim. "I'll talk to her. I don't want to worry her."

"Dad, you need to accept that we're dealing with..." I can't say it. I can't. My eyes dart around, hoping a better-sounding reality will materialize out of thin air. "A serious illness. You need to let us all in. You can't shut us out." The last words reverberate around the room, bouncing off the wall and mocking me. "You can't shut us out. I won't have that. Not again." Tears of anger gather behind my eyes, but I blink them away. *Not again.*

Dad extends his arm. I've never been one for

displaying affection, but I squeeze his hand. To reassure him. And me. Of what? I don't even know.

"I'm glad to be here, Lo."

I kiss his forehead. "Okay, I'll try to be back in two, three hours tops. Paris will come soon to stay with you. Is there anything you need before I leave?"

He opens his book and waves me away, like I'm intruding on his personal time. That's for the best, perhaps.

Of course I'm lucky enough to run into Patagonia leaving Dominic's apartment. He nods, his eyes cold and distant. No snarly remark, no greeting. He shuts the door, and it feels as though he closed it right in my face. Okay then.

Can he possibly be upset I sent him away on our date? Not a date. It wasn't a date. There was no kissing. What? I didn't want him to kiss me. Even my mind is out of control when it comes to that jerk.

"Good morning," Patagonia chirps, digging for something in her large backpack.

"Morning," I growl. "So, you're a researcher?" Why? Why do I ask her that? I don't care. She can be his whatever.

She looks up and smiles, extending her hand. "I'm Patty. I'm a law student and Dom has been kind enough to help me out. I share a three-bed with five other people, and with my job at the club, I get little sleep or room to study."

I shake her hand, marveling at the speed of her speech. Is she high or just generally perky like this? "A club?" Not sure why my mind assessed her verbal vomit and gripped that particular crumb.

"Yeah, I work at Roxie's in Chelsea. It pays for the school." She widens her eyes, as if surprised by how well it pays. "That's where I met Dom." She yanks her headphones out of her bag and plugs them into her phone.

The elevator comes, and we get in and don't talk anymore, aside from the cheerful goodbye she offers.

Despite myself, I pull out my phone to find out what Roxie's deal is. Of course, he found his *researcher* while getting a lap dance or more from her. Fuck him. And *he* is judging *me*?

* * *

By the time the car pulls up in front of the Madison Club, I'm determined to cut all contact with Dominic fucking Cressard. Even if I have to move.

The hostess ushers me into the dining room. Gio is not on his phone—instead, a sleek laptop is perched on the table in front of him.

"Good morning." I plop down and ask for a coffee.

Gio nods his greeting but keeps his eyes on the screen. "Why did my mother call five times this morning?" His voice is laced with annoyance.

It's not that Gio doesn't get along with his mother. He's a good Italian boy, respecting the matriarch as much as anyone else who grew up with a strong mother, but he doesn't let Bianca meddle in his affairs. Not as much as the others.

"If you answered, she would tell you." I cross my arms over my chest, scanning the room.

He sighs and closes his computer. "What's going on? And be fast, the lawyer is here in two minutes."

"Dad wants to live with me while he undergoes treatment."

I don't know what Gio thinks about this because his face remains unmoved. He adjusts his cufflinks and licks his lips while looking at me. It's kind of intimidating. I don't think we've maintained eye contact this long since we were children having staring contests.

"I'm glad I didn't answer then. Good luck with that."

I'm oddly deflated by his response. "Okay." I don't tell him some form of support would be appreciated.

An energetic woman waltzes in. "Mrs. Lowe, I'm Mia Huang."

For a slender, petite woman, her handshake is

commendable. I clench my fist a few times and smile at her.

Gio opens his laptop again. He called this meeting, but he doesn't care to take part in it.

"I'm afraid I don't have good news. We need to wait. The city has thirty days to respond to your objection. Unfortunately, people on the inside are telling us they won't take that long."

"But isn't that good news?" As soon as I speak, the implications hit me. "Shit."

"Exactly. So, while we can raise objections, Mrs. Warren secures her interests and there isn't much we can do about that." Mia Huang stands up.

"Wait. What are my options here?" I glare at Gio, trying to get him engaged.

"Unless you're willing to play her game, I don't see how you can win."

"Can we expose the corruption?" I hiss, and Gio pins me with an impatient look.

"Lo, by the time we got any proof, Warren would be breaking ground. You might uncover deep-rooted corruption at city hall, but one insignificant head would fall and nothing would change. You're better off moving the hospice."

"You know how hard that would be? We finally build up our facility to serve those people in a dignified environment, and now I should start from scratch?"

"Don't make a scene, or this is the last time I invite you here."

I inhale sharply, my heart pounding in my temple. A few eyes are on us, some with raised eyebrows.

"I'll outline possible legal steps in an email to you, but it would be a waste of time. It was nice meeting you, Mrs. Lowe." Mia strides away.

"She is efficient," I growl.

"That's why I'm paying her. Let's go. I need to get to the airport." He stands up.

"Wait. What? Where are you going? Scratch that. What am I supposed to do now?" I grab my purse and follow him.

"Find a new location, or endure the noise and disruption for a few months." He shakes hands with someone, but I don't really pay attention. Can I get a meeting with the mayor? Can I expose Warren? What did Dominic say at the event?

Mrs. Warren might find a different property to develop to keep certain information about herself out of the public domain.

I don't want to ask Dominic for help. Especially not when he's probably using tactics that are like Warren's.

"Lo." Gio frowns at me. I didn't realize he wasn't talking to the other man anymore. "I'm going to the restroom. Will you wait? I can give you a lift to your office."

I nod. Not sure why, because I have my driver waiting for me. Probably circling aimlessly around until I call him. What a waste of gas, and not to think of the environmental impact. I text the driver to tell him I won't need him for the rest of the day.

I should just downgrade to Uber permanently. Would he miss the job? Probably not. I don't even know his name. He might miss the paycheck. Does he have a family?

Commotion to one side grabs my attention. A young man in an expensive biker jacket stumbles through the door and dashes to the elevators, his helmet dangling from one hand. He's in his twenties, very good-looking. Could he be a member here?

The concierge rushes up to him and whispers something.

"Let me be, old man. I'm going, okay?" The elevator dings and he enters, flipping a bird at... I guess all of us. Definitely not a member.

"Ready to go?" Gio stops beside me.

"Sure. What's in that section?" I point to the double door with card access. Perhaps he was an employee?

"It's the private, members-only area." Gio presses the call button. "Gym, pool, whiskey bar, bedrooms."

"Bedrooms?"

He rolls his eyes and checks his phone. "Yes, bedrooms."

"For members to nap?" I can't believe what I think he's telling me.

"Seriously, Lo, do I really need to spell it out for you?"

"Like a brothel?" Okay, the idea kind of thrills me.

"What the hell, Lo? It's not the nineteenth century anymore. Exclusive escort services are included in the membership."

I think he tells me because he knows I won't be scandalized. And I'm not. I'm interested. "Do you use those? Oh, no, Jesus, TMI. Sorry. I don't want to know you have sex."

"Just shut up. Now." He rolls his eyes and enters the elevator.

Just before the elevator closes, the private door across from me opens and Felicia Warren walks out. I almost put my foot between the sliding doors, but I freeze when I see who follows her.

My neighbor, Dominic fucking Cressard.

By the time we descend, a thousand scenarios roam through my mind, and several conflicting emotions flood my bloodstream. He was home when I was leaving, and he squeezed in a quickie while I had the shortest meeting in the history of billing lawyers?

And why do I care?

* * *

At the office I go through the motions, organizing my week so I can work from home and spend time with Dad. Normally, I would be packing for my annual adventure, so there aren't many appointments to cancel or reschedule.

It still takes me an unreasonable amount of time, because my mind continues to disappoint me by remaining at the private floor of the Madison Club where the members bang.

Is Felicia a member? I've seen a few women there before and always assumed they were guests, but maybe there isn't a rule against female members. Especially ones who wear pants, literally and figuratively.

A couple of hours later, I finally pack up everything and shuffle away. I take an Uber home. Maybe Gio or Massi would want to hire my driver.

When I step into my apartment, I bristle. I drop my purse and march through the living room, my heels echoing. This can't be. I don't have to see him to know he is here.

Dominic fucking Cressard is perched at my dining table, playing chess with my dad.

Chapter 8

London

"What's going on?" I try to keep my attitude under control for my dad's benefit.

"Oh, darling, you're back early. I ran into Dominic and he has been keeping me company. And beating me in chess."

"You ran into him? How? When? You're supposed to rest." I feel like an intruder in my own house. Only minuscule remnants of sanity remind me I'm being ridiculous, but when have I ever listened? Especially not when annoyance blinds me.

Dominic rakes his gaze over me in his irritating, self-assured, seductive way. It doesn't work. It doesn't work. Now I'm lying to myself. Great.

"Your dad opened the door for a delivery and got dizzy."

"Are you okay? What happened?" I dash to my dad and put the back of my hand on his forehead.

He recoils. "I'm fine. I got a bit lightheaded, but I'm feeling great now."

"And you conveniently came to the rescue?" I glare at my neighbor.

"I was coming back from the gym. Just happened to be there." Dominic raises his arms in surrender.

Gym? Sure. *Warren wouldn't like you calling her a workout.* Why do I care?

"That must have been a strenuous day for you." My snarl falls flat as neither of them understand I know Patagonia is not a researcher, and that I saw Dominic at Gio's club.

Morning sex, mid-morning sex and the gym. Maybe I'm a little jealous he's getting laid while I've been burning up the batteries of my vibrator.

"Lo, darling, what's up?" Dad squeezes my hand as I glare across the table. "It's not like I let a stranger into your house."

"You don't know him." Not sure why I'm arguing that point, but the last person I want polluting my personal space is my neighbor. It's enough that my privacy is currently non-existent.

"You danced with him at the fundraiser." Dad looks at me like I've just insisted the Earth is flat. He's not wrong, wondering about my absurdly irritated reaction. I should be concerned, but I'm too busy trying to shoot lasers at Dominic with my eyes.

"I can go. I don't want to intrude." Dominic's words might sound like an innocent suggestion, but the challenge is written all over his face. He's taunting me. Not a chance.

"Nonsense." I give him a smile worth a medal for the best performance in pretending. "I'm sure Dad is winning." I pat my father's shoulder and he chuckles.

"Not by any stretch, but that can change." Dad frowns at the chess pieces in front of him.

Dominic gives me that cocky grin, and while my father's attention is on the chessboard, he continues attacking me with his gaze. Languidly, his eyes burn a trail down my skin, and to my dismay my core clenches. I fucking *clench*. Involuntarily, but still.

I'm a hundred percent sure his interest isn't sexual. He gets off on riling me up. And God help me, he's succeeding. As my body tingles with the need for his attention, my mind is on the opposite side of the spectrum.

Dominic returns his focus to the game, and my father leans back and winces. He should be in bed, resting.

Madeleine's emaciated face on the large pillow flashes in my mind's eye. When she could still speak, she told me how much she missed dancing. She had stopped to hopefully recover some of her body's ability, but in the end, she'd have preferred losing her battle while dancing.

I need to give my dad all the joys he can still experience. Even if one of them is a chess game with my neighbor.

I storm out of the kitchen and shut my bedroom door with a bang. I hear muffled voices, but I can't make out what the two of them are saying. The hushed conversation is followed by laughter.

I'm not a sensitive person, but at this moment I feel like a complete outsider. In. My. Own. Home.

Channeling my frustration into work, I call Finn van den Linden. He avoided me successfully at the fundraiser and I'm prepared to leave him yet another message, but he shocks me when he answers.

"London Lowe, to what do I owe the pleasure?"

"Really, Finn? I've been trying to reschedule our meeting for weeks now." I pace my room, half of my attention outside the walls where my dad is betraying me.

"Look, London, I admire your dedication to the research and care for those who need it and I support it, but the research project isn't an investment I want to pursue. It's too risky. Really a donation I'm not ready to make."

"Finn, they have government support already. A

public-private partnership could see the research progress faster."

"Now, while the government involvement may suggest the risk is lower, faster doesn't mean there will be something to bring to market."

"New treatment," I snap.

"Or not. Decades of research could easily come to nothing. That's not where my business interests lie, but good luck." He hangs up.

If I had known how today would go, I would have never gotten out of bed this morning. Before I can try another desperate begging mission—because my fundraising efforts sometimes feel like that—another round of laughter rings out from the kitchen.

I march out to see what's so damn funny. Dominic is at the door to the guest room. *My* guest room. Okay, technically, it's Dad's room now, but still. *Make yourself at home, asshole.*

"Are you leaving?" Finally.

"Do you want me to stay longer?" He smiles and my dad shuffles toward us.

"Dom, here you go. I'm sure you'd enjoy it." He hands over a book.

Dominic smiles and I swear the room gets brighter. His dental hygienist must be a millionaire.

"Thank you, Mr. Lowe. I look forward to the rematch. You're a worthy opponent."

Dad chuckles. "You got lucky today. And call me Micah."

They shake hands and Dominic turns to leave, but a bang on the door stops him. Only my family is cleared to bypass the front desk and come straight upstairs.

As I walk past Dominic, his masculine cologne wafts into my nose. I don't know how it's possible for an entire body to react to a scent, but in that moment, that's what happens.

I don't want to analyze the goosebumps, another involuntary clenching or the raised hair on my nape, and I refuse to acknowledge that my entire apartment smells of him. How is that even possible? The man just melts into surfaces.

I cross the room and yank the door open. My Dominic-motivated mood takes a back seat as Bianca barges in.

"Where is he?" my stepmother snaps, but keeps a relatively cool composure. She is not the warmest person, but she is always classy.

I sigh, more for Dad than for me. "For the record, I was trying to talk some sense into him." I gesture with my head, and Bianca glances over and sees both men still standing by the guest room. Dad is leaning against the doorway with a faint smile.

Bianca straightens, her chin high, and takes the

three steps down from the entrance. "Micah Nathaniel Lowe, what were you thinking?" She stops. "Who are you?" Though he was standing beside my dad the whole time, she apparently missed Dominic at first.

He introduces himself and tries to leave, but my dad stops him with one look. I don't particularly want him to witness any domestic drama, but I'm kind of proud my dad found his mojo and used Dominic to deflect the storm Bianca brought in.

Bianca crosses her arms over her chest and glares at Dominic, then at me, and then she finally lands on the offender. My dad.

"Paris called me to say you're staying here during the treatment. Why? And why wasn't I consulted? What treatment? You told me you're in remission."

I can see how uncomfortable she is with Dominic's presence, and it doesn't look like he feels any better about it. Then her words sink in.

"What?" I press my hands on the banister, still standing near my door. "You underwent treatment already?"

Dominic clears his throat. "I should probably—"

"Stay," my dad barks, and I'm about as stunned by the command as Dominic is. "Bianca, love, I can't commute while I'm getting the treatment."

"Then let's rent a room at the Four Seasons," she says.

Why are we not talking about the remission, or the lack of it? I knew Dad didn't tell us right away, but he's been dealing with it for a while?

"I don't want to spend my... time in a hotel. I want to be home." Dad stumbles and Bianca runs to him. He puts his hands on her shoulders and kisses her forehead.

"This is not your home," she whispers, her voice trembling. She's the strongest woman I know, and I've never seen her overcome with emotions like right now. It pisses me off, because her being emotional is like admitting she doesn't believe Dad will be okay.

"You can both stay here with me." My words surprise me, as well as everyone else in the room.

"Are you sure?" Bianca arches her eyebrows.

"Of course. Soon enough Dad will be done with the treatment and you can return to your home." I pretend I believe that with all my heart, while the doubt and worry blossom in the deep shadows of my soul.

"It seems we can spare you any further drama, young man." Bianca dismisses Dominic as though he were there of his own accord. Dad pats his back and shrugs.

"Of course. Nice to meet you, Mrs. Lowe." Dominic takes Bianca's hand and kisses it.

"I'm Cassinetti. Bianca Cassinetti." She spares no

more time for him and wraps her arms around Dad's shoulders to walk him into the guest room.

Dominic joins me by the door. "If you—"

"Just go," I snap. The last thing I need is to breathe the same air with my father's new chess partner.

"Before I do…" He is the hardest person to get rid of. "I wanted to tell you Felicia Warren is no longer a problem for your charitable endeavor."

"Really? You think your dick is magical, don't you?" I can't believe the destiny of my hospice center was part of their pillow talk.

"Why thank you, it is magical. Though I'm not sure how *you* would know that or how it's pertinent to your case."

"Don't lawyer-talk me. You're in cahoots with her. I saw you at the Madison Club." The words pass through my teeth with a bitter aftertaste.

The smile that spreads across his face pushes all my buttons. "You're jealous, sweetheart?"

"Fuck you."

"Any time, but let me remind you it was you who cut our date short due to your sensitivity." His drawl digs frustration up my spine. "Back to the topic at hand, whatever you think you saw this morning, I don't give a fuck. But perhaps a thank you would be nice after I solved your little problem."

I glare at him. "I'll thank you when Felicia Warren officially withdraws her project."

"I can't wait, neighbor."

Two days pass, and Bianca and I don't kill each other. We've always had a good relationship. Its strength is reinforced by the number of times we see each other in a year. Which is not many.

I love my stepmother, but neither of us is good at compromising. I have to give it to her, though, she's taken off her crown now that she is away from her castle.

Dad hasn't suffered any major symptoms after this round of radiation, but he's weak and rests a lot. When Dominic comes over each day to play chess with him, I either leave the apartment or stay in my room.

I'm on my way to my office to avoid him again. I wish he hadn't become a constant fixture in my family's life.

But Bianca is practically in love with him, and Dad enjoys the small semblance of social life too much for me to cut them off from the *wonderful* Dominic Cressard. Fucking lawyers know how to talk themselves into anyone's graces. Not mine.

I arrive at work and Ashley welcomes me with the

biggest smile. I frown in response, because, well, that's my default reaction.

"What are you so happy about?"

She rolls her eyes. She's never taken my shit, which has made her the employee of the month since she started.

She shoves her hand in front of my face, practically blinding me with a huge rock on her finger.

"You got engaged?"

The smile on her face can probably be seen from space. "Yes. Yes, I said yes." She bounces in glee.

"Congratulations." Tying yourself to one person is the recipe for guaranteed heartache, but even I know it's not appropriate to offer condolences right now.

"Thank you." She walks around to her desk. "Oh, and Mia Huang called you."

I forget about everything else and run to return the call.

"Ms. Lowe, thank you for calling back. I'm due at court, so I'll be brief. My sources at city hall informed me Felicia Warren has withdrawn her application. She's no longer going to develop that real estate. In fact, I hear it's for sale."

Dominic was right.

I stare blankly at my desk, stunned. And... grateful? I'm still irked by how he achieved the win, but I'm so relieved. And I have him to thank for that. Damn it.

"Thank you. That's great news."

"Hopefully someone more considerate buys the properties." She hangs up and my initial relief disappears.

I call Gio to find out who's interested in buying the real estate and end up leaving a message.

I discuss a few items with Ashley and leave. On the way home, I think about the ways I can acknowledge Dominic's help without getting steamrollered by his ego. What was his motivation for helping me?

I come home and Dad is staring at the chessboard, but there is no Dominic. I'm oddly disappointed, but I shake off the unreasonable feeling.

"Where is Bianca?"

"She had some errands to run. Dom had to leave too, so it's just you and me, darling."

He says it as if *Dom* is a part of the family, but I don't let the irritation creep in. Not today, when I have a good reason to celebrate. When I called Zelda at the hospice, she almost cried.

"What do you want to do, Dad?" I'm happy to have him to myself, and mad at the same time that I have to think of our time together in terms of numbers. How many more smiles will he give me? How many conversations do we still have? How many memories can we still create?

"I'd like to go out for a walk." He stands up, slowly, but steadier today.

"Are you sure? We can just—"

"I need fresh air more than anything. Even if we end up only a few feet from your building." He shuffles toward the front door. I help him put on his coat and bundle him up in a scarf. He puts on his woolen flat cap and we venture outside.

The November chill hits us as soon as we step out. The doorman greets us politely. It annoys me that I now remember his name. I shove the thought away and focus on my dad.

We cross the street and slowly make our way to the park.

"Why are you so upset, darling?" Dad gestures to a nearby bench.

"I'm not upset." Other than about his illness. And a few other things in my life, but that's normal.

"I don't want you worrying about me."

"Dad, we're all worried about you, and you can't control that." I help him sit then plop down beside him.

"That's true, perhaps, but it's different for you. I feel you've been hanging on to this anger since Kyle."

I almost snap my neck as I practically jerk away from him. Why would he go there? We've never talked about it. If he thought I was upset before—

"Lo, darling, the reason I'm staying with you at this point in my life is because out of all my children, you're the one who believes that saying goodbye to someone you love must be done holding their hand till the last minute."

No, no, no. Tears prickle my eyes and my initial reaction is to bolt, but I can't leave him here. That's why he wanted to come outside. Ironically, it was to trap me.

"I can't speak for Kyle," he continues. "I don't know why he decided to deal with his last days the way he did, but I can suspect. If it was me... and let's not pretend, it *is* me now... do you think I need you to hold my hand on my deathbed? Do you really believe that is the most important thing to me?"

I swallow a few times, blinking the tears away, but it really just propels them down my cheeks. I want to speak, but the words are suspended in some strange vacuum where my brain can't access them.

"It would be nice, but it's not what matters at the end." His voice is calm and soothing, in contrast to his words. "What matters in my last days or years in this life is the memories we created together. Your first words, your first steps, that god-awful goth look you wore for two years when you were fourteen. The day when I taught you to ride the bike. When I watched you speak at your first gala. Just a series of simple things that make up the mosaic of our life."

I'm crying now—a full-blown break-down in the middle of a public park. And while I hate the topic of the conversation, a part of me is swelling with gratitude. It's sad but empowering. Both tragic and uplifting. The courage my father has to even broach the topic.

"What I am trying to say is that you holding my hand when I won't even be mentally present anymore is not the point, Lo. It's nice and an appreciated gesture, but in the grand scheme of things, you've already given me all I cherish."

We sit in silence as he holds my hand. His words sit with me like an uninvited guest who turns out to be welcome company. Important company.

My heart constricts when Dad breaks the silence. "I'm sorry you had to cancel your travels on my account."

"God..." I breathe out, stifling a sob. I lean my head on his shoulder and he reaches around and wraps me in the best dad hug. Oh, how many years have passed since we shared a moment like this? "There is nowhere I'd rather be, Dad."

"That's good, because you're stuck with me. I don't know for how long, but time doesn't matter right now. I only hope I'll still be here when you finally let yourself fall in love."

Chapter 9

London

Letting myself fall in love? Dad's words play in my head during dinner. For once I'm glad Bianca is taking charge of the conversation because my mind is too agitated. I don't want to fall in love. But I don't want Dad to worry about me. I'm perfectly fine.

I lost Kyle when we were so young. I've carefully created my life to live fully while minimizing the potential of experiencing that horrible pain again. When you wished you were dead as well. When the universe tested you with suffering instead. Abandoned by those you trusted and needed the most.

Not getting hurt is already a challenging mission because I have seven siblings, I lost my mother when I was very young, and my father's health is in danger right now. The likelihood of loss is high enough without letting myself fall in love.

Why is me protecting my heart such a problem? Is Dad trying to make sure there is another man in my life once he's gone? That's bullshit.

But still, the way he lowered his voice and uttered those words in the park, like the future of the world weighed on his shoulders... his words sounded like his last wish. Can I deny him that?

Bianca talks about her shopping and her lunch at Massi's restaurant with her teenage grandson, but I'm only catching a word here and there.

"You're quiet tonight." She squeezes my hand. "Is everything all right?"

I smile. "If you guys don't mind, I'm going out tonight." I kind of surprise myself. I didn't plan on clubbing while Dad is staying with me, but I need to get out for two reasons. My head could use a reset, and it's time to potentially find myself a boyfriend.

Not sure how to execute the latter. I'm perfectly capable of picking up a man, but those are men with no expectations. How do you get a man who wants to date? God. Last time I was in a relationship was... my first time. The damage has been permanent.

How long would I need to keep the man around? I guess I can break up with him after an appropriate time once Dad sees I have, in fact, fallen in love. On paper.

"But of course. Don't sit around with us old folks." Bianca stands up and starts putting away the dishes. At home she has a cook and a housekeeper, even though it's just her and my dad, but despite her status she's never shied away from housework.

"Don't feel like you have to entertain us. I'm ready for bed anyway." Dad stands up and kisses my hair.

Thirty minutes later, I leave the apartment ready to hit the town. And, of course, Patagonia is leaving Dom's. What? Since when do I call him Dom?

I should talk with him about Warren's withdrawal of her building application. Well, now is as good a time as any other.

I nod a greeting to Patty and raise my finger, trying to stop Dominic from closing the door. "Do you have a moment?"

He gives me a lazy smile. "But of course, *Lo.*"

The bastard has now adopted my family's name for me.

"*Dom*," I growl, and his smile widens, practically splitting his face. If he didn't look so hot, it would be so much easier to hate him.

He lets me enter and I realize this is the first time I've been in his apartment. It's the same layout as mine, and it doesn't necessarily have more furniture. But it looks more lived in.

Nestled in the middle of the living room is a large, white leather couch with throw pillows and a fuzzy blanket. And while they are black and gray, they still provide more accent than anything in my plain decor. The sofa faces a wall with a gigantic screen. Of course, that's such a man thing.

His dining table is perched in front of the window wall, but I doubt he eats there because it looks more like a desk. Books, stacks of papers and documents are strewn across the glass surface and on the chairs.

"Sorry, we've been working," he says, following my gaze. "Can I offer you anything?"

"No, I'm going out. This will be short."

I turn sideways, so I'm not looking at his living room. His space has a pull I can't explain, and I irrationally wish he would give me a tour.

"Okay, what's up?" He shifts his weight to one foot, crossing the other at his ankle. He pushes his hands into the pockets of his jeans. His simple white T-shirt stretches over the expanse of his torso.

He's bulkier than when he first moved in. More in shape. His skin is darker, tanned-looking, which is ridiculous in New York's November. I guess he's just healthier, recovering from his burnout.

"Felicia Warren is selling the property. Quite a

dramatic change of heart..." I came here to thank him for his help because it wasn't Gio's lawyers making this happen. I doubt Felicia made a spontaneous business decision. I know it was him. He told me as much. Just like that, my blood boils. He took care of it, probably while fucking her at the Madison Club. But why?

"Why do I feel you're upset about the development? I thought that's what you wanted?" He cocks his head.

We're standing in the shadows, the only light coming from a standing reading lamp and another one on his dining table/desk by the window.

The lighting makes him even sexier. I should have had this conversation over the phone. I'm not even following my own script, for God's sake.

"I came to thank you for your help. I can't help wondering, though, why did you help me? And how?" I take a step back. I have to distance myself physically, hoping my body gets the message.

Distance. Distance. Distance.

But Dominic steps forward, his movement not a covert operation like mine. He invades my space, and while I'm not yet plastered against his door, I do feel cornered. That's bad. But worse, I don't mind. Or my body doesn't.

He is all heat and muscles and manhood. I'm

suddenly breathless, unreasonably warm and itchy. I swallow and crane my neck to look at him.

I won't wilt under his scorching look. I'm not a fool, I know he's toying with me. Reminding me of that stupid moment of weakness when I used his boxes as a punching bag. Asshole.

When my eyes reach his, I don't know if he wants to kill me or fuck me. Or he really is teasing me and I'm the one who doesn't know if the plan is to kill or screw. Both acts stem from anger. Hate.

"As for the why..." His voice washes over me like a soft blanket. "While I got involved uninvited, I always finish what I start. As for the how, I think I told you that already."

His breath on my skin should elevate my annoyance, but it does the exact opposite. I need to get away from him, but I'm not giving him the satisfaction of taking another step back.

"So this would fall under the five percent?" The venom I try to infuse into my retort falls short even to my ears. One corner of his mouth twitches up. He remembers our conversation.

Someone has to defend the criminals. I won't apologize for doing that, or for being damn good at it. And ninety-five percent legit about it. That's what he said the night he brought over the Indian food for our not-a-date.

"Why do you need to know?" He feels even closer now, his breath eliciting goosebumps down my spine. The good kind that trickle down into my center. Goddammit, I hate the power he has over my body.

"Because I don't think our moral compasses are calibrated the same way." I swallow hard.

I spend my days practically begging people for money, and I've never felt this uncomfortable having a conversation. I shouldn't have worn the turtleneck. It's a sleeveless piece, but my neck is burning up under the fabric, making me hot all over.

"Don't tell me you don't like winning." He is not touching me, but every millimeter of my skin burns for him. As though this is foreplay with a promise of things I don't want to contemplate.

Do I really need to resist this?

But I have rules for a reason. Also, lately he's not only my neighbor, he's a friend of the family. My panties don't go into that territory. Ever. This fortifies me a bit, while my core keeps clenching.

"Of course. I love winning. That's the problem, in this case. I enjoy the idea of Warren losing to me, and I worry you may be the magnet to my moral compass." There, I said it. I've never believed the end justifies the means, but in this case, I can't argue that it did.

"Are you worried I'd corrupt you, London?" he drawls.

We glare at each other—or rather I hope I glare while he fucks me with his hooded gaze.

His eyes drop to my lips. And, of course, my tongue darts out of its own accord. I lick my lips and look away quickly. Jesus.

"Your girlfriend didn't take care of you tonight, or is your appetite insatiable?"

He steps back. Thank God. I try to ignore the coldness he's left behind. My body is seriously malfunctioning right now.

"She is not my girlfriend, and you should drop the jealousy act. At the end of the day, I can sleep with whoever I want. It's none of your business." He isn't casually standing and smirking anymore. His default overconfident stance has changed, and he seems pissed now.

"I wonder how Felicia feels about Patty," I bark.

He winces. "What are you talking about?"

Oh my God, I can't believe I just went there. It's not like I have the moral ground to challenge him on this matter. Right now, I don't have solid ground anywhere. I stumble back and hit the door.

Yet, I don't back up. I should, but my brain and common sense have taken a day off. "I saw you with her at the Madison Club. Leaving the private wing where the bedrooms are."

"And how do you know, sweetheart, there are bedrooms at that club?"

Arguing with a lawyer is maddening.

"Fuck you. I came here to thank you for helping me out. I don't want to know what you did to have her back off the project. And I don't want you to ever help me again." I whirl around and march out of his apartment.

I push open the door to the stairwell because I won't wait for the elevator with his gaze on my back. Though he shuts his door loudly enough for me to know he had no intention of doing that.

I storm through the lobby and the doorman rushes to open the door for me. "Have a lovely evening, Ms. Lowe."

Is he provoking me as well? I growl at him with something unintelligible, but he seems unaffected. And I feel even worse than before.

I walk like a madwoman for several blocks before my head functions reasonably again. My anger slowly gives way to embarrassment. God, why do I act like an idiot around him? I might need to move out. Perhaps if I fucked him I might get my sanity back. Or I need to screw someone else.

That's the whole point of going out tonight. I need to find myself a boyfriend. I'm not letting my dad worry about my lack of a love life.

I have plenty of sex life. Well, not lately, but that's always the case leading up to a fundraiser when I'm the busiest, and I haven't had a chance to rectify that. There must be someone willing to extend the sex part beyond the bedroom.

I hail a taxi and make my way to a club in SoHo I've heard about. I don't go to any of my usual places because I don't need to run into anyone I know. It might still happen, but chances are much lower.

Three hours later, I'm slightly drunk and definitely nowhere close to finding a man who could serve as my boyfriend for the next few months so I can pretend to fall in love. For my dad.

The poor bastard beside me is droning on about some stupid game he's developed. He settled into his monologue after I gave him a series of yes and no answers in response to his dull questions.

This is the third guy tonight to buy me a drink, and the conversation goes in the same direction as the other two. Boring me. Seriously, I should pay for my own drinks instead of listening to this shit.

I'd have to spend time with my boyfriend outside the bedroom. Hence the conversations. Or a very pathetic attempt at it. Why are all the fun men either playboys or incapable of commitment? Or rather uninterested. I know why, because unattached is way more fun, but for the time being that's not an option for me.

I look around, stifling a yawn. A group of men saunters in. They reek of money and entitlement. Perhaps a better option than the hipster beside me. One of them is Finn van den Linden. Shit. He's a catch. I mumble something semi-rude to my companion, thank him for the drink and make my way to the five men at the bar.

Finn notices me and his face falls. "London, don't ruin the night with your charitable causes. Come on, everyone, pull out your checkbooks and put your money to a good cause."

They holler, but all of them oblige. I laugh. Well, dating him would be more fun than I hoped I'd have with *my boyfriend.*

Finn collects the donations and puts them in my hand, swaying slightly. He's drunk and kind of obnoxious. I grab the checks and shove them into my clutch.

"Why thank you for your contribution, gentlemen." They all cheer and I face Finn. "I wasn't going to ask you for money. You said no already, but thank you. I just wanted to have a drink."

"Of course, what are you drinking?" He slurs his words a bit.

While he turns to get my cocktail, I realize there are several women already engaged in conversations with the rest of the group. All of them smiling at the men and glaring at each other.

"Here you go, London." Finn hands me the margarita.

"Cheers." I raise my glass. "Are you celebrating something?"

He snorts. "Surviving another day at the office, avoiding my father." He downs his drink and sways a bit.

Okay, he really is drunk. I'm not that desperate, am I?

"Do you want to get out of here?" He studies me with glassy eyes.

Now, I might need to get laid, but he might fall asleep on the way to the bedroom. I smile brightly. "Another time, Finn."

He winks, or maybe just squints, and turns to chat with one of the girls.

I nurse the drink for a moment, but the spectacle of female hunting bores me quickly. I don't bother to say goodbye to the group.

I take a cab but get out two blocks away from my building. The city is as crisp as expected at this time of the year.

It's lit up like a damn Christmas tree, because aside from its usual lights, the holiday decorations are everywhere. Each year they sneak up on us sooner. Next thing I know, they'll erect the tree at the Rockefeller Center in the middle of summer.

Today, everything irks me more than usual. Perhaps there is a reason I always travel somewhere right after the gala.

As the chilly air crawls under my jacket, I laugh at the idea of spending my annual leave in the Arctic. What was I thinking?

As much as I want the walk to help me with my current dilemma, the conclusion is underwhelming. I don't think I can get a boyfriend fast enough for my dad to see how happily settled I am. Ugh! Just the thought of settling makes me sick.

Even if I run into an acceptable candidate right now, it wouldn't be real. But it doesn't have to be. I can fake it. For Dad, I can definitely fake it.

Now that's an idea. I don't need an actual boyfriend, because there is no way I'm going to fall in love anyway. I just need a fake one.

I pull out my phone and scroll through my contacts. Shit. I don't have a close enough male friend to ask them for this type of favor. Most of my acquaintances are busy people, and just coordinating our calendars to deliver on such a charade would be impossible.

Deflated, I turn into my building and take the elevator. On my floor, I automatically turn toward the door across from mine. Maybe I left my inhibition at the bottom of my last drink, but suddenly Dominic seems like a solution to my problem.

He's available, my dad likes him, our schedules work out, and he wouldn't have to invest much time since I'm just across the hallway. A convenient fake boyfriend. Yes, I hate him, but even that plays to my advantage because I can be sure there won't be a heartache.

I look at my home and then back to his door. Before I lose my cool or realize I haven't considered why on Earth would he agree to this, I knock on his door. It's time to get myself a fake boyfriend.

Chapter 10

Dominic

Though I'm trying to find a precedent to help with another case—this time for Cesare's neighbor—my mind keeps coming back to London.

She's like a dragon, spitting fire all the time. It's a mask she formed at one point like a protective wall. Why? It's like she imprisoned her happiness in a stone tower and lost the keys.

Her father and stepmother are nice people. Bianca is a bit overbearing and intense, but they are lovely. Certainly more supportive than my parents have ever been.

And she gets along with her siblings. So why would someone who grew up in a loving, supportive family turn into such an angry ball of energy?

Micah alluded to something in her past. Something

filed the edges of her personality too sharp, but he said it's her story to tell. And that only made me more intrigued.

What made her so angry and inconsiderate of others on the one hand, and so involved in helping on the other?

The more burning question is, why do I care?

I groan. As much as I hate her dragon act, it's a turn on. She despises me or pretends to. I'm pretty sure she regrets that she kissed me.

The woman's need to be in control is perhaps greater than mine. I want to unwrap those protective layers and see her naked truth. And her naked body.

My cock jerks behind my zipper. I haven't had sex in two months and two weeks. Yes, I'm counting. Normally I would assume it's the absence of sex making me horny around her, but that's not the case. My arousal only correlates with her presence. Case in point, the embarrassing lap dance from Patagonia.

Who would have thought that Dominic 'The Player' Cressard could grow immune to lap dances? Poor Nia almost started crying because she worried she would get fired, and she really needs the money. That's what got us talking, and I ended up offering her my place and the job.

Lately, I'm offering help all the time. It kind of goes against my decision to take a sabbatical, but I can't help it. That day when I started working on Alonso's, then London's cases was the first day I felt really alive. In the longest time.

London's case was a mistake, though. Instead of thanking me, she comes and accuses me of sleeping with Felicia Warren? Not even if she was the last woman in the world.

For one, she likes boys young enough to be her sons—the reason I was at the club in the first place, to confront her about her vapid affair—but more importantly, she is as feminine as a rock. And quite a bitch, as I learned from T's and Nia's research.

Is London jealous? She seems to hate me. Though her lips tonight, those full dark pink lips, didn't seem on board with the hatred. Her body shivered under my prowling gaze. She was fighting it, but she wanted me at that moment.

I won't lie. I want to fuck her. She is hot and she excites me, and I want to fuck her to get back into the game.

She is not a delicate flower who would demand a relationship, and even if it was a hate fuck for her, I don't care. I need to get back into the saddle, and if it's the always annoyed neighbor who can boost me there, then so be it.

My cock hardens at the idea. Shit. The only problem is she's been fighting it so hard. Silly woman.

The idea of wearing her down pleases me more than it should.

Challenge accepted. I'm going to screw London Lowe before Christmas. And maybe then I'll be able to return to my life in Chicago.

I almost fist my cock to jerk off to the idea of it when someone knocks. What the hell? It's past midnight and only Nia and my housekeeper have free access to get inside the building.

I open the door and, well, well, well... speak, or in this case think of the devil.

"You're not asleep. Good." She pushes the door open and walks past me. "I have a proposition for you."

"I thought you came to apologize." I close the door.

We're standing where we did a few hours ago, and the air is immediately filled with tension. Sexual tension. She steps back. Again. Just like the first time tonight when she came to glare at me.

"I'm sorry about earlier. I came to..." Suddenly she looks unsure. She bites her bottom lip and shakes her head. "You know what, this is a stupid idea."

She grabs the doorknob, but I lean in, putting my arm above her, pushing into the door, preventing her from opening it. With my front to her back, my arm looming above her head, she inhales sharply.

Her body is warm against mine, feeling too good for me to step away like a normal person would. Her scent washes over me, drawing me to lower my head and inhale more of it.

"You can't storm out of here twice in one night, Lo. You came again, so own it. Tell me your proposition, because I'm telling you right now, sweetheart, I don't mind being propositioned by you."

My voice is low and full of seduction. As much as she pretends she doesn't want me, I'm going to have her.

She breathes heavily, her back brushing my chest when she inhales. It's not like I'm giving her the option to turn, standing like a wall behind her.

All of my self-control is required to keep me from pinning her against my door and shoving that short skirt up to her waist.

I reach around her to lock the door, and as my hand brushes her arm, I swear electricity zaps between us. It's so potent we both freeze, our chests heaving like we've just run a race.

I'm not sure what London is fighting, but it takes all the willpower I've never known I had not to grind my pelvis into her back.

Then the woman I got to know is back and she snarls, "For fuck's sake, step away if you want to hear me out."

I take that step, because while I'm a bastard with very few scruples in my darkened soul, I'm not depraved, or that desperate. Well, maybe I'm a bit desperate. A part of me wants to push her further to see how long she'll pretend not to want it.

We glare at each other for a beat, the wave of frustration floating between us. Mine is purely sexual, but I think London is fighting way more.

Clearly her stopping here on the way back from wherever she went—judging by the faint smell of alcohol on her, it wasn't the library—is not a booty call.

"Come in. Do you want coffee or anything?" I take the three steps down and walk to my kitchen. London remains on the landing, but when I arch my eyebrow, she rolls her eyes and follows me.

"Just a glass of water." She sighs, as if it pains her to accept my hospitality.

As she gulps it down, her eyes roam around my kitchen. Like in hers, white cabinets line one wall, but mine is less tidy.

While London's surfaces are spotless and void of anything, my counter has a toaster, a coffee machine, a few books, a scrunched-up towel, and cups that didn't make it to the dishwasher. It's not dirty, but definitely not tidy.

"You don't have a housekeeper?"

"Did you come to judge the state of my apartment?" I crack my knuckles and she flinches.

"I hate when people do that." She squirms at my

hands.

"Okay, go home, London, I don't fucking care about your opinions." Seriously, this woman is as attractive as she is infuriating. Surely there must be another woman who gets me off and doesn't drive me crazy in the process.

"Sorry." Her tone suggests otherwise. "Okay, hear me out. And I'd like the court to note that after stepping inside, I realized this is the worst idea ever." She stops, looking surprised by her words, and then giggles.

The sound shocks me. If someone told me two minutes ago London was capable of such a sound, I would have laughed in their face. She must be tipsier than she looks.

"Duly noted. What's your proposition?" I lean against the counter and cross my legs at the ankles.

She exhales a long breath. "I'd like you to be my boyfriend."

I wait for the punch line, a twist, a jab, a snarl, but when she remains quiet, I wonder just how much she's drunk tonight. This is rich. My mood improves. I crack my knuckles a few times before I react, enjoying her squirming.

"Sweetheart, did you have to get drunk to ask me?" I erase the distance between us and wrap my arm around her waist. I have no idea what the hell she really wants, but I'm sure going to have fun with it.

She pushes me away. "That's not what I mean, asshole. I need a fake boyfriend. Look, it's important to my dad that he sees me fall in love. I'm not going to do that, but I can at least pretend. He might not..." She swallows hard and blinks a few times. "He might not live..."

She can't finish, and in that moment she looks so vulnerable, all the joking and teasing loses its attraction. I might be an asshole, but I'm not a bully.

"Let me get this straight. You want me to be your fake boyfriend? You want me to lie to your father who, mind you, I've grown to like and respect?"

She shakes her head and starts pacing, or distancing herself from me, stopping by the window, staring into the night. "You say it as if I didn't love or respect him. It will be a lie, but he would never know, so it's not a betrayal. It would make him happy."

I don't know if it's my newly acquired streak of helping others or rather a new level of insanity I hit unexpectedly, but I surprise us both with a simple "Okay."

London whips around. "Okay?"

"Yes, okay." Perhaps being her fake boyfriend is the fastest way to sleep with her and finally get back on the horse. Also, dating someone would prove to Rocco he's been wrong about me the whole time.

"Just like that." She is so genuinely taken aback

that it makes me question the whole thing. Why would she come to me if she expected me to refuse?

"Yeah." I nod.

She narrows her eyes. "Why?"

Jesus, enough with the twenty questions. "Do you want me to date you or not?"

"Fake date me." She folds her arms across her chest. "Yes, I do. I just feel I'm missing something. Why do I never understand your motivations?"

"I guess that would be another why you won't understand." I walk into the living room. "Let's discuss the rules."

"Rules?" London appears from the other side of the wall between the living space and the kitchen.

"Of course, we can't fake it without some sort of code of conduct. I'm not taking you on dates, dinners, or movies. We stay either at your place, or occasionally mine, for the benefit of your parents."

"God, and here I worried you were a romantic. Fine. That works for me. Frankly, I have no desire to spend time with you."

Her remark stings more than it should. After all, I share that desire with her. Minus the need to fuck her.

"We should go on pretend dates though," she adds.

"That's what would happen here," I insist.

Again, I'm not sure why I'm even laying down the rules, but frankly her company isn't pleasant enough that I want to spend more time than necessary with her. Unless it's with my cock buried inside her.

"Okay, fine. Anything else?" She collapses on the other side of the sofa, as far from me as possible.

No problem. Over the course of our next few pretend dates, I'll get her into my lap. Preferably straddling me. My cock twitches at the idea.

"I'm good. What is our origin story, then?" I move sideways to face her, placing my elbow on the backrest.

"Before we agree on that, I'd like to suggest a few rules." She doesn't wait for me to object. "It doesn't look good that you have a young woman coming in and out of here all the time, so I think we need to make sure my dad and Bianca buy into the researcher idea and perhaps meet Patty."

"How many times do I need to tell you that Nia works for me and occasionally uses my guest room to study?" I roll my eyes. "But fine, as far as I'm concerned, we can have dinner with her at your place. She works for me." I bark the last sentence, irked by London's insistence that I'm dating the girl.

"Okay, it's just the optics. You can fuck her as long as no one knows. I'm not excited about this boyfriend idea as it is, but I don't want to be made a fool when my fake boyfriend openly cheats on me."

"Let's move to the background story. I'm really done explaining Nia to you." I turn and tilt my head to the back of the couch, closing my eyes. I've been her fake boyfriend for five minutes and I'm already regretting it.

"Okay, well, I guess we met in the hallway, you invited me to your place, and we fought the attraction for a bit but realized it's stronger. I'll tell Dad I'm dating you tomorrow morning. There is no one else we need to officially announce it to, anyway."

I open my eyes to look at her. "So how long do I need to do this?"

London winces as my words land between us, much harsher than I intended.

"You know what, forget it. I don't want to inconvenience you." She stands up.

I shouldn't have agreed to this. Why do I keep blurting out these weird commitments?

"Sit back down," I growl. I don't expect her to oblige, but she does, glaring at me. "I didn't mean it that way, but we will eventually break up. I'm moving back to Chicago in six months, hopefully sooner."

She cackles. "God, Dominic, I don't want to date you for that long. Three months. A decent time to make my father believe I fell in love and for us to break up."

"What would be the reason for the breakup?" Why do I even care?

She huffs. "We'll come up with something."

"As long as I'm not the villain in that story." This might be the most ridiculous scheme ever to get into a woman's pants. I can't believe I'm even contemplating it.

But then, perhaps the seemingly unattainable is what I need to snap me out of my lethargy. The challenge. The fight. The race.

"Okay, Dominic, your reputation as Prince Charming will stay intact. Anything else?" London cocks her head, unimpressed.

"Should I have a pet name for you?" I just want to see her roll her eyes again.

And she does. "Sure, call me 'honey.'" She shrugs.

I raise my eyebrow. "More like chili."

She glares at me, shaking her head, and I must say her annoyed and pissed off is so much better than me feeling the same.

"What?" This time I shrug and shoot her an innocent smile. "You're hot, and definitely not sweet."

She exhales an exasperated breath. "Again, as I said, I'm regretting coming here tonight. I'll claim temporary insanity."

"Should we practice kissing now?" I ask, because why not, but also because I enjoy way too much the mixture of frustration and disdain on her face.

"We're done here. I'll tell Dad about our relationship tomorrow morning, and stay home for your chess match so we can pretend to like each other, and maybe we can have our first date tomorrow. I'll sneak my laptop in here, so we can both work while they think we're out together." She stands up and I follow, walking her to the door.

"Well, *Chils*, not only have I helped you with your legal case, but now I'm going to lie to your father, who is a great guy. You owe me big time." I put my hands into my pockets and hover on the last step, not making the move to unlock my door.

"Why am I sure I won't like the payback?" She drums her nails on the banister. Her polish is bright red, the only real color on her, shining against her black clothes and dark hair. How I want to fist that mane and make her scream my name.

"Chils, no worries, by the time we're done, you will have paid me back with interest. I'll think of my price overnight. See you tomorrow, sweetheart."

I hoist myself up to reach her at the landing and kiss her forehead. She smells so good I almost lick her.

She jumps back like my lips stung her. I chuckle and unlock the door.

As I watch her ass moving across the hall between us, I smile to myself. This is going to be a lot of fun. Or an absolute headache.

Chapter 11

London

Dad was entirely too excited to hear that I'm dating Dominic. Obviously more than me, or Dominic for that matter, but still a bit too much. He likes the man, and I don't like that he likes him. Frankly, now that last night's cocktails are out of my system, I'm regretting the entire idea.

Seeing Dad gush about how wonderful Dom is—has he even met the guy?—laced my nerves with guilt. I'm lying to my father. But it will make him happy. It already has. Damn it.

In the light of a new day, I hate this scheme that was induced by alcohol and desperation. Another unnervingly persistent question remains: why did Dominic agree?

He helped me with the developer issue and now he

is helping me give my dad something I'm not really capable of offering.

When did I become a coward who can't stand up for her beliefs to her father? Was it his diagnosis? Or should I blame Dominic for this as well? Ever since those boxes appeared in the corridor, I've spiraled from one poor decision to the next.

I don't need to go to the office today, but I had to leave the house. To collect my thoughts. And to avoid my neighbor.

I call Paris and wait for her at a coffee shop, nursing my extra sweet spicy latte. *I'll call you chili.* Asshole.

There has to be a silver lining, right? Maybe fake dating is a great exercise in self-control. The man is insanely hot, and I've suggested to him already—unintentionally, but still—how my body feels around him.

The way he was devouring me with his gaze yesterday, I know he'll continue to provoke me.

"Hey, sorry it took me so long. I had to finish something. What's up, Lo? Are they driving you crazy already?" Paris slides onto the stool beside me.

While we're very different, or perhaps because of that, my identical twin has always been the best sounding board for me. Often she doesn't agree, but she never judges or tries to push her opinion. She simply listens, and I think better when I voice my conflicting feelings and views.

"Actually, Bianca has been very respectful of my space, and Dad is..." I swallow. "I'm grateful for our time together." The air grows somber between us, weighing a ton with the unspoken worry we pretend not to have.

She raises her finger and dashes away to get her order, and I'm thankful she broke the moment.

Not that the situation can improve by avoidance, but that's what we have right now. I don't have time to compose myself before she comes back with her mug. "I'll stop by later this week. How is he doing?"

"He's good, considering. If I didn't know better, I would have more hope." I shrug and decide to change the topic before helplessness takes over. "I need to tell you something."

She arches her eyebrow and I explain the situation —omitting a few intimate details. I don't tell her about kissing him or wanting to kiss him again. Or about him doing God knows what to scare Felicia Warren, but I tell her about our newly-forged fake relationship.

Even speaking about it doesn't clear the mess I fear I jumped into head-first.

Paris scrunches her lips to the side, digesting the information. "But you hate him." She frowns.

"Yeah." I called her to talk, so I won't lie to her.

"Why him?" She fidgets on her stool, pulling her woolen dress lower on her thighs. Always so proper.

"Desperation." I let out a long breath full of frustration and capitulation. I don't give up. Ever. But right now, I'm so unbalanced that I don't even know how to approach everything.

Dad's illness hit me hard. Coupled with the lack of funding for the research project and my inability to go and let loose in Scandinavia, I've been dragged against my will into a territory I don't particularly want to explore.

I feel lonely and needy. And desperate. Christmas looming around the corner doesn't help.

"Don't be ridiculous, you know lots of guys—" Paris narrows her eyes and bites her lips. "Oh."

I nod. She must have pictured the type of guys I usually spend time with and jumped to the same conclusion I did last night. None of them is boyfriend material, not even as a fake one. And none of them would have a reason to do it.

"But why did he agree?" She picks up her tea and observes the street, thinking about the answer.

"Beats me, but he did. I got myself a boyfriend." A bitter laugh makes its way through my throat. "Swear not to tell anyone else."

"Pinkie swear." We hook our small fingers as we used to when we were young.

"I needed to tell you because it all looked simple last night, but this morning it freaked me out. I don't even know how to date, Paris."

"You're not really dating, so don't worry. There is no manual, anyway." She sighs.

People outside carry shopping bags and briefcases, braving the frost and fog.

"What's your next bucket list item?" I move to a safer territory. The current attention on me is more than I care for. Paris's ridiculous bucket list might just pull me out of my funk.

She lowers her gaze and whispers, "A one-night stand."

I snort. "What? That's like the opposite extreme of what you've been doing."

Scowling, she takes a sip of her drink and fidgets with her dress, then clenches her fists before drumming her nails on the sides of her cup.

"What? I'm just saying you have a tendency to get a bit needy right after the first date."

She gasps, heat rising to her cheeks. "That's not true."

"I mean, you sleep with a guy once and you start taking care of his dry cleaning the following day." I shrug.

She huffs. "What's wrong with helping people?"

I love my sister, but we don't live on the same

planet. "I'm helping people, but I don't let them make me into their doormat." I raise my eyebrows. "But you know what, have a one-night stand. It's a good challenge for you. Not to get attached. Enjoy it."

Even though it's on her bucket list, she looks hesitant. If my brain wasn't occupied by the fake dating situation, I'd take her out to score a potential hook-up.

We sip our drinks and discuss Christmas plans. This will be my first Christmas at home since Kyle died. Yeah, it's definitely the holiday throwing me into this mood.

Dad will need another round of treatment in a few weeks. He and Bianca might move back home for a few days, but then they will be back again, so we agreed to have a small, low-key lunch at my place.

Work gives me something to focus on while I walk home. The situations I deal with make me angry, but the solutions, however tiny, make life slightly better, more purposeful.

But as I approach my building, the dread returns and I start to question every decision I've made in the last twenty-four hours.

As soon as I enter my apartment, I can smell my *boyfriend*. As usual, larger than life, he sucks away all the air and his musky scent penetrates the walls. Today, a tantalizing aroma of food mingles too.

Dominic and Bianca are in the kitchen, cooking

together. They haven't heard me yet, so I stay by the front door, trying to control my breathing and tame the pulsing echo in my cars.

Dad says something and they all laugh. Bianca berates Dominic for doing something wrong, and he takes it with a delightful dose of self-deprecation.

They are having a family moment. Without me. In my own house. The little domestic scene raises my hackles. How dare he?

"Hello, everyone." My greeting sounds like an accusation as I walk in and lean against the edge of the partition wall, glaring at Dominic.

"Darling, Dom and Bianca are making lasagna for dinner." Dad chuckles like it's some inside joke.

"I can see that." I force a smile. *Don't be a bitch, London.* This is priceless boyfriend behavior. If boyfriends monopolized your family and invaded your space.

"Did you have a good day, Chils?" Dominic saunters over. He raises his arms, like in surrender, to prevent him from soiling my clothes with flour. So fucking considerate. He kisses my cheek and strokes it with his finger.

"I had a wonderful day." *Until now, asshole.* "I still have a few emails to catch up on." I walk over and kiss my dad.

"You have a good forty-five minutes before dinner,

Lo," Bianca informs me, not even trying to pull me into the cooking fun. She gave up on that a decade ago as a result of my lack of interest.

I don't have emails or anything to do right now, or the head space to attempt something productive. But I'd still rather just stew in my room.

Fewer interactions with my neighbor, fewer reasons for my dad or Bianca—and let's face it, that woman has a sixth sense—to suspect the charade.

That's what I tell myself, anyway. It sounds better than admitting I feared I would dampen the mood with my attitude. Not that I'm apologizing for it. It's who I am.

Somehow, over the course of the past several hours, I became the grump in our fake relationship. Because fucking Dominic is all sunshine. Whatever. I catch my reflection in the mirror. My cheek is smeared with flour. Asshole.

I wipe it away and collapse onto my bed. Hiding, I spend the next half an hour staring at the ceiling.

After a knock on my door, Dominic sticks his head in. "Are you okay?"

"What are you doing?" I hoist my legs over the edge and push up to a sitting position.

He doesn't wait for an invitation and enters, closing the door behind him. He casually walks around the bed and plops onto it on the other side of me, his hands laced under his head, resting on my pillows.

"I repeat. What are you doing?" I enunciate every word with care.

"I came to check on you. We should wait before we both return, pretend to make out." He winks and I roll my eyes. "To maintain the ruse. Or we can make out for real." The corners of his mouth curl up.

"In your dreams," I deadpan.

"It would be more believable if you came out with your hair messed up a bit..."

He lowers his voice, and somehow I can feel his breath in my hair, which is physically impossible.

"Your cheeks flushed..."

Heat spreads over my face.

"Your lips swollen..."

On instinct, I lick my lower lip.

I hate that my reactions are so visible. At least he can't see me clenching between my thighs. He can't hear my heart thumping against my ribcage.

I desperately try to control my breathing, because now the picture of him ravishing my mouth is stealing all the available oxygen.

A grin spreads across his face before he bounces off the bed. "We should help set the table." He ruffles my hair and opens the door for me, effectively shutting me up if I don't want my parents to hear me snarling at him.

"I'm so glad you invited yourself to dinner." Fake honey laces my words, and Dominic chuckles. He enjoys this way too much.

"And I cooked for you, Chils." He squeezes my ass right as we turn the corner, forcing me to swallow a yelp and keep the chain of invectives in my head.

Dinner is picture-perfect because no one at the table can hear my internal commentary of "fuck him," "here we go again," and "screw this, I'm confessing to my father."

Aside from those silent remarks, I also do a lot of gesturing—in my mind as well. Among the top three is eye rolling, head shaking and bird flipping.

I join the others in gushing over the culinary mastery, which pisses me off further because the meal is delicious. But then Bianca led the project, and she bakes a mean lasagna, so there is no surprise there.

At least my rectangular table has room for one chair at each side and Dominic sits across from me. Otherwise I'm sure he would continue manufacturing affection with his arm around my shoulders, his hand on my leg, or squeezing my hand.

Who knew fake dating was so hard? Luckily, as soon as we finish eating—which takes a painfully long time since *Dom* practically gobbles down half of the dish, asking for two servings—my boyfriend announces he has a call and needs to leave.

"Walk me to the door, Chils." He grabs my hand and pulls me up.

I avert my face, so Dad doesn't see my expression.

With his hand on the small of my back, Dominic pushes me toward my front door. I don't want to feel anything, but I can't help it. His touch, warm over the thin layer of my blouse, sends conflicting feelings through my body. Conflicting only for my mind because my body feels no confusion, just pure, shameless need.

"This was nice," Dominic says, his voice carrying across the room to reach the kitchen. "You need to pick up your game, Chils," he whispers into my ear.

I was so focused on getting rid of him and on the sensation his touch caused, his closeness surprises me. His breath, like delicious sin against my skin, sprouts goosebumps on my neck.

I would secretly marvel at the thrill of it, but he enjoys too much what he does to me, so I revert to annoyance.

Again, distracted by my useless internal fights, he catches me by surprise when he grips the back of my neck with his large palm and coerces my face to him before crashing his lips against mine.

My arms fling up, like I might fly away, but with

his free hand he pushes one of them down, grabbing me tightly around my waist. "Come on, Chils, show your dad what a great girlfriend you are."

I drop my other arm, but don't give him the satisfaction of relaxing into his embrace. My lack of cooperation doesn't deter him at all. Dominic teases my lips with his tongue and the traitors part for him.

The faint taste of thyme and garlic somehow makes the kiss more enticing. Mingled with the flavor of manhood he carries around with such confidence, the kiss explodes on my lips with a burning, consuming intensity.

This isn't the aggressive release I sought when I kissed him the first time. This kiss is gentle, yet firm. Vicious and delicious at the same time. I don't even know how, but my arms fly up again, this time to coil around his shoulders as I hold on for dear life while he takes me on a ride full of promise, threat, darkness and sin.

He doesn't move beyond my lips, but I feel the kiss in every hidden crevice of my body, awakening nerve endings I didn't even know I had. I lose myself in the feel of it, deepening the kiss with my tongue, allowing my body to savor every moment. A growl rumbles up his chest as he welcomes my invasion.

Time, place, frustration and animosity cease to exist, floating only as a faint memory in my foggy mind.

I'm aware of the silence in the kitchen, but it's inconsequential. My heartbeat drums in my temples, swelling my head and muting the world around me.

I lose the ability to think, but my other senses go into overdrive, making me hypersensitive to his smell, his touch and his taste. And the sound when Dominic groans against my lips again. It's like junk food. I know I've had enough, but I can't help it. I should stop us, but instead of a protest, a moan escapes me.

Dominic takes it as an invitation and the tenderness is replaced by urgency. He is devouring me now with need, passion, dominance, and I surrender control to him. He takes charge and I let him. It feels... liberating. What?

His length hardens against my stomach as my hips shamelessly grind against him. He swears under his breath, brushing my lips before diving in again. This time it's deep and fast.

Dominic pulls away and cups my face. "Perhaps a sleepover, Chils."

The idea excites me beyond reason. And the consequences douse that excitement with a mountain of ice.

We're both panting. I don't want him to know I'm as wet as he is hard. I don't even want to know that. This is a disaster in the making. Just a few hours ago, I thought this would be an exercise in self-control. And here I am, letting him dominate my will with his kiss.

He's a good kisser, but that doesn't make hooking up a good idea. I muster my determination to ignore the pang of disappointment at cutting this short.

"Enough pretending for one night," I growl, unreasonably proud of getting the upper hand.

He raises his eyebrows. It's just a microsecond of surprise before he rearranges his face into his usual arrogant grin.

"You're right. Nia is waiting anyway. I better go." He calls his goodbyes to my parents again and leaves me.

I stare at the door. Fuck him. What did that mean? Is Nia waiting to work with him, or has he been lying about their relationship and they are screwing?

His words left *my upper hand* blanketed in anger, which is my default feeling, so I should feel safe. But today it's coupled with sexual frustration and, to my utter dismay, jealousy. I hate how he makes me feel.

I hate him.

Chapter 12

Dominic

While we make frequent appearances in front of her parents, London and I barely speak for the next two weeks. We stick to pretending. Not just in terms of the fake dating, but also stubbornly ignoring the heat between us.

Our kiss after dinner with her parents was a promise, but she stomped all over it with her words. *Enough pretending for one night.* I don't believe for one moment she was pretending.

Since that night, however, "Chils" is no longer short for hot chili. My pet name for her now signifies chills. My angry, fake girlfriend transformed from a dragon into an ice queen.

I'm thinking about it all too much. I don't accept failed missions. I don't fail.

Tonight, however, there is no escaping *us*. Bianca gave us tickets for a Broadway show.

I yank at my tie, frustrated with the knot. I try to form it again. I haven't worn a suit since the day I collapsed. It feels strange. Like putting on a second skin that doesn't fit anymore.

My three-hundred-dollar tie is a noose around my neck. The premium cotton dress shirt prickles like barbed wire against my skin.

The last thing I want is to spend an evening with Chils while my wardrobe is attacking my senses.

An incoming video call buzzes from my living room and I make my way to answer.

"Isn't it the middle of the night over there?" I tilt the screen up because I can't sit. Too much nervous energy jiggling through my veins.

Rocco sits on his sofa with the baby in his huge arms. The thing is so tiny he is stroking her back with his index finger and it still covers half of her body.

"Yeah, dipshit. Newsflash, babies don't give a shit." He yawns. "Why are you wearing a suit?"

I briefly consider lying, but what's the point? "Going on a date."

Rocco chuckles while he continues to gently stroke his daughter's back. "You know that getting a lap dance in a club is not a date?"

"Fuck you, asshole. I'm dating my neighbor. We

have tickets for a show." I shove my hands in my pockets.

"You're dating? For real? That's... that's good." He draws the last word out longer than necessary, undecided. Jerk.

"It's a fake dating arrangement." He's about to say something, but I continue. "Nevertheless, it would prove to you I can maintain a relationship."

"Okay, I can see how your competitive ass is doing it to prove something to me—not that I care much—but why would *she* agree to that? What's wrong with her?" The baby fidgets in his arms and he kisses her head.

His tender action is at odds with his usual asshole behavior. Seeing him like this stirs something inside me. It feels like envy, but that makes no sense, so I file it away.

"Nothing is wrong with her," I growl, defending the angry woman who hates me a little too eagerly. "She needed a fake boyfriend and I obliged. It's good practice to find out what you keep promoting, dickhead."

"Fake relationship is nothing like an actual one. Nothing is at stake. You don't worry about losing her."

"Well, if nothing else, I'll prove relationships are boring." Kissing and provoking London Lowe is far from boring. The dynamics would change if we were a couple.

I'm not even sure why her refusal impacts me this much. Okay, I like to win. And yes, I don't remember a woman refusing me. Ever. But she isn't even pleasant company.

Rocco might be right—I'm not capable of a relationship. I'm already failing at the fake one.

"Are you sleeping with her?"

His cat jumps into his lap. He used to carry guns, run clubs where the girls fulfilled all our fantasies and more, and now he's an exhausted man with a baby and a cat. What's so attractive about that?

"No, I'm not. Yet." I regret adding the last part as soon as it leaves my mouth.

His eyes shine as he grins like a Cheshire cat. "She hasn't put out yet." Then he goes completely serious. "You lost everything in that courtroom." His voice is grave, but his expression is mocking.

"Why am I even friends with you?" I growl as he tries to swallow back his laughter. I wish the baby would wake up now and scream into his ears.

A knock on the door prompts me to check the time. "Shit, I'm late. Go be a parent while those kids are innocent enough to not understand what an asshole their dad is." I snap the laptop closed.

"You're late," London snarls the minute I open the door.

My retort dies on my lips when I take her in. Her

usually straight hair is curled in loose waves, falling around her face and past her shoulders. I've only seen her in a ponytail and suddenly I'm overcome with an intense need to fist that mane and coil it around my wrist.

She is wearing a short white fur cape. A black skirt flares out from her waist to her knees. I roam down the length of her legs and land on red stilettos. They match her clutch and her lips. I want to lick that lipstick away while I get her naked, keeping her in those heels only.

"Sorry, I was just finishing a call." I grab my keys and wallet from the console table by the door and yank my coat off the hanger.

"Why are you staring at me like that?" she asks while we wait for the elevator.

"I'm surprised you clean up so nice, Chils." I chuckle, pushing away the fantasy of riding her in those heels. And failing.

"I guess that's as good of a compliment as your small brain allows." The door slides open and she steps into the cabin, allowing me a perfect view of her behind, a seductive secret under the flowing lines of her skirt.

"You must be running low on ways to insult me." I stand beside her, avoiding another look because the first one already runs like a feature film in my head.

"It might be a misconception that lawyers are

smart, but let's face it, your brain has been eaten up by your ego. I'm shocked it fits in here with us."

"Oh, don't worry, Chils, I always make it fit." I put my hand on the small of her back under the hem of the cape and lead her off the elevator.

She growls instead of responding to my innuendo and I chuckle, earning me a shove in the ribs with her elbow. Perhaps tonight will be fun after all.

I couldn't have been more wrong. The ventilation in this place must be broken and my suit continues its performance as a scratchy blanket. London keeps frowning at my fidgeting.

To make things worse, our seats are in the middle of the damn row. My knees are practically pushing holes in the back of the man in front of me. This is why I never go to the theater.

I don't mind being an uncultured asshole if it means I get to avoid these atrocious, uncomfortable seats. The minuscule personal space and my discomfort are only mildly offset by the occasional accidental brush of London's arm against mine, or her scent wafting in my direction.

It's nothing, however, compared to the entertainment we came to witness. I think Bianca deliberately wanted to torture me. Meowing cats, crying babies and nails dragged across rusty metal combined would provide a better artistic experience than the weird musical happening on the stage.

The intermission comes way too late. When they finally draw the curtain for the break, I can't rush to the foyer fast enough. I don't even care if London follows. Fuck me.

"Not having a good time?" She catches up with me outside as I loosen my tie and unbutton my shirt's collar. Amusement laces her voice.

I study her, trying to come up with a smart remark, but God help me, if I have to return to that hellhole... I open my mouth, but before I can try to manipulate her into leaving, she surprises me.

"This is the worst play I've ever seen." She shakes her head. "And I fit into that seat." The corners of her lips quiver.

I exhale. "Thank God. Let's ditch it."

She laughs. "That's the first good idea that has ever come out of your mouth, Cressard."

"My hooking up suggestion beats it," I quip and offer her my arm.

"And the rare moment that I actually enjoyed your company is gone." She heaves an exaggerated sigh, curling her slender arm through mine, and bumps me with her hip, but it's a halfhearted protest.

We get our coats and end up in a small bistro eating nachos and having cocktails. Well, London is having one.

"You don't drink." It's not a question, but she expects an answer as she studies me with those sultry eyes.

The lighting here is low, and it lends her this enticing veil of seduction. Her feet with those damn heels are under the table, but her lips remind me of them, and my stupid cock keeps pressing against my zipper at the idea.

Fuck. London Lowe yells at me, refuses me, growls at me, insults me, and leads me to develop a shoe fetish.

"I stopped drinking six months ago."

"Why?" Her voice is husky, humming with seduction. It must be because she isn't barking her words. Yeah, that's the only reason I hear her differently.

"When I started losing interest in my life, I dropped alcohol and drugs. I used drugs only occasionally, but alcohol had become a daily occurrence over the years. I thought that with my mind cleared I'd have a better chance at identifying the problem."

"And how is it going? You look much better than when I met you." She takes a sip of her drink, her eyes pinned on me. Does she know how sexy that is?

"Are you giving me a compliment, Chils?"

Her jaw ticks before she forces a smile. Even her

fake smile is beautiful. "I'm saying you no longer look like the ghost of a lumberjack. New York's lovely winter weather suits you, I guess. Perfect conditions for your dark soul."

"Obviously." I throw the insult back at her.

She sighs. "My personality comes out warm to people who deserve it."

"Like our doorman?" I don't even know why I'm poking at her.

"You know nothing about me to judge," she snaps.

Shit. This conversation went south pretty fast. "Well, we've established that I'm an asshole."

"Finally, something we can agree on." She leans back in her chair.

"We agreed on the quality of tonight's entertainment." I smooth my tie. The suit has grown more comfortable since we left the theater.

"Jesus. What was Bianca thinking?" Chils shakes her head.

"That we'd enjoy audio and visual torture."

London laughs. And just like with her shoes, it immediately becomes an obsession. I want her to laugh more around me. I'm probably the last person she wants to laugh with though.

"Or after all these years, I suddenly discover my stepmother has weird artistic tastes."

"I only met her recently, but I have a feeling

Bianca thrives on perfection in every aspect of her life. And succeeds."

"Do you have a secret crush?" London pretends to look scandalized. "My poor father." She puts the back of her hand over her eyes in an over-dramatic gesture.

"Did you think I was coming to your place because of you, Chils?" I taunt her.

She straightens, biting her lip, but the glee reaches her eyes, and she fails at her pretense to look offended. "Well, of course you're only coming for chess, I'd hope."

"Is this a fishing expedition?" I lean in closer and she mirrors my move. "Do you want to hear I'm coming to catch a glimpse of you, Chils?" I drop my eyes to her lips and she parts them, inhaling sharply.

The air between us zaps with an unspoken need. The mood shifts and deepens into the realm we seem to always touch but never fully explore. She may fight this all she wants, but she craves me as much as I lust after her.

"I always leave when you're around to avoid you." Her words are meant to smart, but the tone is pure seduction.

I quirk my eyebrow and roll my lips, suppressing a grin. "Because you can't control yourself around me."

"London, am I interrupting?" A beautiful blond

approaches our table. And yes, she is interrupting. Fuck.

We jerk away from each other.

"Violet." London stands up to greet the woman. "We missed you at the fundraiser."

"I'm so sorry. The kids were sick..."

I tune her out. The man beside her glowers at the world around him, while simultaneously eating her up with an intense look. At first glance he looks like a bodyguard, but his eyes clearly claim the woman, so he must be more. Her husband, perhaps.

But there are bodyguards around the room, I notice. Who are these two? The woman seems familiar.

"Dominic." London's voice snaps me back to the conversation. "May I introduce Violet Mathison and her husband, Art?" London shoots daggers from her eyes. I might have ignored the initial attempt at an introduction.

"I'm sorry. Nice to meet you." I stand up and shake Violet's hand. Hearing the name, it's all coming back. I've never met her, but she was with Rocco's wife when Vanessa got stabbed.

I turn to shake Art's hand. The fucker has a mean handshake, but otherwise he just nods. Five years ago, this man made evidence disappear in Vanessa's incident with impressive efficiency.

He glares, probably recognizing me as well.

"Art, manners." Violet puts her hand on his chest and his features soften immediately. "It was nice to run into you, London." She smiles at us.

"Have a lovely evening." London beams. This is her outside persona I've seen at the gala. She plays it so genuinely, it's hard to believe it's just a mask. Or is the snarly Chils a mask for me?

"Will I see you at the hospice on the twenty-sixth?" London asks before the couple leaves.

"Yes, count on me like every year. And please, when you see him, give Andrea a nudge. I've been hunting him down for years now."

"I'll talk to him. See you soon."

The couple walks away to their table.

"I thought you said you don't talk to Andrea." I wish we could jump back into the previous intimacy, but that moment left with the Mathisons.

"Oh, I talk to him. He doesn't talk to me. I'm surprised you remember." London takes another sip of her drink, leaning back, taking her warmth and scent with her.

"I listen." I cross my legs and relax against the chair.

"Andrea is an artist. We used to be close when we were younger. I was the only sister willing to sit still for him when he was practicing drawing. When he had his first exhibition, I bought all his work. Fifty pieces. He got really mad."

"Didn't he get noticed after having sold out his first show? He should be grateful."

"Yeah, he got the recognition he deserves. Violet owns a gallery in SoHo and she's been trying to work with him. The stubborn prick thinks his start was a cheat because I bought it all."

"That's bullshit." For some reason I'm pissed at her brother for not appreciating her gesture.

"Yes and no. You've seen the pieces, they are on my wall in the living room. He's gotten much better since." She chuckles, but her eyes remain cold.

"So your brother doesn't speak to you over mediocre drawings, but you still keep them?" This woman is full of contradictions.

"I keep them to remind myself that not all good intentions are for the other person's benefit. It keeps me grounded in my work, so I don't fall for the pity trap. The people I'm trying to help deserve more than that."

I uncross my legs and lean forward, interested in this new layer of her character.

"How did you become involved with the foundation? Who was Kyle West?"

Chils stiffens and looks away for a moment. I can almost hear the war in her head, debating what she wants to share. Her hand reaches for the pendant on the chain she's always worn between her breasts. So Kyle West wasn't a random kid. She knew him.

She gestures for the server and orders another cocktail. "Kyle was the love of my life," she starts, and her words fall like a punch to my guts.

Love of her life? Shit.

"He was diagnosed with leukemia. I was scheduled to go to Paris with Paris." She snickers. "We'd just turned eighteen and we were planning our big three-month trip. Kyle didn't want me to miss out on that opportunity, and he downplayed his diagnosis so I would go." She sighs and looks away, blinking. "He wasn't... he died before I returned. I didn't get to say goodbye."

The cadence of her speech suggests she might have decided to share but doesn't want to relive the memories, rushing through her words with detachment.

That's why she so freely offered her place to her father and Bianca. And the hospice. She's creating for others what she didn't get a chance to experience with her boyfriend.

"I'm sorry." Fuck, I don't even know what to say. "You started the foundation in his honor?"

She shakes her head slightly, as though ridding herself of the memory, and turns back to me. "Yes, I started the foundation to raise funds for research and support. We award two to five fellowships every year. We also have another nonprofit that focuses on services for those who are diagnosed and their families. The hospice is a part of that. People can apply for support with anything they may need due to high medical bills or loss of income, etc."

She is animated now, the love for her work seeping through her eyes, body, and tone.

"That's a lot of work and goodwill." I reach for her hand and rub my thumb on the soft skin around her knuckles. She tenses but doesn't recoil.

"Never enough, Dominic, never enough." She sighs, and I realize that in her line of work, every win is just a small step in the right direction. It's only a stepping-stone to move to the next issue. How must that feel?

I thrive on getting shit done. Yes, there is always another case, another client, but I get satisfying closure with each case. London hangs between a small step forward and a thousand steps remaining to be taken. No wonder she carries so much frustration with her.

"Okay. What about you? There is so much good one can do in the world, so why would you choose the opposite?" It's a jab, but she asks with a curiosity that doesn't carry a critical undertone.

My hand is still on hers and the burn of the simple touch is sending signals all over my body. She leans closer, her eyes full of attention. And somehow, even though the topic is darker and the mood is heavier, we find intimacy again.

"Not everything is black and white, but in my case I can honestly confirm I made my choices for selfish reasons," I drawl, speaking into her ear. Goosebumps sprout on her neck and I want to trail my tongue there.

I keep my face close to her profile, unreasonably satisfied when her breath hitches and she swallows a few times.

"That's a dose of unexpected self-reflection." She drops her other hand to my knee. "I must say it's somewhat attractive to see you admitting your failures."

I snort. "Oh, don't mistake my words, Chils. I never fail." My lips brush her ear as I whisper the words, a challenge and a threat.

She sucks in a breath and her nails dig into my skin through my slacks before she relaxes them again. I glance at her heels and fuck me, my cock demands attention.

She fidgets a bit and notices the growing tent in my crotch.

Our eyes lock and she raises one eyebrow. "Aroused much?"

Chapter 13

London

Since when is a conversation about someone's shitty career a turn-on? The way he's been looking at me since he opened the door earlier tonight has my body taut with arousal.

The man has this miraculous ability to hit all my sensitive spots at the same time without even touching me. I got to his door earlier annoyed by his lateness, but he shifted the mood immediately.

His body emanates energy that sucks me into a vortex of lust. The lack of self-control is driving me nuts. I hate not having control. And with Dominic Cressard, I'm barely hanging on to it.

His eyes are full of intent, the almost violent desire of a predator. It shocks me that I want to play that game. I want to be his prey, because somehow my body knows I will enjoy every minute of it. The idea is outrageous. Outrageously appealing.

The elevator has never felt this small. It's just me and Dominic, and if I move, the car will explode.

My body is charged with want. No, not want, with an all-consuming, burning need. We stand beside each other, but he might as well have me cornered because I'm trapped.

I was grateful for Violet's interruption earlier. Without my permission, my eyes were pulled to his full lips, and the last thing I want is to complicate things between us. I don't care how much my core clenches in disagreement.

Do I engage in casual sex? Yes.

Do I find Dominic physically attractive? Yes.

Do I want to run into him all the time afterward? No, says my head. Yes! Yes! Yes! screams my body.

We get out of the elevator and I angle toward my door. "Good night, Dominic."

He chuckles, the bastard, and doesn't bother responding. He knows I'm running. It's one thing not being able to control myself around this man. It's completely different—in a horrifying way—that he knows about it.

I don't look back, but the task of retrieving my keys from my minuscule clutch proves impossible. Dominic, on the other hand, opens and closes his door a bit too quickly.

I tilt my head, pressing my forehead against the door and letting out a long, loaded breath. The next breath doesn't fill my lungs with enough oxygen. I vibrate with need and lust while the person who can help me is only a few steps away. Within reach.

No. No. No.

My vibrator will have to do. I close my eyes, and the images of Dominic in his bespoke suit immediately flash through my mind.

The fabric hugged his muscles like a second skin. I see men in suits all the time, but I swear, no one wears it with Dominic's charm. It's like sex personified in dark blue fabric.

What do I do every year around this time? I travel and enjoy life with an open mind. Fully. Unapologetically. Recklessly. Getting myself lost in adrenaline sports and crazy adventures.

A bit of recklessness here in New York can't hurt.

With my fake boyfriend.

Right. Fucking. Now.

I cross the distance to his door and knock. *Open up quickly before I change my mind.*

He does, and Jesus, it was worth it just for that look. His eyes darken. He rolls his shoulders and cracks his neck. He's the tiger and I'm the hare, and while I want to zig-zag and hop away, my heart hammering in my chest, I know I can't escape.

He took off his jacket already and loosened up his tie, and this slightly undone version of him is even more attractive.

"Aroused much?" He throws my earlier words back at me.

"This was a stupid idea." I'm not letting him humiliate me. Before I can turn, he grabs my arm and pulls me inside, kicking his door closed.

My back hits the wall and Dominic's mouth crashes against mine. He tastes like lemons and sin, his tongue pulling me into a dance that gets my body into a tug-of-war with my head. The head is losing miserably.

He fists my hair and angles me to deepen the kiss. I drag my nails down his chest to his waistband and yank at his belt, fiddling with the buckle until he lets out a guttural sound that has my core clenching again.

I gyrate my hips and try to unfasten his belt at the same time. Desperate. Needy. So not me. Damn it.

I wince when Dominic pulls away, whips me around and pins me against the wall, holding both my hands behind my back.

"What the fuck?" I snarl, trying to get away, but his grip never loosens. I wrestle even as I enjoy the inability to move. This is so confusing.

He leans into me, the expanse of his spectacular

torso solid against my back. His shaft hardens against the small of my back. I'm trapped between his heat and the cool wall. Between the need to take over and the arousal, his dominance spreads through my veins.

"My house, my rules. I'm in charge, Chils."

His words scrape my skin like sandpaper, absurdly igniting more heat. The resulting fire is partially my reaction to his breath amplifying my lust, and partially the anger brewing in the back of my mind. Who does he think he is?

But all my fight leaves me when his hand rakes up my leg, under the hem of my skirt. He cups my center, the intrusion violent and fantastic. I gasp.

Somehow I free my hand and grab his arm, not to remove it from my sensitive flesh and not to encourage him further, just grasping for some balance. Physically and mentally.

I dig my nails into his forearm. Dominic groans, grazing my neck with his teeth, probably leaving love bites all over. Branding me.

"What are you doing?" I try to jerk away and the bastard chuckles. Oh, but how that rumble in his chest, his scent and his heat on my skin reverberate through me.

I don't like the situation on principle, but my blank mind doesn't have the power to push back against this pleasure.

With one yank, he has my tights and underwear down to my knees. I don't even get a chance to move, and Dominic is covering my body again. I try to push off the wall, but he doesn't budge.

"Fuck—" My fight dies again when he pinches my clit. I gasp, arching my back, my butt pushing into his erection.

He chuckles again. "That's what I thought."

I want to battle for dominance. God, I want this to happen on my terms, but my body is too far gone to care. I moan as Dominic continues stroking and pinching between my swollen lips, the tingling already building in my stomach.

"You're so wet for me, Chils. I can't wait to fuck you with my tongue, my fingers, my cock." His voice covers me like a seductive blanket, and along with his hand between my thighs, they push me out of my head. My ability to think vanishes.

"Be a good girl and spread those sexy legs for me."

And to my shock, I do as I'm told. I'm rewarded when he plunges not one, not two, but three fingers into my wetness, stretching me and driving me crazy with need. He starts moving, and the friction of his palm against my sensitive bud is too much. The sensory overload turns me into a puddle in his arms.

But before I collapse, he snakes his other arm around my waist and holds me up.

"Fuck, Chils, you're so tight. Beautiful. Don't you love it when I'm in control?"

"Keep dreaming, Cressard." I don't even know how I strung those words together.

He removes his hand and I moan, mourning the loss.

"Bastard."

"I'm in control. Even if it's just for tonight. You're mine to drive crazy. Mine to fuck. Mine to punish if you keep fighting me."

I should be appalled by his words. A part of me wants to jerk away and run. That part is overwhelmed by the pulsing need between my legs, the strung-out nerve endings craving release.

I hate him for his dominance, but somehow I know surrendering would be worth it. As the cold air bites into the sensitive skin of my pussy, I relent and push my hips against him.

"Say it," he orders.

"I hate you, but okay, yes, you're in charge." As much as I've opposed this, relinquishing control to him brings on relief, and another wave of arousal. Tomorrow we can go back to pretending.

Dominic twirls me around and locks his eyes with mine. "You see, Chils, I'm in control, but I have no problem getting on my knees for you, baby."

He traces my bottom lip roughly with his thumb,

letting me taste myself. Then he drops down, his intense gaze stealing the air while sending my heartrate into the stratosphere.

He rips my underwear and tights off so he can hoist one of my legs over his shoulder. Lifting my skirt, he buries his head between my thighs, trailing a series of kisses and bites up to my core.

I'm wild with a burning ache, unable to stay silent. Balanced on one leg, but supported by the amazing solid wall of his muscles, I manage to grind my hips forward.

He lets out a low laugh. "Greedy girl."

My only answer is a long moan as he spears his tongue into me. He alternates between my pussy and my clit, setting up a punishing rhythm that pushes me higher, only to slow down again, savoring me like a delicate dessert.

I'm plastered against his wall, completely at his mercy and loving every minute. His talented tongue makes up for the macho bullshit he's just pulled. And as I get closer to the edge, I realize how much I enjoy not being in charge. Perhaps that's what I needed.

"Dominic," I gasp as he sinks his teeth gently into my delicate nub. As the pain mixes with the burn pulsating through me, I nearly climax.

He grabs my ass and pushes me up, hoisting my

other leg over his shoulder. He supports me with his brawny arms, his large hands digging into my behind.

My head falls back as the orgasm rams through me. I thrash against his mouth and shake all over, screaming his name. Dominic continues to suck and lick like he never plans to stop. I'm going to die in bliss here.

By the time I come down, I've clawed flakes of paint off the wall. He lowers my feet to the ground and stands up, looming over me, practically vibrating with his own need.

He cups my face and kisses me. I taste my arousal on his lips as I continue trembling with aftershocks.

"Seems like you enjoy my lead, Chils." The asshole is proud as a peacock.

"You better stop talking, Cressard, because I'm leaving right now."

He throws his head back and laughs. He fucking laughs. I push him away and somehow surprise him enough to get away.

But for some incomprehensible reason—it must be a hormone-induced bout of stupidity—I run farther into the room instead of to his door.

My attempt is laughable, and he catches me before I get too far. He lifts me up with one arm like a vise around my waist. I kick at the air but I'm like a doll in his grasp. It's pointless and strangely arousing. The short chase and him manhandling me gets me vibrating with anticipation.

"You leave when I say you leave, Chils." His threat sends thrilling goosebumps down my spine. I heave as I try to fight his hold. And the more I struggle, the more aroused I get. And he must know it as he bends me over the backrest of his sofa.

I'm still wearing my fur cape, and it covers my head as my body tilts forward. I stretch my arms forward and slip it over my head, panting with the effort, but finally get free of the garment that has turned into a furnace.

I step out of one shoe and Dominic locks me with his pelvis. I don't know how the sofa is still standing in place because the man is strong as a bull.

"Keep your shoes on," he orders.

Any thought of protest flees, replaced by a tantalizing need to please him. I tap my toes around to find the shoe and slip back into it. All the time, he keeps me pressed against the soft leather of his beige couch.

"Good girl."

I'd never willingly admit what his words do to me.

Dominic rolls the skirt up to my waist and traces the curves of my ass. The touch is light, almost non-existent, but it echoes through me with craving. Again, I'm completely vulnerable, with my body over the sofa, my bare behind exposed to him. And again, the thrill is winning.

I push against him and feel his erection. It kicks me with a jolt of accomplishment. There is a lot of power in surrender.

As if Dominic knew the only way for me to truly climax was to let go. I should be concerned about his ability to see through me, about his unapologetic mission to break through my carefully built defenses. But I'm not. Now *that* should definitely concern me.

As he continues caressing my ass with painfully slow strokes, I fight with many conflicting feelings about our current power game. It might seem that I've lost to him, but it doesn't feel that way.

A vicious slap yanks me out of my head.

My skin burns and I gasp, the pain spreading through me violently. I can't even find my voice, because I want to protest, but damn it, I'm enjoying it too much.

"You leave when I say you leave, Chils." His hand connects with my stinging skin again. "Do you understand?" Another slap. I yelp this time, digging my nails into his sofa and biting my lips to cope with the burn. And hide a smile. Jesus.

I anticipated that Dominic would be a satisfying partner, but he plays me like a violin. I don't remember the last time a man got me out of my head.

He forces my leg up, bending my knee and holding

it against the backrest. I'm crazed with want and I keep jutting my ass toward him.

Dominic caresses my burning skin for a moment and then he straightens, and the loss of his touch pushes a whimper past my throat.

"Don't move," he orders. I'm spread for him, and God I'm dying for his touch. I hate how he commands me around and leaves me exposed,

But as I sift through my confusing emotions, I'm shaken by the realization that I trust him. I'm letting him lead because I know he will take me where I need to go.

Where that security came from is beyond me, but acknowledging it, I allow a crack in my defenses. And it fills me with relief. And an equal amount of dread.

And that's how far I get, because Dominic steals my focus again when he stretches my swollen folds with two fingers and growls an approval.

"Your pussy is a piece of art." His praise hits me right in my core, attacking all my senses. I hear a wrapper rip and then his head nudges at my opening and I sigh.

He sinks in and the burn takes my breath away. Fuck, he is big. I wish I could look, but from my position I can only sense. And that is so much better.

More intense. More consuming. More overwhelming.

It takes him a few thrusts before he's all the way in. Filling me. Stretching me. He keeps murmuring words of praise that attack me with a strange reverence. I know this is typical dirty talk, but God I need someone to validate me. This man is slowly chipping away all my walls.

He moves slowly at first before gaining a piston-like tempo. I moan and groan as our bodies slap against each other. Dominic fists my hair again and rides me like this is the last time we'll get to do this. It is the last time, after all.

The sofa slides forward with every thrust, and Dominic curses before he lifts me and lowers me to the floor, pulling my waist up so I end up on all fours. He plunges back into me, his momentum reaching a punishing pace.

"I'm close—" I pant, and Dominic withdraws completely. "What the hell?" My snarl comes out as a whimper.

He fists my hair and pulls me to him. My back smashes to his chest. How are we still both clothed?

"You will come when I tell you to." He bites the crook of my neck, strong enough to send a pulsating energy to my core.

"I hate you," I growl, but my words fall short because I'm rubbing myself against him like a horny teenager.

He laughs and spins me around, sitting back on his heels. I wrap my legs around him and he lowers me down, filling me again.

Cupping the back of my neck, he captures my lips. I attempt to grind my pelvis against him, but he grips my waist tightly, denying me the ability to move.

He chuckles against me when I groan. His tongue attacks my mouth, his hand pulling my hair painfully, but the bastard doesn't move. He is infuriating. Annoyingly skilled at driving me mad. I'm desperate. Yet, somehow, I'm wonderfully elated.

"Dominic, I swear to God," I warn, and clench around him. He sucks in a sharp breath and starts moving. Gripping my hips, he controls the pace with such power that I'm completely defenseless. And pretty sure I'll be sporting bruises tomorrow.

He moves with a languid fluidity and I want to scream, but at the same time the resulting heat is so rewarding I give up again and let him lead.

And he does. Sucking on my lips and rolling his pelvis, he drives me to the point of madness.

"You can come, Chils."

He reaches between us and pinches my clit. I don't know how, but his command and this last wonderfully painful touch send me over the edge. I fall with an intensity that erases my mind and elicits screams that scratch my vocal cords.

But I don't care, because as I clench around him, Dominic lets out a series of curses, jerking inside me as we both reach the orgasm that crashes over us, breaking us and putting us together at the same time.

It takes us a moment, or a day, to recover. My body liquefied, I cling to him and hate it, but there is no way I can move.

Dominic, on the other hand, somehow still has enough strength to stand up while holding me. He drops me on the couch without finesse and goes to take care of the condom.

Water runs somewhere inside his place, and he comes back with a washcloth. Not many situations can render me speechless, but this does. I want to snarl that I'm perfectly capable of walking to the bathroom and cleaning myself up. *But am I?*

He drops to his knees and wipes me, and I insist internally that the goosebumps sprouted due to the cool contrast of the cloth against my skin. Definitely not because I'm strangely touched by his care.

I open my mouth, because it's time to regain some dignity here, but I don't get a chance to speak.

"Shut up, Chils. I'm still in charge." The tone is matter of fact. He drops the cloth to the floor and squeezes my thighs. I gasp, the pain mixing with pleasure again.

"About that—" It's time to set him straight, because

I may have had a weak moment earlier, but no way I'm giving him more cocky self-confidence.

He pulls my hair and I whimper as his lips crash into mine. He devours me with the same dedication that brought me not one, but two orgasms earlier.

I melt under his rough handling, and for the second time tonight I come to the same conclusion. Sometimes surrendering empowers.

He drags me to the edge of the sofa and unzips my dress. "Let me see those beautiful tits, baby."

I wiggle out of my sleeves. My dress is now a scrunch of fabric at my waist. The throaty rasp that passes through his lips at the sight of my bra makes me spread my legs wider. Okay, I'll find my dignity later.

Dominic pulls down both cups at the same time, freeing my breasts. He flicks his tongue over one peak and his finger over the other, and I arch into him.

"Fuck, Chils, you're beautiful."

And I feel like a goddess. Not something I searched for. I don't have body image issues, but Dominic's praise is easily addictive. I hope there is an antidote, because there is no way I can survive this without getting another hit.

I want to take control, if nothing else for my own sanity, but his skilled tongue has me wriggling under him again.

"You're mine tonight. Stop fighting it, Chils." He

bites my nipple and I yelp, the burning ache spreading like a wildfire. The way he insists on marking my body is infuriating, but I'm past caring.

"Only tonight," I manage, though my voice shakes.

Dominic looks at me and his lips curl into that smug grin of his. He hoists me up and carries me into his bedroom, and shows me how letting go of control is good for me. The best.

It doesn't take long before I welcome his dominance with abandon. For this one night, I'm truly his, and it's so liberating I fear I won't recover.

Chapter 14

Dominic

I jerk awake. It must be still the middle of the night because the darkness is deep. I turn my head to follow the sound that woke me. The sheets rustle as London attempts to stand up unheard.

"Sneaking out on me, Chils?" I roll on to my side and prop my head in my hand.

I didn't expect any less of her. She's someone who craves control. She needs it in her life and there is nothing wrong with that, but she manages too much, especially when it comes to her own feelings.

I thought she was just an angry, bitter woman at first. But I can see now how anger is her go-to defense mechanism.

I needed to get her out of her head, so she could experience the fun beyond her carefully built shields. But I knew it would spook her. Like an animal captured in a cage—though she constructed the cage herself—she tasted freedom last night at a level of exposure unprecedented for her. And now she is running.

"I'm not doing the walk of shame once my dad is up." She pulls the sheet and wraps it around her while looking around for her things.

"There's no shame. We're dating." I smile at her pathetic attempt at modesty as she trips on the sheet sheathing her naked body.

"We shouldn't be doing this. Don't forget this is a fake relationship." She stops fidgeting around and faces me.

A cone of the street light casts shadows across her face. It's beautiful, hiding some of her features in the darkness and softening the other half with a yellow hue. Just like her, half shielded and half shining through. But I can see the shield growing stronger again.

My eyes roam down her long neck and smooth shoulders. Her skin was like silk under my fingertips last night. My cock stirs. This woman got me back in the saddle and it was fucking nirvana. To dominate London Lowe while she struggles and fights against it —at least mentally—was too satisfying.

"There was nothing fake about the way you screamed my name last night." I reach to turn on the lamp.

She sighs. "Don't get too cocky, Cressard. This was a one-off."

"Whatever you need to tell yourself, Chils."

She shakes her head and picks up her dress and shoes from the floor. "So, shoe fetish?" She dangles them on her finger, biting her lips but failing to stifle the grin.

"I didn't know about it until you showed up last night." I check my watch. "Come back to bed, Chils. Your dad won't be up for a couple of hours."

"I still need some shut-eye." She angles toward the bathroom.

"Whatever for? It's Saturday." Her need to leave is cute. Cute? What the hell? Since when do I care about cute? Also, why am I asking her to stay? That's a first for me.

I rarely bring women to my home. Mostly because when I'm at their place or in the club I can leave freely. It must be the months of unwanted celibacy that have me this possessed.

"I have people waiting for me in the hospice," she calls before she runs the water.

I flop back with my hands behind my head, grinning. I'm actually grinning. Well, I have reasons to celebrate since my virility is back.

With my few pro bono cases, a healthy lifestyle and returned libido, I might return to Chicago sooner than planned. Who would have thought that changing the scenery really works?

London comes out of the bathroom wearing her dress, her shoes still in her hands. Her hair is tucked into the back of her dress neckline.

"Are you sure you don't want to stay?" I pat the spot beside me.

She narrows her eyes, her typical mildly annoyed mask back in place. "I don't do sleepovers." She turns. "See you later."

Rolling my eyes, I jump out of bed and follow her. She picks up her cape and takes the three steps to the landing where we discarded her underwear and tights. She sighs and kicks them to the side.

"I'll get you a new pair," I offer.

"Don't bother." She turns and makes a face. "You're naked."

"You didn't mind earlier." I jog up and corner her by the door.

Cupping her face, I seize her lips. I devoured that red lipstick hours ago, but that changes nothing about the way I enjoy her lips. She smells like sex, and a hint of mint. She must have used my toothpaste in the bathroom.

She moans against my tongue, and I fist her hair.

"Dominic." She drops the shoes and grips my shoulders as I deepen the kiss, exploring her mouth.

She tastes like a combination of everything forbidden, the sinful pleasures you know you shouldn't have but still indulge in. And once you get a taste, you can't stop.

My hand wanders down the length of her beautiful body, cursing the dress that covers her skin. I lean in to reach the hem of it when we hear a commotion behind the door.

"What's going on? Oh my God. Dad." She pales and spins around to open the door. Paramedics are in the hall. Fuck.

I rush to grab my sweatpants, but by the time I get to the hallway the paramedics are gone, and Bianca and London are retreating inside. London is shaking her head and Bianca wraps her into an embrace.

"What happened?" I try to push the sense of hopelessness to the darkest corner of my mind. I've just regained my usual drive—I won't sink back into that fucking emotion.

Bianca gives me a tired, weak smile. "Fever." She explains how Micah's temperature hiked rapidly. There is always a threat of infection looming when someone's immunity is weakened by a disease or the treatment, so she called the paramedics. "He refused to go to the hospital. Hopefully it breaks by the morning. I'll go sit with him."

London dashes across the hallway toward me, her nostrils flaring. "I knew this was a bad idea. He needed me and I wasn't there." She digs her finger into my chest.

I grab her wrist. "Stop it. His fever would have spiked regardless of your whereabouts."

"But I should have been there." She yanks her hand away, but I close my grip tighter.

"Stop making yourself a victim. You should have been there? Nothing would have changed. The outcome would have been the same."

"But I would feel better. I should be with him. Support him." She wiggles her hand again, but my grip is unforgiving.

"To make yourself feel better? Listen to yourself. Chils, I know you're scared and need to blame someone. Suit yourself and use me for that if you need to. You're doing everything you can to make him feel loved and supported during this time. But if you think he wants you to put your life on hold, you're mistaken."

"That's rich coming from someone putting their life on hold," she snarls.

"Don't act stupid. We both know these two situations are nothing alike. And if you want to blame someone, let me remind you, you knocked on my door."

She raises her eyebrows. "You're right. I only have myself to blame, so please let me go so I can do just that, asshole."

We glare at each other. She's set on punishing

herself regardless of what I say. Our mutual frustration trembles through our bodies, and I want to fuck it all out of her.

I don't know how long we stand there, silently steaming with the energy that is nothing like what we shared hours ago, but similar.

Our earlier heat brought us release. The heat now brings nothing but a bitter aftertaste.

"Let. Me. Go. I need to check on Dad."

I drop her hand and watch her leave.

Fuuuuuuuuuck.

* * *

London's contradictions keep me awake for the rest of the night. She punishes herself, but by doing so she punishes those around her, keeping her distance.

With everything she does, she is the winner and the loser at the same time. She wraps her good heart in a red layer of snarl.

Her survival mechanism is ridiculous. And apparently ridiculously effective as I find myself knocking on her door the following morning.

I tell myself it's to check on Micah and make sure they don't need anything. Well, I've never been above lying. But to myself?

"Dom. How are you?" Bianca ushers me in.

"How is he doing?" I follow her to the kitchen and she gestures to a pot of coffee, her usual hospitality abandoned. I pour myself a cup and sit across from her.

She nurses her tea, lines of exhaustion marking her face. "The fever broke. Doctor is coming later today to check on him, run some tests and determine the next steps."

We sit in silence, because any hope voiced sounds pathetic in my mind. "How is Chils?"

Bianca sighs. "Lo takes on all the burden in the world and faces mortality on a daily basis through her work, but this is too close to home. Has she told you about Kyle?"

I nod.

"She's never accepted that he chose to die alone because he wanted her to enjoy her trip in Europe. She channeled that guilt and disappointment into something great, the foundation and other charitable endeavors. She also grabs all the opportunities to have fun. To live fully because she believes she needs to do it for Kyle. To experience everything he didn't have a chance to. So she spends her money on adventures. But it's been years now, and instead of finding closure and acceptance, she's learned to live with the guilt.

"She controls her environment carefully to ensure she doesn't get attached. But this is different because it's her dad. She lost her mother, her first love, and now..." Bianca reaches across the table and squeezes my hand. "I'm so glad she has you now. This is not a situation she should face alone."

I swallow the acid ball forming in my throat and squeeze back gently before removing my hand. I'm a fraud. A damn fraud.

I can't change the terms of our arrangement, but I can play her fake boyfriend so Chils can sort through her feelings. Even if it's through yelling or a hate fuck. I owe her at least that much after she unintentionally helped me out of my slump.

Her company, the case with Felicia Warner and, well, last night have contributed to my recovery. The least I can do is to stand by her at this difficult time.

"She should be out any minute. She's just getting dressed. You should go with her to the hospice. It's a humbling experience, but also empowering." Bianca takes her cup to the sink. "If you don't mind, I'm going to lie down."

I stand up, feeling strangely lonely in the middle of London's kitchen, knowing she doesn't want me here.

"What are you doing here?" She appears before I have a chance to consider what to do next.

"Good morning to you too, Chils. I'm waiting for you." I smile. She's dressed in black jeans and a light brown sweater that seems a size too big. It covers her curves like a promise. Who knew a baggy sweater could be this sexy?

Her pale lipstick makes her skin glow in contrast. Her hair is pulled into a ponytail. I clench my fists, remembering the feel of those strands in my palms.

"Why?" She pours a cup of coffee and leans against the counter, watching me. She looks exhausted, the dark shadows under her eyes profound.

For some strange reason I want to take her in my arms and figure out the way to make everything better. What is it with this streak of compassion?

"To accompany you to the hospice," I say, as if I was planning it to begin with.

She cocks her head. "Why?"

Fuck me. *Because I want to see you doing what you love so much. Because I feel like I just lied to Bianca and I want to redeem myself. Because I enjoyed last night, even before you knocked on my door.* "Is why the only word in your vocabulary this morning?" I ask instead.

She narrows her eyes. "Charming as ever, Cressard. Let's go then."

"I'm sorry I lashed out last night." Her shoulders are practically touching her ears as she sits tensely beside me in the back of her car. She's been watching the traffic outside with ridiculous dedication since we entered the vehicle.

"Understandable." I don't mind that she used me to channel her frustration, but her rationale behind it and her stubborn belief she's done something wrong don't sit well with me.

"Are *you* going to apologize?" She faces me now.

"Whatever for?" I frown.

"For calling me stupid, holding me hostage, not understanding the words let go, for..." She trails off because there isn't much she can accuse me of.

I scoot closer and she tries to recoil, but there isn't enough room. "Listen, baby, I'm happy to give you all the orgasms you need." My lips brush her ear. "Be your punching bag when you need to release your anger and frustration, or even hold your hand through this difficult time, but I won't apologize for any of it. I'm a wonderful fake boyfriend."

Her scent in my nose mingles with the warm air in the car. Her breath is a silent whisper around me. She closes her eyes, and her throat bobs up and down.

She groans. "Okay, don't apologize, but back off." Her voice lacks determination. "*Please*," she pushes through her teeth.

I chuckle and move away. She glares at me and then turns away. Escaping. Distancing. I lean back into the leather seat and don't taunt her anymore for the rest of the ride.

As soon as we arrive, I understand the appeal of Warren's investment in this street. While a bit rundown and in desperate need of revitalization, the street has charm, and some amazing real estate.

One side is lined with low rises, mostly housing mom-and-pop shops with apartments above, though many of them seem abandoned. The other side has brownstones with trees flanking the sidewalk.

I follow Chils up a flight of stairs leading to one of those houses. "How did you end up getting this building?"

"I got it a few years back. Gio helped me find it. I think it belonged to a friend of his who'd inherited it but didn't want it anymore. It's sad, this street seems to get less and less traffic, so most of the businesses have closed. Hence the developer's interest."

We enter the foyer with a small reception area. Two staff members greet Chils. I was expecting a gloomy place, wrapped in despair and grief, but this place feels... I don't know... cheerful. Or pleasantly peaceful.

A large staircase with a wooden banister coils up the back of the room and London leads me to it.

"So, are you going to shadow me or do you want to help out?" Her eyes challenge me.

I think my idea of this place was as wrong as my image of London here. I pictured her flowing in like Jackie Kennedy, shaking hands and making people feel more important than they are. I didn't think she did any actual work.

"What do you want me to do?" I sense it won't be legal advice this time, but what the hell. I've been working pro bono, I might dip my feet into volunteering as well.

We reach the upper landing. The floors are carpeted, and the walls are lined with mahogany wood paneling. Each side of the hallway has mostly open doors.

Classical music pours from the other side of the hallway, interrupting the beeping machines. If I didn't know better, I would assume we were visiting an elderly uncle. The warmth spreads through the decor.

Chils walks to the library shelves across from the landing and takes a book and a chess set. She leads me to a room.

"London, darling, how are you today?" an old man rasps, and starts coughing.

"Ralph, I see you're better than ever," London chirps, and I stare, wondering where my angry, bitter Chils disappeared to. "This is Dominic, and he knows how to play chess. I thought you two could give it a try while I'm with Maddie."

Ralph coughs again and points to a table and two wingback chairs in the corner by the door. London drops the chess box on it.

"Be good." She walks out.

"I'm always good," he calls out, only to catch another bout of coughing. Fuck. I hope he's not contagious.

"I was talking to Dominic." London sticks her head back into the door and winks at him. She fucking winks.

"She is something," Ralph rasps. "The kindest person I've ever met."

I scan him, wondering if his mind has been affected as well as his lungs. He chuckles.

"Okay, young man, she's hiding it really well, but that heart is bigger than most. And well protected. Too well, if you ask me. I tried to woo her." His shoulders shake with suppressed laughter.

I chuckle. "So do you want to play chess?"

"Can we watch porn on your phone instead?"

I've seen shit in my life, and not much can faze me anymore, but I find myself gaping. "Isn't that something you should do in private?"

"They blocked those sites on my phone. I shouldn't get too excited." He shrugs. "You would think, in a hospice center, they understand I'm waiting for death, so why would they refuse me a little peek at a nice pussy?"

"That seems fair, but I don't think I want to get into trouble my first time here."

"I see you're a pussy, just not one I'd like to see." He shuffles to the chair, parks his oxygen tank and plops down. He opens the chess box and the pawns topple, and some roll to the floor. "Fuck."

"Okay, I'll let you watch for a bit, but let's at least pretend we're playing." I sigh and slouch in the chair across from him, unlocking my phone.

"Lower the sound. Maybe next time you can bring headphones." He extends his shaking hand and snatches my phone.

While he chuckles, I set up the board.

"Papa." A voice startles both of us and Ralph drops the phone. It lands with a clank. "Oh, hello, I didn't know you had company."

"Dominic, this is my daughter, Leticia. Dom and I are playing chess."

Leticia smiles at me and then frowns at the chessboard. I move a pawn like that could save anything.

"Whose phone is that?" She leans to pick it up and the old bastard chuckles. Leticia's eyes widen. "Papa!"

I snatch the phone from her and close the app. "I should leave you alone probably." I clear my throat.

"Nonsense, sit down," Ralph orders, and I sit,

because what else can I do? "Leticia, what did the insurance say?"

She sighs and sits at the edge of the bed, fidgeting with her ring.

"The assholes don't want to pay out my disability claim," Ralph explains.

I turn to Leticia and fire off a series of questions to clarify their situation.

Before I think better about it, I say, "I might be able to help."

Chapter 15

London

I close the book and watch Madeleine sleep. Her breathing is labored but I still rejoice in her vital signs, despite the devastating knowledge that it won't be long before she moves beyond this life.

Dad's complications last night—though very typical in cases like his—weigh on my conscience, eating up my energy and determination to stay strong for him.

I should have been there, but Dominic is right, I can't be by his side all the time. The situation was nothing like, and yet so similar to my absence at Kyle's side. I lashed out because that's the only way I know how to deal with fear and hopelessness. And there is too much of the latter in my life.

This morning, after barely sleeping, I almost canceled my regular visit to the center. Facing my father's mortality on a daily basis while he remains positive and insists on his independence is proving much harder than I thought.

I wasn't really thinking about the emotional toll of my commitment. I'm dealing with life-threatening circumstances all the time. Still, I'm not prepared.

Everything seems to topple over my head. I hate this feeling. It's like my life is suspended in some sort of pilot program to test me. Living with my parents, last-minute struggles with all my projects, no party trip this year, freezing gloomy weather—it's all tearing me apart.

And let's not forget my morally gray, insanely hot and super annoying neighbor.

I shouldn't have had sex with my fake boyfriend. Despite the gravity of my family situation, my mind keeps returning to the feelings he sparks in me.

It wasn't just the mind-blowing orgasms and his talented tongue and cock, it was... Well, I don't know, but while he was ordering me around and manhandling me, I felt safe, cherished, protected, and so fucking good, all over. I was able to relax, to let go, to forget everything else.

Dominic Cressard ruined sex for me, because I've experienced a lot in that area and I still didn't know there was another level. I don't know if it's his skills—and clearly he's honed them over the years, and I don't want to think how and with whom—or just some special chemistry between us. If it's the latter, I'm screwed.

As much as I want to fight it, last night I got a taste of Dominic, and I'm not willing to let go. I fought it and attempted to run, but I can't kid myself. I need another dose. And, selfishly, I need an escape from my current life.

I just wish I knew what he was thinking. Is he considering this a fling to pass the time? An added benefit to his role as my fake boyfriend?

I need to understand his motivations, so I can protect myself, but I can't imagine asking him. How can I handle it without dealing with his over-inflated ego?

Leaving the book on Maddie's nightstand, I walk out. The hallway has a strange energy. It's too silent, no one in sight. This place is usually quiet.

While the versions of the silence are different—afternoon lull, morning calm, painful stillness after we lose someone—I know them all. But this is different. Today is Saturday, when we get the most family visits. It shouldn't be this quiet.

I walk to the other side where I left Dominic, and as I reach the open door of Ralph's room, I hear a murmur.

Several people stand around, chatting. And waiting? For what? I step inside with care, as if expecting a land mine.

Dominic is scribbling something on a legal pad, listening to a woman.

"What's going on?" I whisper. None of these people are residents because most of those are bed-ridden. I recognize a few family members.

"Dominic is helping us," says a young man beside me.

"For free." An elderly lady beams at me.

I move to stand beside him. He is focused on the woman in front of him fully but gives me a mischievous glance. The gesture clamps at my lungs.

"I thought you were playing chess." I fail to sound irritated while ignoring the wings tickling my insides.

He reaches to squeeze my hand. "Chillax, Chils, two more people and we can leave if you're ready."

"I didn't want to play chess anyway," Ralph says, without raising his eyes from a phone.

I step aside and watch the scene. Somehow, the bastard started an impromptu legal clinic in the last hour. And based on the grins and adoring looks, a successful one. I sit on the edge of Ralph's bed and wait.

I could talk to Zelda or visit other residents, but I'm somewhat fascinated by all of this. Dominic keeps taking notes, squinting occasionally. I wonder if he needs glasses and is too vain to wear them.

When he puts the pen down, he takes the woman's hands into his large ones. The memory of his touch last night swirls around my stomach, spreading a yearning ache.

He murmurs something before flashing a blinding smile. The woman giggles and practically bows before she relinquishes her seat to the next victim.

His rapport with these people spreads sweet, warm liquid through me, and I find myself smiling. It annoys me, because there is nothing happy about these people's situations. And because I don't want to feel warm and fuzzy around Dominic. I don't do warm and fuzzy.

And yet, today the usual irritation and anger that propel me forward took a day off. It must be the lack of sleep.

By the time Dominic is done, we're leaving the place like a pair of celebrities, practically applauded by family and staff members. I resent and love the attention he's getting.

"Are you giving unsolicited legal advice to unsuspecting victims? You really are looking to secure that spot in purgatory."

"Don't be jealous, Chils, this is still your baby and endeavor. It was Ralph who didn't want to play chess."

He puts his hand on the small of my back, leading me to the car.

We don't need to pretend here. I don't need someone to protect me on the streets of New York. Yet the gesture thrills me.

I suck in my breath, burying half of my face in my scarf to hide it. "Why was Ralph on your phone?"

"Porn," he says casually while opening the car door for me.

I stop and gape at him. "What the hell, Cressard? Do you have to corrupt everyone you cross paths with?"

"I don't know, Chils, have I successfully corrupted you?" He lowers his voice, and I feel every velvet tone deep inside me. My entire body pebbles at the sound. Or melts.

Swallowing hard, I slide into the seat. "You're incorrigible."

Dominic walks around and joins me. "Guilty as charged, but very innocent this time because Ralph insisted. Give the man some guilty pleasure in his old age." He winks.

"Until he has a heart attack from the excitement?" I glare at him.

Usually, when I leave the hospice, I'm wrapped in frustration and anger to mask the hopelessness. Dominic seems unaffected.

"Correct me if I'm wrong, but Ralph is there practically waiting for the inevitable. I'm pretty sure he'd be fine dying from excitement a few days early rather than continuing to wait for the end bored out of his mind."

I stare. Speechless. It sounds so wrong, yet feels somehow right. Even after all these years, I still have a tendency to overprotect the residents. I don't believe I can play God and prolong their lives, but it's a natural reaction.

Apparently, I need my fake boyfriend to remind me to actually live by my motto. The one Andrea's pictures on my wall remind me of every single day. Not all my good intentions benefit others.

"Let's have lunch, Chils." Dominic gives the driver instructions and I relax into the seat. I don't even mind he's ordering around my driver, not asking me if or where I want to eat.

I'm not annoyed because it feels good to let someone take care of me. I really am tired.

He takes me to a posh bistro in SoHo.

"How do you even know about this place?" I ask as we wait to be seated. The restaurant teems with activity.

"I overheard two women talking about it at the gym." He turns to talk to the hostess.

"You're paying attention to other people's conversations while working out?" I follow him around tables full of delicious meals and inviting aromas.

"I'm paying attention to women."

Of course he does.

He pulls a chair out for me then bends too close to my ear. "Always." A whisper of breath touches me, igniting another involuntary reaction that reaches my core. My body is getting seriously addicted to this man.

"So, what kind of services does your nonprofit offer?" Dominic spreads the linen napkin across his lap.

"Anything they need, but beside the hospice, we mostly help people navigate the system: dealing with appointments, insurance, banks, any part of their life that is impacted by their diagnosis. I have a team of people who call around, source things, apply to programs, look for support groups, et cetera."

"It looks like you could benefit from a legal clinic." He splits a warm bread roll and pops it into his mouth.

"Yeah, but I don't have the resources to start such a project, so we refer our clients to other clinics in town."

"Yeah, but the needs of people with cancer, or any other life-threatening or debilitating diseases, are different. Having a clinic specific to the issues of people with terminal illness or long-term disabilities and their family members could improve their quality of life significantly."

"You're not wrong, but my focus has been research. The support arm of our services is something that sprung up organically based on necessity. And yes, there is way more we can do, but not enough funding or time to tackle it."

"Perhaps I could help." He cocks his head.

"You really are hoping to avoid hell."

He shocked me this morning when he wanted to come along. I thought it was just because he felt bad how we left things last night. I thought it was an empty gesture.

"Why are you so set on reminding me that my practices don't meet your standards?" He shakes his head, scowling.

"They *don't* meet moral, and most times, legal standards in general."

"And yet you seemed to enjoy my immoral tongue last night." He wiggles his eybrows, avoiding the topic. But at least that gives me a segue.

"Talking about last night. I have a proposition. You're here for a few more months—let's enjoy it." I lick my lips.

Dominic leans back in his chair. If his chest puffs up any more, he might burst like a balloon.

The typical grin on his face turns a new shade of obnoxious as he runs his thumb across his lower lip, savoring the moment. Bastard.

"I thought you didn't think it was a good idea." He cracks his knuckles.

"Oh, it's the worst idea, but we're not impressionable teenagers, so we can deal with it. It's not as though we even like each other enough to fall in love. Why not have fun?"

"I like you just fine, and given that you first propositioned me with fake dating and that's not enough, now you're proposing, what..." He gestures between us with his finger. "Friends with benefits? I think you like me too, Chils."

"More like enemies with benefits, and if you keep talking the deal is off."

The server brings our salads and I spear a tomato with unnecessary force.

"Don't be sensitive, baby. I'm all in." He licks his lower lip languidly and I squirm in my seat, because somehow I felt that stroke of his tongue on my skin.

"We should set some rules." My voice is too husky. Damn it.

"Of course." He rolls his eyes and turns his focus to his salad. Thank God. If his gaze continues to fuck me here, I might need a change of underwear before we leave.

"No sleepovers, and no spontaneous getting together. Only scheduled liaisons are allowed."

"Not ready to give up control, Chils?" He chuckles.

"Take it or leave it." This is a terrible idea, but the memory of that smirking mouth eating my pussy overrides any lingering doubt.

"Oh, I'll take it, but I have some rules of my own." He pats the napkin at the corner of his mouth. Jesus, everything the man does is sexual.

"I wouldn't expect any less of you, *boyfriend.*" I lean back, crossing my arms over my chest, ready to negate the whole deal.

"I'm in control, and you'll do as I ask." His words sink into my core, spreading heat, and it takes all my willpower not to squirm as my pulse bounces from my temples to the now soaked area between my legs.

Dominic cocks his eyebrow, his jaw tight, his features dangerous. His look is predatory and threatening in every sense of the word. And so fucking hot.

"Okay." I breathe out my consent, but he hears me because the self-assured grin returns.

"And no condoms."

My fork drops. "Are you out of your mind? I don't know where your dick has been."

"Are you on birth control?"

"Yes, but—"

"I'm clean, and I have no problem getting tested again. I trust you're clean as well. If I'm going to commit to one partner, which isn't really my thing, I want a benefit that makes it..." His pause is filled with a current that zaps through me like fire. "Worth my while." He reaches for my hand and kisses my knuckles. "And yours, of course."

He obviously fucked my brain away last night because my next words are reckless. "Okay, no condoms." I'm so aroused from this conversation, I can't wait to get home and put my vibrator to good use.

"Have you finished?" Dominic gestures to my half-eaten bowl.

"Yeah."

He gestures for the bill.

"Go to the ladies' room and wait there." Pure sin laces his tone, while dominance oozes through his eyes. Goosebumps cover my skin.

"What?" Oxygen hits only the top of my lungs.

Everything around me peaks in intensity. The sounds—the hushed conversations around us, the clanking cutlery, the splash of water somewhere, clinking ice, even the suppressed sounds of traffic outside.

The colors—the bright room seems to dim around me, zooming all its light in on Dominic. The rest of it turns into a blur.

The aromas—tantalizing steak on the next table, fresh lemon in Dominic's water, and his own scent of musk and pheromones. It all hits me as I consider his words. The promise and the threat. The expectation behind them.

"You heard me. Go now, Chils." He growls.

A newborn fawn could walk with more grace than I do as I make my way to the bathroom. I'm not aware of anything around me, and hyper-aware of everything at the same time. It's the strangest state of desire that propels me to action.

A woman washes her hands and smiles at me in the mirror. I pull out my lipstick and trace it over my lips, my heart jerking, probably trying to learn its function.

The bathroom is upscale—marble vanities lit with dim spotlights and a clean lavender smell reminiscent of an esthetician's salon. The dark brown and gold decor gives the small space an intimate vibe.

The woman leaves, and before I can even check if there is anyone else in one of the three cubicles, Dominic barrels in, grabs my arm and pulls me with him into the middle stall.

He locks the door and, moving soundlessly, crooks his finger in the waistband of my jeans and tugs me to him. He unfastens the button, his heavy-lidded gaze eating me alive.

His breath—fresh lemon and carnal hunger—feathers across my face, but he doesn't lean in to kiss me.

"Don't move," he mouths. He squats and yanks my jeans and underwear down to my ankles. I look down, my body shaking as he doesn't move either.

He's not touching me. The bastard is only breathing on my skin, but my body is experiencing a complete shutdown. And a revival.

My mouth is dry, my heart is pounding, my stomach is in a knot, my center is literally leaking and all my nerve endings vibrate with anticipation. I want to lean forward, drag him up and capture his lips before I set his cock free to fuck me.

But his *don't move* order stops me from doing it. I agreed to relinquish control, and stopping myself from rushing into things is maddening in the most wonderful and frustrating way.

Dominic blows lightly between my legs. I gasp and my knees buckle, but he digs his large hands into my ass. I lean into it, using his strong arms as a sort of chair, because my legs are no longer working. And he hasn't touched me yet.

"You're such a good girl, Chils. Show me that beautiful wet pussy." I shuffle to stand as wide as possible with my jeans binding my ankles.

Dominic takes off my left shoe and pulls my jeans off completely. He doesn't bother with the other side and lifts my freed leg onto the toilet seat. This stall isn't big enough, but somehow the mountain of a man fits, kneeling in front of me.

"You better hold on, baby," he drawls and latches onto my clit with such vigor I yelp.

The door clicks and voices reach us. I freeze, but Dominic doesn't seem impacted by the women who now chat at the vanity by the sounds of it.

I grasp Dominic's hair, biting my lip and focusing all my consciousness—and by now I have little left—on staying silent while the heat spreads across my body, consuming me with a need so powerful I might just give up and scream. And not care as long as Dominic continues driving me toward this climax.

Luckily, the women leave before the orgasm hits me. On instinct, I pull away because the sensation is too much, but Dominic doesn't let me escape. He digs his fingers into the flesh of my behind and continues feasting on me as if my juices were the fountain of life.

When he is finally done with me, I'm shaking so hard, I might need to stay here for a few hours before I can exit decently.

He stands up and kisses me, letting me taste myself. I freeze when the door opens and someone else comes in, but my *boyfriend* doesn't care. He keeps devouring my lips while he pulls down his zipper.

Oh my God, I can't imagine keeping quiet if he

continues his assault, and his dark voice confirms he agrees with me. "On your knees, Chils."

"Jesus," someone says. Heels echo through the room and the door clicks again.

"Fuck," I growl.

"You better hurry, sweetheart." Dominic fists my hair and I sink to my knees.

I wrap my hand around his base and take my time, dragging my tongue over the underside of his hard shaft. I swirl it over his head, already sheathed with droplets of his arousal.

Dominic sucks in a sharp breath and I look up before taking him into my mouth. He is breathtakingly beautiful, staring at me with hooded eyes. He plasters his hands on the door behind me. I hollow my cheeks and take in as much of him as I can.

"God, you're so fucking beautiful. Such a good girl, Chils." His words tingle where his tongue was just minutes ago and I grind my hips, clenching.

I brace my hands on his impressive quads and watch as he comes undone while he fucks my mouth.

I'm on my knees, my eyes filled with tears, gagging and struggling to take all of him, yet seeing what my mouth does to him makes me feel powerful.

Someone might have come in again, but I'm so enthralled with his taste, his smell, the feel of him, the look of him, that I tune out the rest of the world.

All my senses are sharply focused on this man. On the way I make him feel and the thrill I draw from it. Never have I given a blowjob and gotten this close to coming myself.

"Fuck," he grits out. "Swallow every single drop, Chils."

Clicks of heels and scandalized curses play in the background as Dominic opens his mouth, swearing mutely, and ropes of his cum trickle down my throat, almost choking me.

He pulls me up so fast by my hair I yelp, but he swallows the sound with his mouth, his lips and tongue urgent. His kisses are never tender, but this time the fervor feels like gratitude, and I take it all with an enthusiasm that is scary and foreign to me.

Dominic helps me get dressed, not even bothering with cleaning up. He unlocks and pushes me out, and I stumble as I see two women fixing their makeup in the mirror. Shit, I didn't realize someone was still here.

What was I thinking?

I wasn't.

For a few ecstatic moments, Dominic erased my constant worry. Just like last night.

I amble to the sink and wash my hands. They watch me. *Okay, bitches, don't be jealous.*

Dominic strolls out of the cubicle and they gasp,

staring at him. He washes his hands next to me and kisses my temple.

"Ladies." He bows his head and leaves, whistling. The bastard. Two pairs of eyes peer at me as heat spreads through my cheeks.

I look down, meticulously rinsing away the soap while my arousal still stains my inner thighs. When I lift my eyes, I focus on the smile softening my face.

And like lightning, trepidation hits me. Not because my very public sex with Dominic filled me with thrill. But it's filled me with expectations, and I wonder just how casual this liaison can remain.

Chapter 16

Dominic

The club is dim, loud and humid, filled with people's sweat and the stench of alcohol. Glowing lights illuminate the dance floor. Bass bounces around the walls and the floor, reverberating through my shoes. Roaming servers dressed in tiny dresses with flickering headbands hand drinks to people who no longer know how to behave. This is hell.

Have nightclubs always been like this? I've never shied away from a party, but I really don't like it here.

I lean against the white bar. The side planes beneath the bar top keep switching colors, not adding much to the decor, but adding to my headache. Someone bumps into me and my soda sloshes over my wrist. Fuck me.

It's an upscale club that boasts an invitation-only

clientele, but it might as well be a pig stall. Either I have to start drinking again or this is my last night at a place like this.

Lesson number one, I hate clubs when sober. Lesson number two, New Year's Eve would be better spent fucking my fake girlfriend.

The girlfriend who is swaying on the dance floor with her twin sister.

How did I ever think they were the same person? They're identical on paper, but they are so not in real life. Right now they are both drunk, and I feel like a bodyguard.

The asshole in a booth to my side, dressed in a three-piece suit, is watching London's ass. My jaw ticks.

I want to admire her rocking hips, but instead I'm darting my eyes around like a hawk, scowling at all these drunken assholes who dare to look at my woman. Well, my pretend girlfriend. But still.

Over the past couple of weeks, London's rules have become loose guidelines. As fake as our relationship status.

She can pretend there is no spontaneous sex, but on numerous occasions she insisted on *scheduling* the session when my tongue was already deep down her throat long enough to soak her underwear. She put it on our calendars mere seconds before I dragged her skirt up.

She won't admit that she's failed at maintaining her distance. Instead, she schedules sex daily. I'm not complaining.

The only rule she diligently follows is no sleepovers. And I'm fine with that as well. The perfect relationship.

I will miss this arrangement once I'm gone. Especially since clubs are my primary spots to pick up women, and it's clear I'm not setting foot in this type of place sober anymore.

The suit is now practically drooling over Chils. He stands up and I put my soda down and walk over to him, cracking my knuckles. He steps back, maybe sensing my energy. Smart guy.

"Having a good night?" I cock my head.

"Do I know you?"

Two of his friends stand up.

"Happy New Year, dipshit. And if you want to celebrate without a broken nose, you'll stop ogling my woman."

He snorts, shaking his head and my fists curl up.

"You better watch her yourself, then." He nods toward the dancefloor.

I look over my shoulder and growl. London dances around a man who looks like steroids are his only nutrition. He leans in and tells her something and she shakes her head and raises her arms, gyrating around him. The asshole yanks her to him and whispers into her ear.

My vision blurs as irritation claws its way through my muscles. I launch forward even before I see his hand on her ass. She pushes him away, but he doesn't budge.

"Get your hands off of her or she is the last thing you will ever touch." Blood is rushing into my temples.

Even over the loud music, I hear Paris gasp. I'm faintly aware the activity around me slows down, but my focus remains on the asshole and Chils. I'm seconds away from ripping him apart.

My warning takes him by surprise and London extracts herself from his roaming paws. Music and some unfamiliar emotions roar in my head.

"Dominic, you came to dance." London stumbles and falls into my arms. Annoyingly cheerful, she's completely oblivious to the tension.

Unexpected affection squeezes at my chest as I feel her in my arms. At the same time, fury and an irrational sense of ownership settles in. Unsettling me. What the hell am I doing?

"I don't dance. We're going home. Now." I twirl her around, so she faces the general direction of the exit, and look behind to get Paris.

London pivots back and collapses against my chest. "But it's New Year's Eve. Don't be such a party pooper." She beams at me. Her genuine smile is like a sucker-punch to my gut.

Lesson number three, it takes six shots and a bottle of champagne for Chils to smile sincerely. Interesting. What's even more interesting is the warmth it spreads through me, and the desire to have her smile at me like that more. For real.

I hate night clubs.

"It's not New Year's *Eve* anymore," I growl. "It's January first. Let's go."

"London, baby, I need to talk to you." The steroid douche tries to get to her. *Baby?*

"Ash, fuck off." London swats at him and dances around me, grinding her pelvis into my hips.

I'm all for a private show, but right now a vein is threatening to burst out of my neck.

Clearly *Ash* has no self-preservation instincts because he pushes between us. "I need your help. I fucked up and Hunter is really pissed—"

His T-shirt rips as I grab him and toss him to the side.

"What the—" His protest is swallowed by the music and the crowd as he staggers backward.

"Let's go," Paris chirps and grabs London's hand, dragging her away.

I throw a hundred-dollar bill to the woman minding the coat check to get us out as quickly as possible.

"You're jealous, Cressard. My lawyer fought over me." Chils giggles, hooking her arm in Paris's as they both stumble out of the club.

I try to control my breathing as I crack my knuckles. Chils is completely oblivious to my mood, which pisses me off more.

"Who was the dickhead, *baby*? And I'm not jealous," I roar. "But I won't stand by while someone ogles and touches you." The irrational, dark energy spreads through me like poison.

"That's so romantic." Paris shimmies her shoulders.

Fucking women. I turn my back on them and look at the sky, but no comfort comes from there, so I whirl back. "Who was he?" I don't even know why I'm insisting on this.

"Who? Ash? I met him when Sydney started dating Hunter." London spreads her arms and sways as though she wants to fly.

I swear to God I'll need dentures if I don't relax my jaw soon. It might be the fresh air or the aftermath of her shiny smile. Or simply the fact we're out of the glimmering hellhole, but my anger dissipates slightly.

It's replaced by the realization I just acted like a caveman. London Lowe inspires this kind of behavior in me. The fact rolls around my stomach like an undigested meal. Why do I care?

I shake my head and assess the street. It's freezing, and the chance of a cab is non-existent with thousands of locals and tourists roaming the streets in celebration.

I look at the two women by my side. Paris is bundled in a long fur coat, but Chils—who doesn't spend money on unnecessary things—shivers in her short fur cape. Fuck me.

"Do you have your driver waiting?" I take off my coat and put it around her shoulders.

"Of course not. I gave him a week off to spend with his family. I'm not some cruel slave master." She wraps her arms around my waist.

I want to ask her what the driver's name is because I'm sure she doesn't know, but I bite my tongue. Now is not the time—or temperature—for arguments.

Also, I enjoy how her warmth spreads through me. A drunk Chils smiles and clings, and I kind of like this version.

It scares the shit out of me.

"Happy New Year, boyfriend," London yells, raising her arms above her head and doing a little dance.

Paris joins her and soon they are both doubled over in a fit of laughter. If I wasn't half frozen, I might enjoy the sight.

Right now, I'm more worried about getting two tipsy women home without catching pneumonia, and ignoring the feelings swimming in my bloodstream.

The club is only a few blocks from our building, but it may as well be on another continent by the time we get there. I doubt even a hot shower will make me feel warmer. Or less annoyed. Fucking Ash, and all the other assholes.

Chils leans into me in the elevator and her body soothes me a bit. I can't help myself and kiss her hair, and she makes a noise somewhere between a sigh and a moan.

"You guys are so cute." Paris yawns.

I look at us in the mirror. Paris is the only person who knows we aren't truly dating, but I have to agree with her, this moment is anything but fake. I don't want to define it.

"Happy New Year." Paris kisses us both before she stumbles into Chils's apartment.

"Thank you for defending my honor tonight." Chils looks at me through hooded eyes, her hands gripping the lapels of my suit.

There is kindness in her eyes, and I want to remember this moment forever because she feels like home. And because there is no way I want—can allow myself—to explore this closeness. I don't do shit like this.

"And thank you for your coat." Her voice is breathy, and I wish I didn't find her so irresistible.

I lower my lips to hers. She tastes like alcohol, but even if she didn't, the kiss is intoxicating. She moans against my mouth and parts her lips.

I angle her head and savor the softness and warmth of her. I cup her cheeks. They are freezing cold, but still, touching her sends heat through my body.

As always, my mouth on her fills me with need, but tonight it also spreads a new feeling of warmth everywhere. It's different. More intimate. More vulnerable. Definitely scarier.

Abort. Abort. Abort.

"I better go take a hot shower. I'm freezing. Good night, Chils. See you tomorrow."

She pouts. "But we have an appointment scheduled for the end of the year."

"Officially, it's already the first. Go to sleep, sweetheart. No sleepovers, remember?" I shove her gently toward her door. She mumbles a protest, but yawns at the same time and doesn't argue.

I almost beat up a guy or two today, and then a smile and a kiss scare the shit out of me. What the actual fuck?

I need to keep some distance. Two things made last night the worst New Year's Eve ever. First, I felt Chils was mine—mine to protect. Fat lie.

Second, the weird, fuzzy feeling that crept over me when she stumbled into me, smiled at me, wrapped her arms around me, or later when I kissed her good night. I don't do fuzzy.

The gym is still closed, so I go for a run. The frost prickles my lungs like a thousand little needles, but I don't stop. Unlike other mornings when I drag my ass out early for a run, today I don't cross paths with other runners.

The park is littered with confetti, bottles, several partygoers and some poor assholes from the clean-up crew.

My head is littered with unwanted feelings.

Fuck.

Feelings? The worst New Year's ever.

And I don't even count the stupid bar. I need to hit Roxie's to reinstate some balance in my life. To feel like me again. How would Chils feel about me getting a lap dance?

Why do I care?

I run faster, but the Arctic-like air makes me wheeze and I turn around before the much-needed endorphins hit.

I don't feel any better by the time I reach my building.

"Happy New Year, Mr. Cressard." Cesare opens the door and survivable temperatures envelop me.

"I told you to call me Dominic. Happy New Year." I want to get out of here because Cesare doesn't deserve my foul mood.

"If you don't mind, my wife baked some banana bread for you." Cesare dashes behind the concierge desk and pulls out a box.

"Thank you." I take it and turn to leave.

"Share it with Ms. Lowe. It's her favorite."

That stops me. Cesare is clearly observant and noticed that we're spending time together. But that's not what surprises me. The woman doesn't even know his name.

"How do you know it's her favorite?"

"My wife sent her one after she helped me keep this job. She told me it's the best she's ever had."

"Are you sure you didn't speak to her sister?" The story prompts me to walk back to him.

"I know, those two look so similar, but only at first glance." He chuckles. "Ms. Lowe witnessed a woman harassing me for something that was her own fault. She used to live in the penthouse. A bitter woman. Anyway, she tried to get me fired and I would have lost this job, but Ms. Lowe intervened.

"She helps everyone. Her driver sometimes sneaks in for coffee when he waits for her, and the woman really goes beyond and above helping people. You would never know by the scowl she wears on her face." He chuckles again and then goes rigid. "I shouldn't have... I don't gossip about—"

"Relax, Cesare, I'm glad you told me. I think that scowl is permanent damage by now," I joke, but it falls flat, mostly because I don't enjoy making fun of Chils. Unless it's to her face. I thank him again and make my way upstairs.

So, she doesn't know the doorman's or her driver's names, but she still takes care of them. The woman makes sure the wall around her is impenetrable, without forming personal attachments. That's good. Easier for me to stay on the right side.

Maybe last night was just a result of adrenaline and cold. I get off the elevator and consider wishing Happy New Year to Micah and Bianca, but I decide to stay away.

What good would come from growing attached to her family? I'm leaving in three months. Perhaps sooner.

I spent Christmas with them, and it was the best holiday I've had in years. My family doesn't give a shit about inviting me anymore, and usually I just go somewhere exotic.

Bianca hired a chef, Paris talked a hundred miles an hour, Micah didn't feel well enough to play chess. London's brother Gio kept staring into empty space and everyone fussed around him because it was apparently weird that he didn't spend the day on his phone. Overall, it wasn't a great night, and yet the best Christmas for me.

And that's the problem. I'm alone here, so I'm grateful for any company. Perhaps I should head back to Chicago at the end of this month. Right after I complete the pro bono cases I've started.

I can get Nia involved and work with her remotely. I don't need to stay here longer. I'm pretty sure I've recovered.

I get home, take a hot shower, and have several slices of the banana bread. It really is very good. I'm about to open my laptop when someone knocks.

Alarm bells sound in my chest as my eyes land on Paris.

"What's going on?" She looks even more like London without makeup.

"Nothing. Well, London is sick."

My stomach tightens. "You drank a lot last night." But even as I say it, I know Paris wouldn't come over if it was just a hangover.

She shudders. "Don't remind me, but Lo has a fever. It's probably just a cold, but it's dangerous for

Dad. He can't catch anything right now. Can she stay with you? I mean, she is protesting and wants to go to a hotel, but—"

"Of course." I dash across the hallway, Paris on my heels.

I march straight to London's bedroom. Curled in the fetal position, in the middle of her bed, she looks so small. I swipe her sweaty hair from her face and she groans.

"Fuck, Chils, I'm buying you a new coat." I scoop her up and she groans again.

"Leave me be. I just need to sleep." Her protest falls short as she snuggles her face into the crook of my neck. Her skin is like a furnace.

I don't know how to care for a sick person. But that doesn't stop me from carrying her across the hallway to my place. She is sick, but she is breathing, and she is in my arms.

I can protect her. I need to protect her. I'll sort out what those feelings mean later.

"Hopefully the fever breaks soon. I need to go home and pack for my skiing trip, but if you need anything, call me. I'll write down my number, and Sydney's too," Paris says as I stride into my bedroom. "Thank you," she sighs, hesitating in the door. "Maybe I should cancel my trip."

I place Chils gently in my bed and tuck the

comforter around her. "You don't have to. Go ski. I'm sure she'll sleep through this and be better by tonight."

* * *

I couldn't have been more wrong. By the late afternoon, London is burning up.

"Where is my cat?" She pats around her. "I want my Kitty."

Jesus, she's delirious. She doesn't even have a cat. She keeps patting the bed, then falls into a restless slumber.

She hasn't drunk or eaten anything and I'm out of my mind. I sit in the bed with her and hold her because, fuck, I don't know what else to do.

I'm soaked in her sweat, but I don't let go, although my body heat is probably not the best thing for her.

Screw it. I'm so out of my depth here. I scoot her to the side and go to get a glass of water, and my phone to call the doctor I used to have on call for the Da Bonno family.

Her chest expands and contracts as she breathes. The frantic flutter under her eyelids confirms her body or mind is fighting something.

My eyes study the curves of her face. Ridden with her constant worry, fighting the sickness, and so beautiful even as she glistens with sweat. Light from the window dances across her pale skin. I want to touch her, but she looks so fragile.

I wait for the physician, sitting by her side, help-less. I hate the hopelessness taking residence in my heart. I'm lost here. Unable to help her, but also scared shitless by all the emotions.

This morning I was sure I would start pulling back from her. But the universe laughed at me and threw me into this situation, challenging me to prove I don't care. But I do. I fucking do.

The doctor leaves me with strict instructions to keep her hydrated and to take her to the hospital if her fever doesn't break. So much for help.

I search online restlessly and text with Rocco, who is luckily awake with his own care-taking shit.

London is thrashing in my bed as if she is having a nightmare, and I'm pacing around like a caged animal. Fuck this shit.

I follow Rocco's advice, only because it was suggested in one of the online forums as well, and wet a large towel. After pulling London's T-shirt over her head, I wrap her in the cold towel and then in a thick blanket and the comforter.

And I wait. And sit. And pace. And sit again. The fifteen minutes lasts an eternity, an endless road stretching before me to a dark place littered with dread.

I slowly unwrap her while she moans and, shit, I would give anything to switch places with her.

I repeat the process three more times before the fever breaks. I force her to drink a bit of water and she swallows and falls asleep again.

Without protesting or fussing, which would be great if this was anyone else. Obliging London only intensifies my dread. *Please just get better, Chils.*

Seeing her without any fight left in her is up there with collapsing in the middle of the courtroom. A gut-wrenching realization of potential loss. Is this the feeling London lives with every day? It's so fucking lonely. No one should feel this lonely.

If there was a moment in the last few months I needed a drink, it's tonight. Instead, I climb in beside her and watch her sleep. She is finally breathing peacefully.

This definitely breaks the no sleepover rule.

Not much faking is left in this relationship.

Chapter 17

London

I open my eyes, but the room doesn't come into focus immediately. I close them again because I feel like a steamroller flattened me in my sleep.

I feel like I haven't moved in ages. Wait a minute. I open my eyes again. I'm at Dominic's. Goddammit. No sleepovers.

I sit up, but my head swims so violently, I have to close my eyes again and lean forward. Doubled over, I groan. My mind wanders while my head stabilizes. I was sick, and Paris made me stay at Dominic's because of my dad. How long have I been here?

A few disconnected images flash through my foggy mind. Dominic pacing the room, wiping my forehead, putting a glass to my lips, murmuring words to me, holding me. Caring for me. Fuck.

"Good morning, sleepyhead." His voice startles me.

I look up, ignoring the vertigo. "What time is it?" I squint at him because my head is so congested it might explode.

"About eleven. How are you feeling?" He walks around and jumps on the bed. It reminds me how he did the same the first night we started fake dating.

It feels different this time, this familiar move I've seen him do many times. He puts his hands under his head and crosses his feet at his ankles and winks at me.

I lower myself back to my pillow, facing him. "Thank you for letting me stay."

"Of course, I'm glad you're feeling better." He touches my forehead with the back of his head. "For a day or two I was really worried."

"A day or two? What do you mean?" I frown. He carried me over on the first.

"It's the fourth of January, Chils." He tucks a strand of hair behind my ear.

"I've been here for almost a week?" I sit up again, but the rushed movement was a bad idea, so I collapse back.

"Three nights, don't be dramatic." He chuckles. "Enough time for me to figure out why you don't do sleepovers."

I turn my swimming head slowly to face him again.

His grin suggests I'm going to hate what's coming. Dominic reaches in between the large pillows and pulls out my stuffed cat.

"You would miss this little tiger." The toy dangles in front of me as he holds it by its tail like a captured rodent.

I snatch my cat from him and hide it under the covers. "I'll fucking kill Paris."

"So what's its name?" His voice is playful.

"Kitty has an emotional, personal value."

I wish I didn't feel this weak because I want to march out of here. Though I have no idea where I'd go since I need to avoid my place for a day or two more for Dad's sake.

Dominic laughs. "Understood. Kitty looks like she's seen a lot." His eyes twinkle with mischief.

"She has. I got her from Kyle, so she is special, even though old." I tell him about Kitty's sentimental value only to make him feel bad about teasing me. Geez, this head cold took away my mental sharpness. I can't even retort properly.

"Is the necklace from him as well?" His tone loses its playfulness. The cocky grin I've gotten so used to is gone as well. Puzzled by his need to know and my hesitation to tell him, I touch the pendant without even thinking about it.

The intensity of his gaze penetrates me with an

odd feeling. It scares me, yet I can't look away. Consumed by the sheer weight of his look, I struggle with a reply.

It feels like there is only one right answer and I might fail if I don't get it on the first try. It's ridiculous, yet my heart gallops.

"Why?" I try to avoid the answer, because as much as I don't want to admit it, I don't want to hurt him. But that's what I see in his eyes.

The fever must have killed more gray matter than I thought possible. And why do I fear my answer might hurt him?

"You never take it off. I figured it's important to you." His eyes rest on my hand, squeezing the charm. I'm relieved he moved the attention from my face, but it's only momentarily before he looks up again.

I nod, hating how this feels like a double betrayal. To Kyle and to Dominic. It shouldn't, though. Goddammit.

Dominic's face hardens. He studies me for a beat longer and I want to recoil. Or apologize. Or run. It feels like an important moment has just passed between us, but I'm too exhausted and scared to understand its significance.

He swings his legs off the mattress and stands up. "I'll warm up some soup for you, but you should at least brush your teeth, Chils."

I cover my mouth. Shit, this morning is a walk through a garden of humiliation. Frazzled by his gaze and questions and everything in between, I find some semblance of my typical mood and lean into annoyance, glaring at him.

"I'll shower as well." I look down and realize I'm wearing his shirt. It shouldn't surprise me.

Dominic smirks and saunters to his closet and brings out another one. "Here. Are you sure you're strong enough?"

I nod.

"Don't lock the door," he warns.

I take my time cleaning up, and it's not only because the floor occasionally shifts around me violently.

Something has shifted between us. It challenges the control I have over this arrangement. Whatever we have is starting to feel more like a relationship, and I don't know how to navigate that.

How to steer the ship back to its harbor where I can jump off safely. Where I can hide again. His piercing look a few minutes ago warned me there is no hiding from Dominic fucking Cressard.

My stomach growls as I wash my hair, and then again when I dry myself with a large, black towel. When I finally make it to the living room, I slump onto the sofa, exhausted.

I pull a soft blanket off the back and snuggle into it. Dominic comes over and leans in to kiss me.

"That's better," he murmurs. "Here, drink this." He hands me a small plastic container with a ginger shot.

I down it. "I hate these things."

"The taste is strong, but it should help you." He misunderstands my comment.

"I'm talking about the product itself. Look at this tiny, cute cup filled with five dollars of ginger juice. A prime example of consumerism. You can buy ginger root and make your own for a fraction of the price. Someone packaged the convenience and now it's the new trendy shit to drink."

I speak too passionately, not only from my conviction but from the need to maintain inconsequential conversation instead of addressing the tension between us.

Dominic walks to the kitchen, and I hear dishes clanking. "Saving time is a good business proposition. Do you envy the person who gets rich on their idea, regardless of how stupid it is?"

He comes back with a steaming bowl and sits sideways beside me. He folds his large leg under him, carefully balancing the dish in his hands.

"I'm not jealous," I scoff.

The tantalizing smell of the strong broth makes my

mouth water. Dominic puts the spoon to his mouth and blows on it before he moves it to my mouth. He is fucking feeding me.

I want to protest, but as my lips part he shoves the spoon inside, and the warm taste of home and comfort explodes on my tongue. So much for avoiding the feelings' exploration.

"Why are you so angry about the stupid ginger shot?" Dominic puts another spoonful into my mouth before I can answer.

The topic of the conversation does nothing to lessen my confusion over all of this. Over the intensity of his gaze unraveling me. Over his care of me. It's too much. Too touching. I'd prefer to fight over the world's injustice.

"It's the money people spend buying this bullshit. It could be used better."

I swallow three more spoonfuls before he answers. The soup spreads through my stomach, but the feeling reaches further. I forgot that simple chicken stock can have healing properties.

I try to ignore the scene by itself. Intimate. A simple yet profound moment. Dominic slowly puts the spoon in my mouth, his eyes lingering on my lips. I'm weak and congested, but I feel so beautiful, important, and cherished as he takes care of me.

"It could be used better?" He studies me. "Like

paying the medical bills for all people who didn't prevent the flu because they didn't drink ginger?" He shrugs, a lazy smile curling his lips, and silences me with another spoonful.

He puts the bowl on the coffee table and leans in, cupping my face. "You don't have to be angry all the time, Chils. You've been changing people's lives. Even if it's not enough, it still is a hundred percent more than what it would be if you didn't care."

His words wash over me, tasting and sticking like honey. Dominic captures my mouth, gently nibbling on my lips, trailing his tongue across them.

I open for him, starved for the tenderness I didn't even know I needed. Unsure what to do with my defenses as he chips at them.

The kiss is decadently slow and I want it to last forever, but my congestion forces me to pull away. "I can't breathe."

And I can't, but not only because of my sickness. I'm overwhelmed by the whirlpool of emotions stirring inside me, suffocating me.

Dominic grabs a tissue box from the table and tosses it in my lap. "Talking about doing more, I have a surprise for you." He walks over to his dining table and grabs something from the top of the pile.

"Why don't you set up an office in your spare

room?" Every time I'm here, more books and folders are strewn around.

"I won't be here long enough to go to the trouble."

He walks over to me with the document, but I have to look away because his casual mention of the tight time-line for his stay makes my stomach squirm with dread.

Why? I always knew there was an expiration date. I welcomed it because it made this whole fake dating ploy feasible. Stupid head cold.

He kneels, sinking his knee into the sofa beside me, and holds out the document. It's a request for a title change. I scan the words.

"This is the building beside the hospice?"

"I bought it." He beams at me. A warm smile, rather than his typical cocky grin, his eyes glistening with expectations.

"You what?" *How does that align with him leaving?* "What are you going to do with it?"

An array of emotions swims through me as I try to comprehend what he is telling me.

As I try to adjust to the mischievous but hopeful look on his face.

As my lack of comprehension crashes against my growing apprehension, because either he's sending mixed signals or I'm still impaired from my fever.

"What are *we* going to do with it? I thought I could

run a niche legal clinic for the people with illness and disabilities on the ground floor." He waves his hand, as though dismissing a minor detail, and I try to fight my excitement because this makes no sense.

His initiative, while very beneficial, is so at odds with the man I know. This right here is scaring me. This right here screams long-term.

He stands up and gestures, all animated. "And we can refit the rest of the building into small apartments for people from out of town who come for treatment. Your dad can stay with you or easily afford a hotel, but this option will be affordable or subsidized by the charity. We have to figure it out."

He paces in front of me and continues. "And the top floor with the terrace could be rented out to an architect firm, or someone like that. The lease would help with the maintenance of the property. I only ran a few numbers, and obviously I have no access to the Kyle West Foundation's finances to find the best way to get this off the ground, but we can figure that out together."

My heart hammers against my ribcage, pumping fear and excitement equally through my veins. And a dose of disbelief so large that I don't even start to dissect it.

"You own the building?" is all that comes out of me.

He shrugs. "Let's just say Felicia Warren had a good reason to accept my offer. What do you say?"

"Why are you doing this?" There is a long list of questions swarming in my head—mostly logistics on how this can work—but they are insignificant until I understand his reasoning. Uncharacteristically, I rein in the bubbling anger—my safety. I could lash out and all this would go away.

"My ticket to purgatory." He winks. "What do you say, Chils? We could be like Melinda and Bill Gates, a power couple spending money meaningfully."

A power couple? If he proposed to me right now, I would be less stunned. His proposal is in some ways bigger than a marriage one would be. This would tie us beyond the sham of a relationship we've been enjoying.

This would mean so much more for my work, but it would expand our current—very temporary—relationship, and fear at the idea is edging around my chest.

"But you're leaving soon."

The fever must have left parts of my brain incapacitated. His proposal is daring and fantastic. The woman in me wants to run. She regrets ever meeting this hurricane of a man. The altruistic me, so used to fighting for every win, is rejoicing.

"Look, I'll rent the building to your charity at a minimal charge and write a personal donation every year to cover that rent, so you'll manage the property.

The clinic can be set up and running next week. Nia is our first volunteer and she's recruited two of her classmates. You can figure out the rest later, and Chicago isn't that far. Even after buying a building I can still afford my private plane." He chuckles, leans down and kisses me.

I scoot away, needing to distance myself. "I don't know what to say. I think you're looking for ways to continue this fake relationship, Cressard." I turn to mockery, the second-best response after anger.

"Look, Chils, the pro bono work has energized me, so leaving something behind that truly is meaningful is like a thank you for my time here, when I was able to get back on track." He wraps his arms around me.

Then he whispers, "Get better quickly, because my balls are turning blue," and despite feeling like shit, I shiver with pleasure.

Yet, his words don't distract me enough from his *leaving something behind* comment. It's not only *something* he'll leave behind.

It really only took Dominic two weeks to have the clinic set up.

Our doorman's brother came to paint and fix-up the first floor. We had several businesses donating furniture. And Patagonia's friends started volunteering. Word of mouth spread quickly, and after the first week we are already at full capacity.

Dominic works there actively. In fact, he's there right now while I'm waiting for my dad to finish his treatment.

I try not to think about the personal ramifications of Dominic's actions and generosity. I focus on the overall benefit, but it's not lost on me how much I enjoy working with him.

How I admire his drive and dedication. His ability to solve any problem with a smile. Okay, a self-assured grin, which only adds to his appeal somehow.

Bianca is pacing the linoleum floor, the slap of her soles drilling into my brain.

She sighs and sits beside me, a cluster of nervous energy. I squeeze her hand.

"Your dad is thrilled you've found someone. Dominic is a great guy." My hand dampens in hers.

I didn't think we would have to keep up the lie for this long. Well, I didn't really think it through at all, but it seems harder and harder to officially break up with him because my dad is not doing well, and I don't want him to worry.

Somehow, we've fallen into this rhythm, living as an actual couple. With charity work, my family and his constant proximity, I get little time to myself.

As much as I don't want to admit it, I don't mind it. Buried in preparation for the legal clinic and exploring options for the building, we don't even bicker as before.

We fuck like we hate each other, and I wonder if it's because we enjoy it or because it strips down the intimacy we experienced in the days after New Year's Eve. His caveman, possessive bullshit at the club started it and we both jumped to put the brakes on it.

It's for the best.

He's leaving anyway.

We don't do relationships.

"He's been very helpful with my work." I come up with a lame response and Bianca studies me with her hawk eyes. She's seeing something, but I'm not sure what. What do I need to hide better?

Luckily the nurse comes out, and we go to help Dad into the wheelchair. Walking hasn't been easy for him lately. I help them get out and into my town car before I take an Uber to my office.

"London, the hospice called. It's one of the clients." Ashley puts a to-go cup of tea into my hands and I turn on my heels, forgetting Dad and my neighbor.

"Let my driver know to pick me up there." I rush back onto the street.

I hail a cab. My stomach twists into a poisonous knot I can never really untie. It's familiar though.

The first time I experienced this level of dread was

when Mom died. Then again with Kyle. It doesn't get easier. Ever. I cradle the tea in my hands. It's good, but not good enough to loosen the acid searing my stomach.

As soon as I enter the reception area, I know I'm late. It's the weird level of silence and determined work that gives it away. Like life continues but everyone feels slightly guilty about it. The air reeks of grief.

I don't have to ask questions. Somehow, I know. I wish I was wrong. With all my heart and soul, I hope to be wrong. But as soon as I reach the door to Madeleine's room, I know my instincts didn't lie.

Her bed is empty. They have moved her already. Irritation coils up my spine, and I want to blame Zelda for not calling me sooner.

"She loved dancing. Did you know?" Ralph coughs behind me.

He's leaning on his oxygen tank and smiling at me. It's a knowing smile with a bit of sadness mixed into it. This man knows mourning can have different forms, but we respect the memory of those we lost the best when we don't forget to live.

I do that for Kyle all the time, while I'm still mad he hid so much from me and robbed me of my opportunity to say goodbye.

"I didn't get to say goodbye," I sigh. I'm not talking about Madeleine only, but Ralph doesn't know.

"Let's dance for her. She would like that." Before I can protest, because his suggestion makes no sense, he shuffles closer and puts his arm on my hip, bracing himself as he tries to find his balance.

He is not really leading me into a dance move. Ralph struggles to hold on to me and his tank, but somehow he still pulls me closer to him.

We sway slowly, the only music Ralph's wheezing breaths and the distant beeping of monitors in other rooms. He smells moldy and sweaty, but I don't mind. I don't know what else to do, so I indulge in our silent dance.

Sometimes, comfort is found in nonsensical activities. As we continue the awkward moves, tears start falling freely, and I can't help but wrap my arms around him gently and allow myself to grieve.

"She loved your voice," he whispers, and a loud sob escapes me.

"Your jokes annoyed her." I wipe my tears, but they keep coming.

We go back and forth with insignificant details we know or make up about Madeleine, and soon others join us in the hallway, offering their memories.

Our impromptu memorial comes to an abrupt stop when Ralph catches another of his coughing bouts. I help him back to his room.

"Thank you." I start toward the door.

"For what?" he rasps. A nurse comes in to check on him.

"For being you." In the world where I chose anger as a coping mechanism, Ralph somehow stirred me into a dance.

I descend to the first floor and Zelda stops me with two files in her hands.

"Would you like to help me choose the new client?" She puts a hand on my shoulder.

I shrug. "No, I trust you to make the right choice."

What else is there to say? It seems perverse that Madeleine has just died and we are already focused on the future. Calling the next person on the long waiting list we have. I hate this.

I don't see my car anywhere, so I sit down on a step, sad and overwhelmed. Yet again, useless, aching from the lack of control over situations like this. Squeezing my knees close to me, I lower my forehead and exhale.

The air tastes like a popsicle, a smoggy one. The wind sweeps under my collar, making me shiver. Even in the warm long coat Dominic insisted on giving me, making an unwarranted fuss about me not taking care of myself enough, I'm cold. Too cold. Too lonely.

"You're gonna freeze your ass, Chils."

I look up. Dominic stands at the foot of the stairs like a motorcycle model in jeans and a hoodie with a bomber jacket. It's not fair how good the man looks.

"I gave your car to a family that came to the clinic. They would have gotten lost and frozen. Let me take you home. Uber awaits, my lady." He stretches his arm and I take his hand.

And just like that, I'm not alone.

We drive home in silence. He doesn't ask me what happened. Either he's heard or he doesn't need the details to understand what I need.

Well, I don't even know what I need, but as we get off the elevator at home, he kisses me and then steers me toward his place. "We have an appointment in the books for right now."

His breath in my ear gets all my muscles taut and my core tingling. We have nothing scheduled for today, but I'm not protesting. I need him to get me out of my head, and sex with him does the job the best.

By the time we reach his bedroom, Dominic has shed his jacket and hoodie and he is pulling my sweater over my head. Our pants fall to the floor.

"What do you need, Chils?"

I push him to the bed and straddle him, taking what I need with abandon. His skin is like velvet under my fingertips as I explore the endless expanse of his muscles.

I'm wet the minute I feel his skin against mine. I position him at my entrance, and as I lower myself down, I'm filled with a lot more than just his cock.

To escape the influx of emotions, I set a pace that gets me out of my head the fastest, and when I curl my toes, screaming his name and clenching around this beautiful man, I realize this is the first time he gave me control in the bedroom.

I wish he hadn't.

Chapter 18

Dominic

Chils's climax drags me over the edge, squeezing my cock to the last drop. She collapses beside me, with her back to my side, and I wrap my arm and leg around her.

We're a mess of sweaty limbs and ragged breaths. I've never enjoyed cuddling after sex, but today she needs all my attention.

"Thank you," she whispers. She sounds remote. Her body, warm and damp, is here with me, but her mind and soul are fighting somewhere else. In a place I have no access to, and I shouldn't want to have it. Yet here we are.

This woman somehow unravels me every single time. I don't know anymore if it's still a challenge to conquer her defenses just to prove I can. Because it feels like anything but.

I want her to share with me, which is deranged. Until recently, I believed sharing with a woman was a clear path to getting tied down. Not interested. Then why do I want my fake girlfriend to share with me?

"For what?" I kiss her shoulder.

When I saw her car in front of the hospice, I called Chils, but she didn't answer, so I called Ashley to confirm I could use the car. She told me about Madeleine. I didn't know the lady, but Chils spent lots of time with her.

"For making me feel less lonely."

Her words pull at my heart. Allowing me to see her vulnerability feels as if she left a door to a secret chamber slightly ajar, not protecting herself with anger, but leaning into her pain and the intimacy between us.

I don't fucking know what to do with such trust. I do know, however, at this moment, I don't want to be anywhere else. At the same time, I don't want the responsibility. That's not right. I do want the responsibility, but it's hard to accept that I do.

When I pulled back after the New Year's party, I was sure it was the right choice for both of us. When I carried her sick into my bed just a few hours later, I didn't want to stay away anymore. Out of my mind while she fevered in my bed, I realized I no longer want us to be a ruse.

You got yourself a girlfriend, asshole, don't fuck it up. Rocco summed up the situation when I spoke to him. I don't fuck things up. I don't fail. So I went and bought the goddamned building.

Chils would never agree that this is an actual relationship, so I need to find a way to stay close and let her come to the same realization as me. To accept we're good together.

There is more to our partnership. Being more involved with her work these past two weeks, I figured out a way to make sure we stay close even after I return to Chicago.

And before she knows it, she'll be in a genuine relationship. I wanted to tell her today about my plans, but I need to let her grieve.

"Madeleine was lucky to have you. You made her last days here better."

I flip her to face me, but London squeezes her eyes shut, only a lonely tear escaping. I grab her wrists and drag them above her head. Her heart beats against my chest and my erection throbs between us.

I have half a mind to fuck the sadness out of her. To give her all she needs to forget. She lost someone today, and I want to give her the chance to cope.

"Look at me, Chils," I growl.

She pries her eyes open. Scowling. That's my girl.

"Your visits made her happy. Brief moments of

happiness are better than no joy at all. Do you understand?" I bark the last question because I swear the woman needs to break that vicious cycle of not-enough.

She glares at me as the silence ticks away and the sexual tension grows. The way her naked skin feels against my body is addictive.

"Yes," she rasps finally, her chest heaving.

"Good girl." I kiss her gently, but she bites my lip, and the kiss turns desperate quickly.

I grip her wrists with one hand and explore her body with the other. I'm familiar with every inch of her, all her sensitive spots. Like when I feather the hollow around her hip bone with my finger, barely touching her, her nipples harden.

Despite that, it's always new. Every time I touch her, her body responds differently, letting go more. Letting me in more. At least physically.

I pinch her nipple and she sucks in air. Roaming farther down, I slick my fingers through the swollen lips of her wet pussy. Her hips buck and she arches, asking for more.

"Thank you for round one. I needed to feel in control, but can you fuck me now?" She wrestles to free her hands. The fiery dragon is back. She wraps her legs around my waist and lifts her hips, seeking friction.

Something dark and satisfying spreads through me when she asks me to take control.

"I'm going to release your wrists, but you keep your hands up there. If you move them, you get punished. If you move, you get punished." I search her eyes for her consent.

Desire and defiance war in her eyes, but as she licks her lips, I know which is winning.

"You should tie me up then." Her breathing is labored.

"No, Chils, you need to control yourself if you want to come."

Her face constricts into that mask of contempt she wears so well, but her eyes sparkle with excitement. I chuckle and let go of her wrists.

She keeps them above her head and her body relaxes beneath me. She looks almost innocent. Fuck me.

"Good girl. Don't you dare move."

I take my time, slowly trailing her curves with my lips, my tongue and teeth. It hits me that I've never felt this alive with any other woman before. I thought she just helped me find my mojo, but it's more than that.

Being with her is better than winning a case. More thrilling than a new car. Just consuming. Wonderful. Scary. All I never wanted, yet can't get enough of now that I've had a taste.

I've never had a long-term partner, and I appreciate now how the familiar could be more exciting. How taking care of Chils is rewarding for me. I want to be less selfish because her pleasure is mine.

It makes me feel more alive than I'd ever felt before my collapse. When my life was full of things, money, prestige and women. And empty at the same time. Giving seems to be the theme since I came to New York, and fuck if it doesn't feel good.

To her credit, Chils stays still, but she channels her feelings into a series of sounds—moans, groans, exasperated sighs—and colorful invectives to curse me.

But she doesn't move, and I plan to reward her. Delaying her satisfaction for the most explosive effect.

I make my way down between her legs and I tease her sensitive nub with my teeth. This is what breaks her. Chils lifts her hips, eager to meet my face with her beautiful pussy.

I push her down, digging my fingers into the flesh of her hips, probably bruising her. She responds with a sound that is half groan and half whimper. Her hands grab my hair to keep me where she wants me.

I give her what she wants for a moment, and then I lift my head. Our eyes lock and the frustration on her face makes me chuckle.

"You move, you don't come." I shrug. This is fun, but I'm not planning on not finishing the job.

"Just fucking punish me and finish, you—"

Her words get swallowed by a sharp intake of breath as I smack her pussy with the back of my hand. Her eyes widen. I follow with four more slaps in rapid succession.

"Please," she croons. It's not a plea for me to stop. I bet her pussy is burning, throbbing with need, and I give her what she wants, eating her like she's my last meal.

Chils explodes, thrashing and wriggling, and I lift onto my haunches. Hauling her knees over my shoulders, I bury my cock inside her, not waiting for her to come down before I start pumping and get her over the edge again.

This time, we reach the peak together. In perfect unison. Chils gets to abandon the world where people leave her, and I'm sinking deeper into the grasp of this complicated woman who makes me want to be a different man.

"I should go." Chils murmurs against my chest and attempts to push away, but I tighten my hold on her.

We haven't left my bed for hours, and it's not even dinnertime, but she's trying to leave. The no sleepover rule was reinstated right after her sickness. Every time

I feel we've created a connection, she retracts like she got burned.

"You're still in my bed, which means I'm in charge." I kiss the crown of her head and she stays in my arms, but her body isn't warmly languid anymore.

Still flushed post-sex, it's more taut. Like a string, ready to snap, but still hanging by the tiniest thread. She will not make this easy.

"This isn't a good idea." She looks up, meeting my eyes, determined to sway everything her way—fake and as superficial as possible.

We stare at each other, and the room fills with heavy breathing. In the beat of the loud silence, I consider how bad it would be to admit how I feel. It would terrify her. I'm still scared to put those feelings into words. She would run faster than an Olympic sprinter.

Fuck. I don't even know what exactly I feel. It's not fake between us anymore, but I'm not ready to name it.

I know I'm ridiculously jealous of the stuffed cat and the pendant between her breasts, and it pisses me off that I can't do much about that. I can't compete with a dead man. I don't want to compete for her. I want her to want me. For real.

"I should leave," she repeats, her words coming out on a hitched breath. They hit me with a tinge of annoyance. Will she really pretend she doesn't want to stay?

My arm is tight around her. She hasn't moved. She isn't struggling to get away from me. The fire in her eyes is burning, but it might just be her typical anger.

"I should leave." Her voice trembles, weakening her resolution.

"But you don't want to leave, Chils." The air between us zaps with tension. "Do you?" Even the defiance in her eyes is sexy. I roll over, pinning her under me. "Do you?" I growl.

She glares at me, and I can almost hear the argument insider her head. The protective walls sounding the alarm, while the woman hidden behind them is trying to escape.

"This doesn't feel fake to me," she snaps. "I don't want you to get ideas. And besides, we don't do sleepovers, remember?"

"It's hardly a sleepover. It's not even night." But she is determined to run and hide, so I change my tactic. "Let me meet you halfway. We both leave the bedroom and you let me cook dinner for you."

"I should check on my dad." She licks her lips, her eyes darting around, avoiding direct contact.

Oh, but she can't fool me. "Good, let's go and see him together, and the food gets delivered in the meantime."

She frowns. "You just offered to cook."

I kiss her and then jump out of bed, slapping her

hip playfully. "I'd have to learn how to do that first. Chinese or Indian?"

She chuckles. "Do you even have to ask?" She swings her legs over the edge of the bed.

Wrapping herself in the sheet, she stumbles around looking for her clothes. It reminds me of our first night, and for some outlandish reason the memory fills me with warm satisfaction. We've come so far, yet we're still carefully discovering the journey.

"Indian it is, my lady." I pull my T-shirt over my head, meeting London's frown. She has her hands on her hips. I raise my eyebrows. "Chop-chop, get dressed. I don't think your dad wants to see you like this."

"Did you just manipulate me into having dinner with you?" She rolls her eyes. "God, I hate dating a lawyer."

"Fake dating, baby," I deadpan. She was scared enough already. I need to make her comfortable before I tell her about my plan.

We visit with Micah, who seems to do better tonight. "It's great you are working together now, but don't forget to enjoy life a bit as well." He pats Chils's hand. Sitting in a wingback armchair Bianca had delivered for him, he looks smaller than before.

Squatting beside him, Chils is trying to remain cheerful, but I can see she's forcing herself to act that way. Today's loss of Madeleine still hovers over her, but I think it's deeper than that. She faces death daily, but she's not ready to face her father's mortality. It will break her.

More than before, I know I need to stay around to help her pick up the pieces. Though I hope that time is still far, far away, and I'll be able to get us to explore this relationship for real before that ever happens.

"I'm worried about Gio," Bianca says. She is sipping her tea on the sofa.

"Why? Because he hasn't been glued to his screen?" London stands up and sits on the armrest, wrapping her arm around her father's shoulder.

"No. Well, yes, but there is more. He's stubborn and doesn't want to talk to me. You need to find out what's going on." Bianca takes a sip. It's funny how her request almost sounds like a plea, or a suggestion, but it's said with such finality, no one would dare to protest.

"Okay, I'll talk to him." London shrugs.

"I'm going to get ready for bed." Micah pushes to standing, but almost collapses. I rush to help him and accompany him to his bedroom. Fuck, the man suffers from his loss of independence more than from his disease.

The women follow us, and we say our goodbyes and return to my place for dinner.

* * *

"You're insane." London jabs her fork in my direction.

"Why? Didn't you say you'd like to expand what you do to other cities? The building would suit us. And you can get the upper crust of Chicago to donate just like you do here." I push my plate away.

There's no reason not to expand her work to Chicago. I found the perfect property, suitable for a hospice and a support center with a legal clinic.

"Suit us? Since when has all my hard work, years of building something, become 'ours'? You bought the building here to make yourself feel better, but I don't want you to go behind my back and plan my expansion. I take on as much as I can handle. Sorry if it's not up to your standards." She drops her fork.

Glaring at me, she folds her arms across her chest. Can't she see this is a great plan to help more people? Is she really going to protest on principle?

"What the hell are you talking about? What if I did do it to feel better? Who cares about my motives as long as they benefit others? Let's not forget you started helping others to repent for what you foolishly believe was your failure." I stand up, my chair rocking back on two legs before dropping back down with a loud thud.

The minute my words come out, I know I've pushed too far. But damn it, I don't care. I'm not someone who commonly loses my temper, but this woman is infuriating.

She stands up, her nostrils flaring as she clenches her fists a few times. "Don't you judge my motivations. I have done nothing wrong intentionally. Not something you can say."

Here we go again. "Of course, I'm the villain here. Just like you, I can't fucking change the past, but I can try to atone. Or whatever it is I'm doing. People will benefit."

My breath is fast-paced and shallow by the time I finish. It takes all my willpower not to pounce on her. I don't even know if I want to shake her, spank her, or just fuck some sense into her.

I've trod so carefully to keep her around, to make her see how good we are together, and now I may have lost it. If she leaves, I have only myself to blame.

"Chils, I can make a few phone calls and get people lined up to donate enough for you to get things rolling." I lean against the counter to soften the combative stance.

"I won't launder money for your shady clients." Her face is flushed, the vein in her neck pulsing. "The means do not always justify the end. Regardless of how kind or generous the end is."

Is she for real? "What the hell? Why is anger always the first weapon and shield you grab? Always so damn angry. A mask you put on to deal with shit. Here you go, all victim because you didn't get that one last chance to say goodbye to your boyfriend. You pour yourself into all this noble work, but it's all fake."

Pushing off the counter, I throw my arms up. "Because while you spread hope on one side of the city, you make sure you spit fire on the other. Angry at everyone, cold to those who try to get close. A victim and victimizer at the same time. The polarity is kind of exhausting. Decide who you fucking want to be, Chils."

I pace around, unable to look at her, pissed and... goddammit, disappointed. I don't get disappointed. My therapist would be thrilled. Isn't disappointment a direct result of desire? Mission accomplished. I came here to quieten down and re-discover my desire. It fucking sucks. All these feelings are horrible.

"Why are you doing it all?" Her voice startles me. My back is to the kitchen as I stare blindly at the flickering lights of the city. I didn't hear Chils moving, but her scent is close behind me now. Her body is almost touching mine, the heat relaxing me immediately.

"I don't know why, Chils. Perhaps it is for selfish reasons. When I took the first pro bono case here, I felt alive. I have more money than I truly need, so why not?" I turn around and cup her face. "Also, I kind of like being around you, Chils."

She studies me with those large eyes that rarely show her true feelings. There is no coolness in them right now. There is hesitation. But the angry fire is missing, replaced by contemplation.

She opens her mouth and closes it again. I can almost see the war brewing inside her. Part of her wants to accept and get excited about the opportunity, but there is a part of her that defaults to her natural mistrust and consistent refusal of attachment. Or it might be something completely different, but the war is better than a refusal.

We both know the attachment has sneaked in without us even realizing. That doesn't mean Chils is ready to take a leap and accept it.

Perhaps I moved too fast with both opportunities. She got spooked when I bought the building here. I should have waited with the Chicago property. But the opportunity came up, and I didn't want it to pass.

"I want to buy the building, but I realize this needs to be a mutual decision. In fact, such expansion needs to be discussed with your board of directors. But the opportunity is there, within your reach. This could be us."

She swallows and relaxes a bit, and then the lines around her eyes curve up just a little. It's almost invisible, but it's the first time I've seen traces of joy. Perhaps hope in those eyes.

"A power couple?" She bites her lips.

"A power couple." I lean in and seize her mouth.

I think in our very weird way, through an argument and lots of anger, we've just made our relationship official.

Chapter 19

London

The man beside me snores and his head falls onto my shoulder. I should have taken Dominic's private jet, but it felt like an unnecessary luxury. Especially since it's a short flight back to New York, and he couldn't even come with me because of some emergency with one of the clinic's clients.

First-class seats shouldn't feel this cramped. I jerk my shoulder up and the man's head bounces. He utters a choking snore and settles on the other side of the seat.

I glimpse something wet on my shoulder. Great, he's been drooling on me. I find napkins in my purse and try to wipe the saliva from the fabric of my jacket.

The property in Chicago is amazing, but instead of excitement, I'm filled with a weird uneasiness. I agreed to inspect the building because clearly I'm not smart enough to argue with a lawyer.

When Dominic proposed the expansion, I wanted him to shut up and leave me alone. I don't know what I want anymore because he's tilted the axis of my carefully designed life, leaving me exposed and vulnerable, and in unknown territory. I don't want him to return to Chicago, and I want him to return there as soon as possible.

When he looked at me and said this could be us, my initial reaction was pure joy. I think. It's been a while since I practiced that emotion.

And I didn't get to explore it further because as soon as I answered, half agreeing to way more than a professional partnership, a familiar dread settled.

If I expand my work to another city, to his city, we'll be bound. We already are through the property he purchased in New York, but at least that wouldn't require us to talk much.

Things could run smoothly without him being involved. But even if we don't interact closely, he'll forever remain a part of my work.

Another person I'd stand to lose. I can't bear that. The building is perfect, but I won't tell him that. I'll refuse. I can't get entangled in this.

Dominic isn't planning to stay in New York, and I need to distance myself from him before it's too late.

Because I don't want him to stay. I don't. I ignore how much that resolution has weakened in the last few weeks.

The idea of an altruistic power couple has its merits, but I was doing fine on my own. I have no idea when our relationship changed the trajectory. And that by itself is scary.

Maybe Dominic is right. I play the victim and at the same time victimize those around me with my carefully maintained distance. My unwillingness to commit might hurt people, but really, I've never gone far enough in any relationship to make anyone suffer from the consequences of my attitude.

Besides my family, there are only a few people who are a constant in my life. Ashley is one of them. Zelda perhaps. The rest of the volunteers and employees come and go. And I'm fine with that.

Dominic is somehow trying to stay and leave at the same time, and I don't know what to do with that. I'm lost, and I hate being lost. I need to regain control.

My dad would understand we broke up, and I can quickly start dating someone else if only to show him I've moved on after Kyle. Of course, I will have moved on. Just because I choose not to expose myself to more pain doesn't mean I'm stuck in the past.

My stomach constricts as I walk through the

airport and find my car. The driver greets me with a smile and closes the door behind me.

He gets behind the wheel and checks on me in the rearview mirror. Our eyes lock and he gives me a shy smile before he pulls onto the road.

Usually, I dive into my emails and messages when I'm being driven. Today, I surprise myself.

"It's Miles, isn't it?"

He jerks his eyes from the road to the mirror for a moment. I'm not the only one surprised.

"Yes, Ms. Lowe."

I smile, despite knowing he can't see me. "Miles, I don't think I want to pay someone for driving me around. I think I should use Uber."

His eyes dart to meet mine again, full of concern. "I see."

Shit. "Oh no, I don't want you to leave. I'd like you to stay, but instead of driving me around, you would drive the families who come to visit their sick relatives, or anyone who is a client of our nonprofit. Your employment conditions would remain the same, but people who can benefit more would use your services."

I've been agonizing about letting him go, but after Dominic used this car to have a clinic patient driven to the bus station, I liked the idea of transitioning the driver's responsibilities.

I can't pretend Dominic hasn't made an impact

already. Which doesn't mean I wouldn't have arrived at this solution by myself.

The same goes for the legal clinic. I've wanted one for a while. But time, and money... And I just... Starting a clinic was a lasting commitment. Not something I can lean into easily. Buying the hospice center was a huge step for me.

We arrive at the Madison Club. "Miles, I'll discuss things with Ashley to figure out how we'll go about it."

"Thank you, Ms. Lowe. I consider this new responsibility a promotion." Miles smiles at me. He's about to get out.

"Don't. I can jump out. Why don't you take the rest of the day off? And we'll talk tomorrow."

He drove me to JFK early in the morning, so he must be tired. I know I am, but I still have to talk to Gio because if Bianca asks me about it one more time, I'm going to lose it.

He waits for me in the restaurant, drumming his fingers on the table and frowning as I sit down.

"What do you want?" he growls.

"Nice to see you too, bro. Thank you for asking. I'm doing well. I've just come from Chicago and I'm starving. Do you mind if I order something?" I dial up my sarcasm with my most fake smile while I open a menu.

He glowers, but before he can say anything the server comes. I order a coffee and a small salad.

"What do you need, Lo?" Gio loops back to his original question as soon as we're alone again.

"Not much, just a story for Bianca to explain your behavior lately." I lean back and cross my arms over my chest.

"Fuck." He rolls his eyes. "Tell Mother to call me if she wants to talk to me."

It's slightly unnerving when he speaks directly to me, not at his screen. Dark circles shade his face, and it doesn't look like he shaved this morning.

"Would you answer her call?" I raise my eyebrows and he looks away. The whole reason I'm here is because he's avoiding her calls.

We sit in silence, and I wonder if this is a complete waste of time.

"You look like shit, Gio." Not sure if this is the best approach to get him talking. I don't even know if I want him to share. Why on earth did Bianca think I'm the right person for the job? But of course, Paris and Sydney have probably tried already.

"I purchased a retail chain and it's been a lot of work. We're re-branding and planning to open several new stores."

I think he's telling the truth, but I doubt that's the only reason for his weird behavior.

My salad arrives and I dig in with enthusiasm.

"Why were you in Chicago?" he asks with a frown.

I don't know why I decide to get his opinion since I've decided to pass on the opportunity, but I give him the file anyway. "Look at this property."

He scans the documents, then does a few searches and reads something else.

"It's for sale. It seems clean and a good deal. Why?"

"I went to see it today." The only problem with my determination to drop the opportunity is that I've already pictured how we can use it. That was a mistake.

"Why?" Gio's disturbed expression deepens. But what do I know? This might be his normal look when he is not squinting at his computer or phone.

"Potential expansion of my nonprofit to another city. A hospice plus patient and caregiver services."

He nods with something akin to respect. It's just a passing emotion smoothing his frown, but it's there. "That's great. Did you choose Chicago to stay close to your boyfriend?"

I flinch. I keep forgetting Paris is the only one who knows that our relationship isn't real. Though I'm not sure about that anymore. I want to deflect somehow, but Gio has always been good in advising me about my work.

"He found the location. I feel this is a great opportunity, but it's a big step."

"I wouldn't worry about it. You've always played it safe. Relying on your connections here, on my connections, on the familiar environment to ensure you can raise enough money. But you're good at what you do, and you don't need the shield of your family to achieve more, Lo. Go for it. Your work is meaningful, don't limit yourself."

His words warm me up and shake me at the same time.

"Thank you. I guess you're right. But there is a problem. The one you named at the beginning. Dominic."

"I didn't mention him as a problem. I mentioned him as an additional benefit. I think you have a good foundation here to expand to another city. Chicago seems a natural choice since you have personal ties there."

I stare at him. Without all the conflicting feelings, on paper, it really sounds like a no-brainer.

"Are you going to fuck up everything because you're scared?" Gio asks casually.

"I'm not scared," I retort way too quickly.

He raises his eyebrows. "Okay. But you live your life based on what you think Kyle deserves. Not what you deserve. What a guy you loved when you weren't even an adult might have deserved. If that's not fear, I don't know what is. There is a real man here who is willing to dive into your selfless world of helping people... And, if my information and impressions are correct, he's been more into selfish endeavors in the past. Yet, you're going to drop it because you think you owe Kyle an eternity of suffering?"

Every word that comes out of his mouth coils around my stomach, making me push the stupid salad away. Gio uncovers my wounds that have been festering for years.

All this time I thought they were healed, but that was a lie. I'm stuck in the past, making decisions today based on what happened almost fifteen years ago.

Instead of a reasonable response, I unleash my frustration. "Well, since we're giving each other relationship advice, you better figure out what's going on with Mila before she runs for the hills rather than dealing with a workaholic like you." I stand up, and for a brief moment I cherish the shocked look on his handsome face. "I'll tell Bianca you're in love." I have no idea if that's true. I based my retort purely on those looks I spied during the gala, but I'm not far from reality based on his reaction.

"Don't you dare, London." His chair screeches on the floor, but I turn and rush out of there.

How dare he?

How dare he?

How dare he tell me the truth?

I hail a cab and give them the address of a hair salon where I go every year after the gala. I don't have an appointment, but I've postponed my regular visit already and I need to shed some of this weight. I'm sure they can squeeze me in.

I need to do something radical to help me find my equilibrium.

"What the actual fuck?" Dominic cries out when he sees me.

I run my hand over my freshly shaved head. "What? My skull has a good shape for this kind of a haircut. And I did it for a great cause. Someone with cancer will get a new wig. Besides, my hair grows really fast." I must admit I'm kind of enjoying his exasperation.

Dominic erases the distance between us and seizes my lips. We're in his living room, the city lights creating a postcard-like backdrop. He devours my mouth and I love every minute of it. I wish his kisses weren't this primal. Intoxicating. Addictive.

Dominic kisses with everything he has to give. Like there isn't another breath to take after this.

I allow myself a similar reckless abandon every time I travel. Just diving into any activity like it's the last thing I'll get to do.

I moan against his lips, gripping his shoulders and enjoying every second of his possessiveness.

"You're going to pay for this." His voice sends delicious shivers down my spine, and he knows it.

My body responds immediately—goosebumps, trembling, fluttering stomach, hammering heart and soaked underwear. The man winds me up with a few words.

I yelp as he hauls me over his shoulder and marches to his bedroom. He tears my clothes off, and somehow his as well at the same time.

"Hands on the bed and bend over." The rumble of his voice alone can push me to the edge.

I don't comply immediately. I stare at him, trying to look defiant, but I'm probably failing miserably because I'm so aroused.

Dominic clenches his jaw, his features darkening as he steps closer. We're both naked, squaring off like fighters in a ring. I step back without even making the conscious decision to do so.

"Chils," he growls, and I lift my chin.

I don't know why I'm pushing back, because I know in the end I'll gladly submit. In fact, every fiber of my body is already screaming in surrender.

He closes the short distance between us. It's not even half a step, but the impact is shocking. He towers above me with a savage look in his eyes.

He hasn't touched me yet, but his scent alone, along with the heat his beautiful body emanates, is enough for me to succumb. Not because he takes power from me, but because I want him so much.

I turn, bend, and my hands don't even reach the edge of the bed when a vicious smack lights up my ass cheek.

I suck in a breath and lower my forehead, dealing with the burn and the spiked arousal, panting.

"Are you sorry?" He smacks me again. I clench and then relax when Dominic feathers my burning skin with a tender caress. "I loved fisting your hair. Say you're sorry."

I have nothing to be sorry about and I want to argue that, but I want him to fuck me more, so I play along. "I'm sorry I cut my hair."

I get my reward. Three times in a row. And with every orgasm, I'm sinking deeper into the world ruled by this man.

Like those stupid boxes he left in the hallway a few months ago. He may have removed them, but he invaded my life with so much more. I don't think I can pretend anymore that getting rid of him would be good for me.

We lie spent between crumpled sheets. I think about the danger of letting myself fall while Dominic draws lazy circles on my belly, occasionally taking my nipple in his mouth. I think he's doing it mindlessly, and still it feels so natural and normal.

"How did my hometown treat you?" He props his chin in his palm, watching me with those observant eyes.

"The entire city is sheathed in black. It's horrible. Everywhere I went, people were crying, building shrines, mourning the loss of you." I cover my eyes with the back of my forearm for dramatic effect.

He closes his teeth around my nipple and I yelp. "Don't make me punish you again. Though I see it's losing its thrill, now that you're enjoying it a bit too much. I have to step up my game." He kisses me with a decadent amount of pressure, suction, tongue and all. It's annoying how good he is at all of this. "What do you think about the building?"

And here we go. The moment of truth. What is the truth, though, is the question. "I don't know. It's not bad, but I don't think it's a good idea."

"What do you mean? Why not? I'll buy the building for you—"

"Aren't you a romantic?" I try to derail the conversation. I need to refuse this collaboration, but I don't want to. I wish I was brave enough to take the leap.

Dominic rolls over me, pinning me to the mattress. He brackets my face between his large palms, and I swear his eyes can see deep into my soul. Deeper than I'd peek myself. I'm not happy that he can probably feel my heart pounding against his chest.

"What are you scared of? Talk to me, Chils."

The simple, honest request forms a lump in my throat.

We stare at each other for a second, or a day, but I can't find my voice. I don't have to justify myself to him. The bitter thought sounds childish and petulant even in my mind.

"You always say you don't do enough. You can do more now." He kisses my forehead, which only makes me feel worse.

My hesitation is not about my ability to expand. Though that scares me too, it's not my biggest fear.

"The pressure to raise the funds is too much." My argument is too weak for anyone, let alone a lawyer used to cross-examination.

He kisses my forehead again. "Just as you have people regularly contributing here, you will find donors in Chicago. I'll help you."

I'm pretty sure he knows my reluctance lies elsewhere, but I'm grateful he plays along. "I don't want to do it." I push out the words, coarse with pent-up emotions.

He stiffens around me. It's like I'm engulfed by a solid coffin, only his blazing eyes shining with life.

The sounds of the city outside blend into the background until I can only hear my thumping heart, and even that probably only exists in my mind.

"I see." Dominic rolls on to his back.

The loss of his heat is devastating. He doesn't leave the bed, yet he's never felt so far. He might be in Chicago already. We stare at the ceiling. Frozen in time. Torn. Disappointed.

I see. He only said two short words, but I heard the hurt in them. I recognize it because I feel it as well.

Chapter 20

Dominic

I pound the pavement with punishing determination, as if I was in a race. I'm trying to tame the disjointed thoughts and my growing agitation. The sharp wind cuts right through my running vest, chilling me to the bone.

I force my way along the path, ignoring the other joggers. Central Park is desolate, filled only with the chilled air and silence ringing eerily in my ears, interrupted by the sound of my shoes on the frosted ground. The trees sparkle with the early morning sunlight, but its magic is lost on me.

Fuck London. Fuck New York. I'm not staying here any longer. The only reason I've stayed this long was some misguided loyalty to Chils and her father. They gave me a false feeling of belonging, but I don't belong here.

I came here to rediscover my drive, and that's where the mission needs to end. I can fix the one last problem in my recovery quickly. To rip off that particular bandage, I'll shower and go to court today. And I'll stay there all day, even if it kills me. Goddammit.

I run faster, fueled by my anger. Chils finally slept over. Thank you very much. We stared at the ceiling like two strangers and eventually I fell asleep, and she must have as well because she was still there when I woke up.

I'm not sure what pisses me off more. That she doesn't feel the same way about this thing between us, or that *I* feel those things.

Rocco's out of his mind, because this is frankly the shittiest feeling of hopelessness I've ever experienced. I feel like a failure, and I don't do failure.

I anticipated she'd be scared to upgrade our relationship. Frankly, I wasn't sure if we could keep it up. Neither of us is exactly experienced in that area. But I expected that through the mutual passion for the project here and in Chicago we would create our own version of partnership. And when she agreed to fly to Chicago, I was hopeful. What a stupid sentiment.

"Good morning, Dominic." Cesare opens the door for me and I jog inside, my lungs grateful for the warmth.

"I'm going to miss you, Cesare." I pat his shoulder and he frowns.

"Are you moving out? I thought you and Ms. Lowe—"

"My stay here has always been temporary. I'll be selling the apartment." I leave him there because I don't want to discuss it further. I'd originally planned to keep the place as an investment property, but no longer. Selling is the right move.

The right move should spread satisfaction through my veins. My veins are plagued with anger today.

It's enough I'll be connected to her through the legal clinic here. I'll have to delegate the property management and the project itself to someone fast.

I open the door and throw my key on the console table. I turn and gasp, startled because I forgot about her shaved head. Chils jumps up from the sofa, spilling what is in her mug and wincing in pain.

"Did you burn yourself?" I dash to her and take her hand into mine. Like touching an exposed wire, the jolt of electricity dials up the sensitivity of every single cell of my body.

Ignoring the reaction, I focus on the already reddening skin between her knuckles and her wrist. My heart bounces around my chest in a weird, disconnected beat.

The last thing I expected this morning was a flood of worry for her.

Or the way the touch sends shivers of desire down my spine.

Or the unconditional need to protect her.

"It's okay." Chils pulls her hand to her. "What spooked you?"

I roll my eyes. "I forgot about your hair."

She bites her lip, failing to suppress her amusement. "I guess I got properly punished for it." She shakes her hand, blowing at it.

A memory from last night flicks through my mind, and I cup the back of her neck. I lower my head but stop myself before our lips meet.

I've never suffered from a lack of rational thinking. Ever. That's why I'm good at arguing a case. That's why I'm the best fucking lawyer. Yet this woman strips me of all of that, and I seem to crave more.

We stare at each other, our chests heaving with the undercurrent of built-up tension. With her head shaved, Chils looks younger and more innocent. At odds with her personality. I was pissed yesterday because I loved wrapping her ponytail around my wrist.

Seeing her now, stripped of my selfish emotions, I see how the lack of hair only accentuates her beauty. She does indeed have an elegantly shaped skull.

Her new haircut highlights her delicate cheekbones and her eyes. With her usual scowl removed, I see how expressive those big eyes are, how they're ringed by the longest lashes. Right now, they are filled with expectation and hurt. There is nothing sexual in her need. Or mine.

As much as we both wish to pretend otherwise, we're desperate for each other. Yet running away from it.

I touch her lips with mine, gently. Chils raises on her tiptoes and seeks a deeper connection.

I give in and we kiss. Desperate, we channel our frustration, pain and fear into intimacy, leaving us breathless and yearning. Chils clings to me as if she fears I'm going to disappear.

But does she? Does she want this at all? Or is she going to hide behind her walls? Perhaps I got it all wrong. Maybe the physical connection with a firmly attached expiration date is all she's ever wanted. Maybe she believes I've infiltrated her work only to stay close. Have I? Fuck if I know anymore.

I squeeze her neck tighter, probably leaving marks, and I plant my other hand on the small of her back, holding her close. I don't let my hands roam, because I don't want us to get sidetracked.

We continue kissing, because we know we communicate best without words. But it's time we accepted that's part of our problem. We fuck or we bark at each other. And then we go and do our own thing. Like me buying a building.

I stepped in here earlier, resolute to pack up and leave. Now I want nothing more than to fight for her. Even though that fight is mostly *with* her. But she stayed here. She didn't sneak out, and that gives me a jolt of that useless, stupid hope that seems to rule my judgment lately.

I pull away. Chils looks at me, startled, and I want to wipe her worries away, but she needs to get there herself.

"Talk to me, London." I use her name on purpose. This is not playful chatter or bickering.

She swallows and slides her arms down mine slowly. She lowers her eyes and stares at the carpet. "I thought you might want to stay here. At the same time, I didn't want you to stay here."

"Chicago is only a short flight away. Nothing has to change." *Between us*, but I don't say that part out loud. It's a miracle she's willing to voice her fears—I can't risk scaring her off.

I'm fully aware of how hard this is for her. She may let me boss her around in the bedroom, but she needs to be fully in control of her life. If her feelings are even remotely as irrational and consuming as mine, she must feel as lost as me.

For some outlandish reason, the vulnerability of the fear we clearly share makes me feel stronger.

"Everything is going to change. I'm staying here. I have to stay close to my family. To my father." She looks up at me, seeking confirmation that I understand what she's trying to say.

"Well, then I'll be flying back and forth, and you can come for short periods of time to take care of necessary work." Even as I utter the words, I know it's not the logistics of our relationship we need to address, but it keeps her talking, so I hope we get there. That fucking hope again.

"It's a reasonable solution for my work if I expand, but what about us? It would be difficult to have you in my life..." She lets out a long breath through pursed lips. "If you leave."

She must be voicing only some of her thoughts, because she makes no sense. "What are you talking about, Chils? I'm not abandoning you."

"You can't promise that," she snaps. "Nobody can promise that."

"What? What have I done to make you believe I want to leave you? If anything, I'm taking all possible steps to keep us connected despite everything."

"We don't always have a choice." Her eyes glisten and she steps back. And it hits me then. Kyle didn't have a choice. Her mother had no choice. Madeleine and many other clients had no choice. Her father has no choice in what's going to happen.

I yank her to me and wrap my arms around her, burying her in my embrace. In her own weird, complicated way, she's admitting she cares about me, or could see herself caring enough, so she needs to step back and protect herself.

I hold on to her, and for a damn lawyer I'm lost for words. I can't promise I won't die.

At last, I venture down a path that might not bring her much reassurance, but I don't know how else to show her. "Chils, do you regret knowing Madeleine?"

She freezes, every sinew in her body taut as a drawn bowstring. But she doesn't move, so I keep holding her, allowing her to hide before she speaks.

A clock ticks away the long minutes. I don't even own a clock, but the time she takes to react is loud in my mind, regardless. Like the countdown to a jury's decision, it coils around me with restless energy, but I can't rush her.

Finally, she shakes her head. Or I think she does. She might be suffocating because I realize I'm holding on to her with a ferocity that matches my need to finally lay the cards on the table, to stop fighting something we didn't want but can't escape anymore.

"She loved listening to your voice," I continue. "There is no difference between you reading to her one hundred times or only once. The joy you brought to her life is priceless. Kyle robbed you of those last moments with him, and you keep giving those moments back to others. Beats of joy. The only person you deny is you. I think you could make people even happier if you allowed yourself the same."

She wiggles a bit, and I loosen my grip slightly so she can look up. Etched into her features are agony and doubt. An internal battle wages in her eyes. For once, I don't think she fights against me. She is grappling with her own fear, her own notion of safety.

Before she can lose that fight, I say, "I'm not promising you forever, because we both know we have no idea how that would work. But even if it's just one day we can spend together, it's better than nothing. It's a hundred percent more than nothing. A brief moment of happiness is better than no happiness at all."

I can't even believe I'm saying the words. Who even am I? Yet they ring true.

She wraps her arms around my waist and rests her forehead on my chest, exhaling a long, loaded breath.

"Chils, you can protect yourself from heartache and live a contented life. Or you can take the risk and reach for fucking nirvana every single day. I rest my case." I kiss the crown of her head. It's not even prickly yet, her hair buzzed too short.

"You make a compelling argument, Cressard—"

I put a finger on her lips. I need to throw in something else before she talks herself out of this. "I challenge you to try. Or are you really that scared?"

She looks up, her eyes widening before she narrows them, glaring at me through hooded lids. "I don't think relationships are built on challenges."

"We can make our own rules, baby." I wiggle my eyebrows. "Chils, there have been many fleeting moments in my life, but this thing between us feels lasting."

Again, I'm shocked by my admission, but I won't shy away because I'm scared. First, I don't get scared. Second, I've just challenged her fear, so I can't admit my own. The words are out there, and I'll own them.

She cocks her head and studies me. Her scrutiny peels at my defenses but doesn't weaken me. It probably peels at hers as well. I'm cocky enough to hope I shook the foundation of her protective walls with my arguments.

"Don't make me regret this, Dominic." Her threat is laced with mirth, but I know she means it. She'll take the leap, but needs to share the accountability. At least at this point.

I have no qualifications to take over liability for a relationship, but if that's what it takes to give her a sense of security, that's what I'll do. She's just given me a key to her heart, and I take it seriously. With responsibility. And the lingering bitterness of panic.

* * *

We spend the morning at the clinic and then the hospice. During a lunch break, we discuss the plan for the Chicago project. We've picked up takeout from a small cafe at the corner, and we eat in a small conference room at the legal clinic.

We considered staying home, but we needed to escape the intimacy the past twelve hours have brought. We addressed many things this morning, but we don't need to resolve everything.

"I'm going to buy the building anyway. Even if your board doesn't approve of the expansion. That property is an excellent investment." I take a bite of my sandwich.

"It'd certainly be a better investment than giving it to a charity." Chils stabs into her salad and takes a small bite.

"Are you trying to dissuade me already?"

My phone buzzes. I glance at the number then flip the device upside down. I've been preparing to return to my former life, but this call is a bit too much too soon. I can ignore it for a day or two. Or so I hope.

"Do you need to answer that?" Chils raises her eyebrows.

"No, I can call them back." The phone vibrates again. "I can invest my money for profit, but I don't need to, so why not a nonprofit endeavor?"

"I got myself a rich boyfriend. The bachelorettes of New York and Chicago will be jealous." She pretends to fan herself and I laugh.

"Yeah, because you'd suffer without my money. You might have a very different relationship with it, and arguably it came to you easily, but we're both filthy rich." I stand up and pull her to me, kissing away any objection she was formulating.

"Are you planning on doing this every time I might have a different opinion?" Her words are just a breeze on my lips.

"Pretty much." I dive my tongue into that beautiful mouth, already thinking about other ways I can enjoy it later.

After last night it would be considered make-up sex. I've never had that because I've never cared to make up with anyone, or to argue with a woman.

Chils moans, and I have half a mind to bend her over the desk here, but there are clients waiting, so I pull away reluctantly.

"I have one more case to take, but I wanted to ask you to help me with something afterward." I don't know if it's a good idea to take her with me on my afternoon mission, but something tells me I'll be less inclined to chicken out if she is around.

"What do you need?" She packs up the lunch and throws the garbage away.

"I'll tell you later. See you here in an hour?" I grab my phone. It buzzes again in my hand.

"Okay, I'll take care of a few things next door and I'll be back at two." She kisses my cheek. So normal. So common. So good.

I look at the screen and decide to take the dreaded call.

Chils squeezes my hand. She probably thinks I'm nervous about our destination. Well, yes, but that's not the only reason. The reason is Corrado Napolis.

Napolis is a ruthless businessman, a descendant of a crime family that has legitimized their operations over the decades, but that doesn't mean their business practices are equally legitimate.

Napolis is not above bribes, extortion, insider trading or other shortcuts in building his empire. He's also a client of mine. I got him off a racketeering and money laundering charge before.

Now he's been accused of murder. I'm pretty sure this is the one crime he didn't commit.

He called me because I'm probably one of a few who can get him acquitted. The only one, most likely.

I wrap my arm around Chils's shoulders and pull her closer. In all our differences and reluctance to make our relationship official, we considered several factors—living in two different cities, our shared aversion to commitment, the fact that we hate each other most of the time.

There is one thing, however, we kind of forgot in the midst of all the pro bono work. My paying clients are shady. My practices are morally gray.

I should talk to Chils about it, but first I called T back in my Chicago office to find out what she can about Napolis. If he really is innocent, as he claims, I'll take the case.

Uber drops us in front of the civil courthouse. The entrance is guarded by the massive stone pillars, so familiar yet so foreign to me right now. I've tried to come here once or twice since I've moved to New York, but the suffocating feeling of drowning in an oil tank attacked me every time.

As if sensing the lack of oxygen and nausea rippling through my body, Chils grabs my hand. This is the first time we've held hands. I draw a long breath.

She looks up at me. "So how does it work? We can just go in?"

"Yeah, we can look up an open case and sit in the gallery." I clear my throat, my palm clammy against her small hand.

"Okay, Cressard, should I drag you in?" She teases me, and I think it's working. I swallow and squeeze her hand tighter before I step on to the first stair.

It's like climbing toward a Himalayan summit—the air seems thinner, sweat drips down my spine, my muscles are trying to give in. I pant, and we haven't even reached the front entrance.

It's not lost on me that I voluntarily chose to have her witness me at my most vulnerable. After the sappy declarations this morning, I don't even recognize myself. The woman cursed me, and I don't fucking mind. Jesus.

Several well-dressed attorneys rush around us, the traffic on the street behind us roars, and my breath echoes loudly in my head.

The only peaceful constant is Chils. She holds my hand and doesn't rush me. Just slowly steps alongside me, giving me all the time in the world with infinite patience.

Finally, we reach the top landing. I glance at her, expecting to see disappointment or mockery. What a wuss I am.

Instead, she smiles at me. There is encouragement in her eyes. The same softness she reserves for her dad or the sick people in her life. It could be mistaken for pity, but I've observed her enough in her interactions at the hospice center to know it's not pity, it's silent support. She just is, and allows others to draw from her strength.

I don't want to fail her. No matter what support she provides, patients in her life have limited time. I want to use her support for something lasting. Even if it's just getting my career back.

I kiss her forehead and step forward.

Chapter 21

London

I wake up to the most amazing sensation. It takes a moment for my brain to fully comprehend the feeling. Mostly because it's so good, I don't try to unravel it. It's unraveling me. I stretch my arms luxuriously, the silky sheets smooth under my fingertips.

My body vibrates with desire and the message finally gets to my brain, and I realize it's Dominic's tongue between my legs that woke me up.

I don't know when I last woke up with a smile on my face, let alone a talented mouth between my thighs. Yet, this has become my typical morning over the past two weeks.

I moan loudly and arch my back. "Good morning." I sink my fingers into his hair and look down.

Oh, the glint in his eyes. "Good morning." His

whisper against my sensitive spot almost pushes me over the edge, but Dominic has other plans.

He pushes up, the biceps bulging around me, and slides inside in one fluid thrust. Mornings are the only times when we make love. All the other times he fucks me like he hates me. I love all of it. Even the lovemaking.

Had I known sleepovers have this kind of ending, I would have made them a part of my life sooner.

I've been practically living with Dominic, and to my surprise, it irritates me less than I anticipated. Maybe living with my parents prior to this honed my cohabitation skills, or maybe Dominic is just easy to live with.

We've fallen into a beautiful rhythm of life, working together, living together, and giving each other plenty of orgasms.

Case in point, I scream his name as we reach the summit together. This is the best way to start a day. Relaxing and invigorating at the same time.

Dominic kisses me deeply and then jumps out of bed. "Good morning, baby. Join me in the shower." He winks, but I know this is not an optional invitation. After all, this is his bedroom, and he is in charge.

Still dazed from sleep and the orgasm, I don't move immediately.

"Chils," he growls, and I find him leaning against the doorway. His eyes darken with the sinful threat.

I don't know when and how I lost my mind, but I stumble from the bed and pad across the room to join him. I get rewarded. Against the sink, watching us in the mirror. And then again in the shower. The man has no limits.

Later, I leave to spend some time with my dad. He's been doing much better. His tests are encouraging and his treatment ended. Now we have to wait and see. They will move back to their house in a few days.

"You look happier every day, darling." Dad pulls me into a hug. He hasn't recovered his former strength, but he has more energy.

We're sitting on my sofa, just admiring the winter shine of Central Park beyond the windows.

"I'm reasonably happy, Dad. I'm glad you're doing better." I rest my cheek on his chest, reveling in the beat of his heart.

What a beautiful vibration. A silent sound of life. My dad got a new lease on life. We don't know how long the terms are, but I'm grateful for every moment.

"I'm not going anywhere. Not just yet." He strokes my back. The list of things I let myself enjoy is growing every day.

"And how is work, Lo?" Bianca comes from the kitchen and sits beside us. "You and Dom have been bickering all the time, but spending more time together seems to suit your relationship."

I straighten up, smiling. She is not wrong. "We work well together. Though Dominic started leaning into real work more, consulting with some of his clients."

"It's a shame you lost the Chicago property. It would have been great for your endeavors and your relationship." Bianca stands up and straightens magazines on the coffee table. The woman can't sit still.

She's right—losing the Chicago property to a higher bid is the only dark cloud over the past two weeks. Frankly, I was partially relieved, because it means I'll be more permanently closer to my dad.

At the same time, it freed up time for Dominic and he picked up more of his regular work, which bothers me. We have been avoiding the topic. Both of us refuse to cast shadows over our carefully created cocoon.

I'm not a fool. I understand he hasn't had a complete transformation, and he won't be fully satisfied taking on small pro bono cases forever, but I would prefer it if he steered toward defending more innocent people. Or moved to New York permanently.

But this relationship thing is too new for both of us, and I'm acutely aware we need time to plan the future. We need to enjoy the present. I'm just not sure how much time we truly have before jumping into changes we might not be prepared for.

"We can always search for another property there." I'm trying to stay vague to avoid being cross-examined by Bianca.

"His firm is still there. Are you going to have a long-distance relationship?" She bores her intelligent eyes into me, and I want to bring up Gio and Mila, if only to escape her attention.

"Bianca, love, let her be. They're adults and they will figure it out." My dad squeezes her hand and she purses her lips, but doesn't interrogate me further.

The worst part is that she's voiced my worries. After I leave my dad I cross the hallway with dread, and a strong need to take back some control.

It's only a few steps to reach Dominic's door, but by the time I enter his apartment, I'm riled up and ready to address the problem. As usual, when I face a problem, all my typical frustration and anger resurface.

The apartment smells like Dominic, coffee and my perfume. It's an aroma of a place that has become my home. As soon as the scent tickles my nose, my resolution softens. We don't have to fight—we can talk.

Dominic is sitting at the desk, his profile to me. God, he's breathtaking. The brilliant winter sun shines behind him, creating a halo around him. If I didn't know him, I would see him as an angel.

If angels had sharp, masculine features, smart and often conniving glints in their eyes, and a ruthless side offset by passion, endless drive and natural congeniality.

I lean against the banister and study him for a moment. He is on a video call, but I can't tell what's he saying. I admire the rhythm of his confident speech, the resolution in his husky voice.

He looks up and smiles as he sees me. "Corrado, I'll have to go now, but I'll see you on Monday at the bond hearing."

I hear only this last sentence, and while I don't want to jump to conclusions, the words wind around my nerves, lacing them with bitter dread.

"Who is Corrado?" I walk down slowly but stop before crossing the living room. Something stops me from getting close. I need my autonomy for this conversation. In Dominic's immediate vicinity, I always suffer a loss of reason.

"Corrado Napolis is my client. How is your dad?" Walking to the kitchen, he smiles at me. That smile caresses my soul.

I feared his immediate proximity could challenge my resolve. Who am I kidding? It's one look from him, one crinkle of a smile, and my anger dissipates. Yet I can't shake the feeling he's trying to swipe the conversation away.

"I remember the name from the news a few years ago. Money laundering?" I move to the kitchen.

Dominic pours himself a cup of coffee and smiles at me again. "Acquitted." He takes a sip and leans against the counter.

He's trying to look casual, but he puts the cup down beside him and cracks his knuckles, gearing up for a fight.

A strange realization hits me. It washes over me with a sobering coolness. I don't want to argue with him. I want to agree with him.

I worry we've hit a topic where the lack of agreement could break us.

"You're seeing him at a bond hearing? Where?" It shouldn't bother me.

I've always known Dominic will go back to Chicago or commute there in some sort of fashion. But going back to Chicago is a different story than going back to his former clients.

I'm acutely aware of every single line on his face, as though I could scrutinize it and get answers before he even speaks.

"Chicago." He picks up the cup and takes a sip.

It might be a simple move, but I know it's more calculated than that. He's adding an air of casualness into our conversation. On purpose. It only increases the significance.

For a moment I regret stepping into his phone call, hearing those last lines. I can't pretend I'm unaffected.

"What has he done?" I don't know why I want to know. The details of the case are irrelevant.

"He's been accused of murder." Dominic lowers the cup and takes a step. I mirror it with a step back.

"Murder? You're going to have him acquitted of that as well?" My words sound like an accusation. Because they are.

A strange sense of premonition grips me, and somehow I know with absolute certainty that if we continue this conversation, the damage will be irreparable.

"He didn't do it." Dominic puts his hands into his pockets. I don't know if it's another attempt to lessen the gravity of this conversation or to keep them from shaking me. His nostrils flare slightly. He's trying to control his frustration.

"Like he didn't launder money?" My voice bounces around the walls with velocity matching its volume.

We're arguing about a stupid case, but all the while that isn't the issue here.

"This time he's been framed." Dominic rakes his hair and walks away. I hear paper rustle and a bang like a heavy book being dropped.

I dash around to his dining table/desk. He's filing papers and organizing his working chaos.

"You are going to leave to defend a murderer?" I shout and swipe my arms over the surface, papers flying around.

"What the hell, Chils?" He raises his arms in question, glowering at me. An angel? Fuck. A god of rage. "Someone has pinned a murder on him."

"And what about the other crimes he's never been prosecuted for?"

"Jesus Christ, Chils, are you for real? This is life. Real life. People do shit and people deserve justice. I'm going to make sure Napoli doesn't pay for a crime he didn't commit. We can talk about the future direction of my firm afterward. I'll be back in a week tops, and I'll stay here to prepare for the trial."

I don't know how to reconcile a man who is simultaneously defending criminals and helping defenseless victims of the healthcare system. I don't want to look away from some of his work.

I've been so proud of all the results he's single-handedly facilitated for the patients and caregivers, the clients of the nonprofit.

I can't condone his work in Chicago. It goes against everything I believe in. Also, it's something that can so easily seep into my work.

I experienced firsthand the satisfaction of getting rid of Felicity Warren. That blackmail resulted in a positive outcome for people who needed it the most.

To influence change at the bureaucratic level requires a lot of patience, and often loads of disappointment.

Advocacy can easily be replaced with bribery for much faster results. For a good cause, the end would justify the means. I know that. But I can't allow that. It's not right.

If Dominic continues donating money and time to my causes, I'd always keep the source of such donations in the back of my mind, questioning what I'm getting mixed up with.

I know I have no right to derail his career. No right to ask him to change what he's been doing all his life. What he's succeeded and excelled at.

Still, I thought...

"It looks like your stay here hasn't changed you much." Disappointment weighs me down, my shoulders shuddering under its mass.

I don't know if I'm disappointed on his behalf or mine. Most probably on ours. Because I let him pull me into this. I allowed him to manipulate me into believing there could be an us.

"I didn't come here to change. I moved here to recover, and rediscover *joie de vivre*." The frustration vibrates through his body. He shakes his head, cracking his knuckles again. "I found that with you." He steps closer and reaches out for me, but I recoil. "For fuck's sake, Chils. I can't just abandon him now. I'm his only option."

The safety and thrill of our morning together flicks through my mind. I could let him do this one last job. But there will always be one last urgent case, and I will always navigate between the acceptable levels of corruption, between all the shades of gray.

"No, Dominic, *you* have another option. You can stay here. With me." Even to my ears the words have a dusting of finality. I didn't start this argument believing I'd go this far, but why postpone the inevitable now?

A flicker of surprise flares across his face, dilating his pupils, but it's quickly replaced by defiance and something else. Anger? "What are you saying, Chils?"

I didn't know that was what I was saying, but I don't have any doubt right now. "I'm saying if you go to Chicago now to defend Napoli, you don't have to come back."

Dominic eliminates the distance between us, and I yelp as he grabs my jaw and forces me to look at him. I won't give him the satisfaction and flinch. Deep down, I know he won't harm me.

His nostrils pulse along with the vein on his neck, but there isn't anger in his eyes. It's more disbelief. He's looking at me as if wondering who I really am.

Glaring, he grinds his jaw so tight that he might crush his molars. "Is this some twisted way to demonstrate your fear that I'd leave you? I'm not leaving you, Chils. I'm going to Chicago for work, and I'll be back."

I jerk away from him. Losing his touch—however brutal—and his scent feels acute, like a fatal wound. "As I said, if you go, don't come back."

"Nobody fucking gives me an ultimatum," he bellows, and sends the rest of the things on his desk flying. At least that's what I think the sound is because I'm rushing to the door already.

I dash home and, relieved my parents are in their room, I lock myself in my bedroom. Sinking down to the floor, I close my eyes and refuse to cry.

I'm not sure what I've just done, but I do know my sense of moral conduct has just cost me the best thing I've had in my life since Kyle.

I told Dominic I feared he would corrupt me, but I didn't expect my refusal to be corrupted would hurt this much.

I collapse into the fetal position. Not crying, just getting reacquainted with the familiar feeling of loneliness. It's like muscle memory and spreads freely through my bones, into the darkest crevices of my soul.

And there, well-hidden, I discover Dominic has never been the best thing since Kyle.

He is the best thing. Period. I love the man. I love him more than anything or anyone in my life.

And I will never get to tell him that.

Chapter 22

Dominic

"**A**re you trying to break the world record for the number of consecutive burnouts in one year?" T leans in my doorway.

She is dressed to the nines in stilettos, a red pencil skirt and a white button-down shirt tucked into her high waistline. There is not a wrinkle on her clothes despite the late hour, and what I would estimate has been a ten-hour workday.

She looks professional, sexy and unapproachable. We used to flirt a lot. Not because either of us wanted to cross the line. She is too good of a paralegal to ruin our working relationship. We just enjoyed the innuendo.

But she could be topless or even naked right now and I wouldn't give a shit.

"I didn't fucking burn out," I snarl and take a sip of

my whiskey. This has been my modus operandi since I returned to Chicago last week.

Eight days ago, to be precise. I snarl instead of talk, and I drink—not in excess, yet, but still.

Chils was right—my stay in New York didn't change much in the end.

It changed everything. Though that's something I'm refusing to acknowledge. *Everything* seems too much. And I still have my work, so it can't be everything.

Some things, just to mess with me, haven't changed. Other things definitely have. Like this office doesn't feel mine anymore. My clients spark only a little drive. T is annoying. That hasn't changed. Or has it?

I don't know anymore, because people around me have lost their dimension. They are like cardboard figures littering my path, there just to piss me off.

The only multi-dimensional person in my life is... No, I'm not going there. She is not in my life anymore, anyway.

"Glad to see you imported New York's arrogance. It goes so well with your charming personality." T walks over and sits in the chair across from me.

She leans back comfortably and crosses one long leg over the other. Clearly my snarling scares off most of my employees, but Theodora is not one of them.

Eight days, seven hours and twenty-two minutes. The time ticks away in a weird state of detachment. I'm not the person who left here months ago. And I'm not the person I discovered in New York. I'm a shell of the two. A pathetic shell.

I never fail, yet my relationship with Chils feels like a gigantic defeat. Unlike with other setbacks, when I simply analyzed and corrected course or avoided the downfall altogether, this time I just want to forget.

It's not working. With every passing day, every passing hour, I feel worse. Like I've made a mistake. Not that I'd know how that feels.

I kill myself in the gym twice a day, and I spend the rest of my waking hours working or tossing and turning in bed. Sometimes I sleep—briefly—on my sofa here. I fucking hate failure.

My house doesn't feel like home. It's cold and empty, only adding to my misery. I'm going to sell it. It has always been too big for me. A smaller apartment closer to the office would make more sense.

Once Napoli's case is over, I'll call my realtor. The seed of the idea doesn't sprout, just dies immediately, failing to bloom because everything around me is a wasteland.

"Is there anything you need?" I glower at T, perched in front of me with her Mona Lisa smile. A bit too comfortable for my taste—or my current dislike of everything and everyone. She doesn't even flinch, which pisses me off.

"The question is, if *you* need anything? You've been working. I think." She circles her long manicured finger around the mess on my desk with a scrunched-up nose, as if it was sprayed by a skunk. "Yet you haven't asked for anything in the past three days."

"What's your point?" This conversation is exhausting. All conversations have been exhausting lately. I hate people.

"I don't know. The last time I checked I was your paralegal. Your researcher. Have you decided to do your own research? Or you don't want me to work on your accounts anymore? Why the hell are you pretending to be Robinson Crusoe all alone on your island?"

Fucking T. Employees shouldn't be allowed free speech.

"I don't know what you're talking about, but if you lack work assignments, you can file the paper-work over there." I gesture to my coffee table, now overflowing with papers, and then I return to scan-ning the file in front of me, without any idea what it says.

"I'm not your damn assistant, Dominic. I don't know what you *caught* in New York, but you better get over it. Napoli needs you on top of your game. If you thought your sabbatical benefited you, it didn't. You're worse than when you left, for fuck's sake."

She is not wrong. Perhaps I shouldn't have come back. Maybe it's Chicago and this shitty office that makes me lose my shit. I don't know anymore. I have no interest in anything I used to enjoy.

Nothing makes sense. Nothing is exciting. Nothing is worth my attention or effort.

"Napoli will be fine. The PI has some info on the actual killer and he's coming in early in the morning so we can take action."

"This might be helpful." She stands up and hands me a manila envelope. She scrutinizes me with her hand on her hip. "I took the liberty of working on the case even without your instructions." She starts to leave.

"T..." I stand up from my desk. "Thank you."

She gives me a distasteful look and shakes her head. "You can show your appreciation with a bonus, boss."

I nod and wish I wasn't looking at her. A glimmer of disappointment passes through her face before she strides away. She was hoping for a verbal sparring match. One more thing I don't do anymore. I don't tease or insult people.

I walk over to the wall of glass where the spectacular skyline of Chicago glows in front of me.

I miss my view of Central Park. Fuck. Of course, the thought propels other images.

Chils's full lips arguing with me over... well, over anything and everything really. I snort. She truly is a person of contradictions. Fierce and sad. Feisty and considerate. Angry and compassionate.

A soundtrack of her sounds has played on an endless loop in my mind. Her throaty laugh when she forgets to sulk and truly relaxes. Her moan when I wake her up with my tongue between her thighs. The volume of her arguments. The whisper of her breath when she sleeps beside me.

She used to play with her ponytail when she read. I guess that's no longer possible. Maybe she runs her hands over her smooth skull now.

I wonder if Micah moved out. If Paris returned from her trip to Europe. If Cesare's wife baked another loaf of banana bread. Has Chils received the funds from the city to finance the new medical equipment in the hospice? Has she started planning her next gala?

Where will she go on her next trip? Have any of the cases in the legal clinic been resolved? Are there new ones they might need help with?

I return to my desk and call Nia.

"Hey, Dom, how are you?" she answers, and I hear the familiar silence in the background. She is either studying or still poring over the files at the clinic.

It's the same silence I discovered in the library as a child. The one I immersed myself in during the long hours of studying for my exams. The peace I usually enjoyed when staying at my office this late. That one has been drowned out by the ongoing b-roll of Chils playing in my head.

"I'm good," I lie. Fake it until you make it. "Are you at the clinic?"

"Yeah." I hear a creak and picture her leaning on the old chair behind one of the communal desks. "I'm preparing paperwork for a case. By the way, we won the insurance claim for Ralph's daughter."

Satisfaction and something akin to pure joy flushes through me. "I knew we would. Good job, Nia. Tell me about other cases."

We talk for over an hour. Nia explains several cases, I give her suggestions, we brainstorm solutions. At the end of the call, I feel... I don't know, I feel alive for the first time in a week.

Perhaps I should open a legal clinic here. It's the balancing of my work and the selfless help that might recreate the missing harmony in my life. Fill the void.

The only cloud over the conversation was the persistent image of Chils in the background. She might have even sat next door to Nia with one of the hospice's clients. It's probably too late for that. Unless someone is leaving this world already. She would be there. Who will help her pull out of those shadows swallowing her?

A message distracts me from the downward spiral of my thoughts.

Rocco: Are you sleeping, asshole?

I don't bother responding and click on the video call. He answers immediately. He's showered, sipping a coffee on his rooftop deck. He looks rested.

"Have you killed the children to get some shut-eye?" Even my jokes are messed up.

"Don't fucking joke about that, asshole. We hired a night nanny. I've been getting eight hours of sleep for a week now. And Ness all to myself, but I'll spare you the details."

He closes his eyes and tilts his head toward the sun, content and happy. Never did I think I'd be jealous of Rocco da Bonno, but right at this moment, I envy him everything, including the eight hours of sleep.

"You certainly look rested."

He frowns at me. "What's wrong with you?"

"Nothing. Why?"

I don't even know why I'm lying. Mostly because I don't need Rocco gloating about my failure. Or to put my problems into words. Chils made her decision. I'm not good enough for her. No amount of dissecting would change that.

"Are you in your office? You're back in Chicago?"

He moves on his chair, leaning forward slightly to give me his undivided attention.

"Yeah, I'm back. Napoli got set up for murder." I recline, pushing the flexible backrest of my chair and put my feet on the corner of my desk.

"Good. I've never liked that dickhead."

Nobody really likes Napoli. Come to think of it, I hate his guts. Yet that has never stopped me from working with him.

The realization hits me like a brick in the head, the aftershocks echoing through my mind. Fuck me. Have I lost the first woman who ever meant anything to me for this?

"It was a setup. I'm going to get him off." The lack of enthusiasm in my statement surprises us both.

Rocco narrows his eyes, as if squinting will let him pick up on my bullshit better. "I don't doubt that. So you're back-back, or just visiting to hit the headlines for your ruthless awesomeness as a defense lawyer?"

"I'm back." What was my motivation to return? The headlines? The fame? The impossible case only I can win? The asshole Napoli? None of that seems even remotely important or exciting. Certainly not worth losing Chils over.

"What about London? I don't think your sex drive can withstand a long-distance relationship." He snorts, pleased with himself.

"We broke up." This is the first time I've said those words. First time I admitted openly that it's over between us. The words leak like acid all over my insides, slowly eating away at me.

Fucking Rocco laughs. "I know you're not relationship material, but guessing by your overall state, I don't think the breakup was a welcome development. What did you do?"

Smug asshole. "I didn't do anything. She didn't like that I took Napoli's case, or the general idea of me returning to my work."

He nods, scratching the back of his neck. "She wasn't for the long-distance relationship?"

"Not with someone who defends criminals." I click my stapler a few times, because discarding staples all over my desk is apparently reasonable behavior.

Rocco takes his cup and inhales the smell of the drink with reverence. "I'm kind of on her side."

"What the fuck, Rocco? You don't even know her." But I don't really blame him. I want everyone to be on Chils's side. She deserves that.

"No, but from what you've told me, the woman spreads good around herself like fairy dust. If you expected her to give up on all her principles for you, you're delusional."

"Screw you. I'm good at my job. I have a successful

firm here. I won't give up everything because of a woman."

The fact that I'm defending my firm and the work I no longer like is a new level of low. Like six feet under wouldn't be low enough for the lies I tell myself. Or my friend.

"A woman?" He snorts, looking at me as if I was deranged.

"Okay, she was probably as close to *the* woman as I'll ever get, but that doesn't matter anymore. She gave me an ultimatum. Nobody gives me ultimatums."

"Sure. Sure." Rocco raises his arms in surrender. "So, you're happy being back?"

Oh, if only I could wipe that haughty grin off his face. Instead, I glower at him, because no, I'm not fucking happy. Because if I didn't see it before from my high horse, I see now I made a mistake. Possibly the biggest mistake of my life.

"That's what I thought." He interprets my silent glare. "Let me just summarize this: you burned out, probably a result of your lifestyle and lack of balance. You took a sabbatical and you found joy in pro bono work, a lifestyle that wasn't killing you anymore. You also found a woman who made you happy. As happy as an arrogant asshole like you can get." He pops a strawberry into his mouth. "And at the peak of it all, you decided to return to Chicago, back to the shit lifestyle and soul-sucking clients. And by the looks of it—exhibit A: the return of the lumberjack beard—it all worked out well." He eats another piece of fruit.

"No, it didn't," I bark. "It didn't, but there isn't much I can do about that."

"You draw the line at the ultimatum? How dare she?" he mocks me. "Listen, asshole, you better grovel until she takes you back. Because she is the best thing that's ever happened to you. And it's your fault you didn't see it and pushed her into giving you the ultimatum."

"So I should just fold and cater to her wishes. This is my work we're talking about."

"Pull your fucking head out of the sand, Dom. She didn't ask you to give up lawyering, she asked you to do it with higher moral standards. Now, don't get me wrong, I don't judge how you've made your money. I've done worse. But I understand how potentially dangerous your clients are."

"London wasn't scared. She just didn't like that I defended crooks." That's a pretty pathetic defense line.

"Fine, even if she didn't mind... The thing is that once you have someone else in your life, it's no longer about you, your fun, the adrenaline of it all. What if the people who are trying to destroy Napoli would want to get to you?"

He pauses, letting that sink in. I swallow. If anyone

hurt Chils, I would kill them. But nobody would want to hurt her deliberately if it wasn't for me.

"I see on that beautiful face of yours that there is some brain left. So let's circle back, perhaps her objections were morally motivated, but safety is a part of it. And I know what I'm saying because someone fucking stabbed Ness, and it was the worst pain I've ever experienced. So, London's request wasn't too farfetched."

He shrugs and grabs another piece of fruit. "But let's explore the selfish part of it all. You don't even like that job. I saw you droning on and on about all the people you helped while in New York. I haven't seen you so animated, so real, since you've made your first hundred mil. Fighting her ultimatum was stupid. An excuse because you're scared. The question is, do you love her?"

I'm about to argue that I'm not scared, but his question strikes me like lightning, buzzing through every nerve in my body. What I find searching for the answer isn't a resolute denial. It's recognition that vibrates through me.

"I think I fucked up." I crack my knuckles.

"You think? It's easy. You need to make her listen, and your argument, or even better your actions need to make it impossible for her to refuse."

"How do I do that?"

"I don't know, asshole, only you can figure that out.

But I would suggest you start by dropping Napoli, and then prepare the best closing argument of your life."

I don't think I ever argued a case with such a volatile potential result, or one where so much was at stake, but for the first time in a week, my entire being is squeezed between dread and excitement.

I'm going to win Chils back. It feels like an impossible mission at this point, but I'll do whatever it takes. As grave as the idea of making her trust me and believe in us might be, I jump up like a winner already. Because Rocco's words provided clarity clearer than crystal.

I love London Lowe.

Now I have to hope she loves me back.

Chapter 23

London

Ralph's daughter silently cries at his bedside. I lean in the doorway, not wanting to disturb her, but unable to move. Last night I gave him my phone to watch porn.

I remember how we danced together after Madeleine passed away, and I wonder if today we should all just watch an adult movie to remember Ralph.

The thought curls up the corners of my lips slightly.

"He loved it here," his daughter whispers.

She lifts her eyes to me, still holding her father's hand. The afternoon sun seeping through the window behind her gives her an almost ethereal look.

She smiles, her face still wet with tears. "You gave

him a gift, London. I hope when I'm at the end of my journey I can find a place like this one."

"I think Ralph would have made the best out of any place or situation." I wipe a tear from my cheek.

"Perhaps, but it was here he could spread the joy, even though he could barely breathe. He was always like that, just a goofball. Maybe we should throw a party to celebrate his life, to remember how much fun he was."

"He would love that." I let the tears wash my face, not trying to suppress them. Ralph would have called me on my bullshit if I tried. "I'm going to give you some privacy. Take as much time as you need."

I wish Dominic was here. Like so many times over the past three weeks, I picture his handsome grin, and how he would pull me into his arms and everything would seem bearable.

How much loss must one experience to cope better? I was a child when Mom died. Losing her was profound, but I was shielded from it by my young age, my family, and later on by Bianca's family.

After Kyle, my heart was broken into a million pieces. Small shards I've never picked up. I've lost many people over the years. Most of them strangers, clients, acquaintances who touched my life briefly.

And yet, grieving the loss of Dominic has scraped me raw. I can't even dive into the stages of grief because I haven't reached denial yet. For the first time in my life, I can't access anger. I'm just numb.

The days pass around me, and I go through the motions, mind over matter. I pretend most of the time, which is fucking exhausting. I pretend for my father and Bianca. I pretended at Hunter's opening of the new gym, and have avoided Syd ever since.

I pretend in front of my team at the foundation, and here in the hospice.

I pretend in front of Patagonia, who has leaned into the unofficial leader's role at the legal clinic, and takes enormous pleasure in reporting every single accomplishment to me.

I'm not sure if Dominic put her up to that. If he did, it's just plain cruel. The whole clinic is like a slap in the face. And I can't just cancel it. None of those people, clients or volunteers, would deserve that.

I head down to the reception area and sit in an armchair by the entrance. After I don't know how long, I dial my office.

"Ashley, I'm not coming in today. Anything urgent?"

I'm facing the front window. It's been overcast since Dominic left. Disgusting slush covers the streets. I wish I was in the Caribbean, or Hawaii. Here, the gray weather just laughs in my face. Thank you very much, Mother Nature, for matching my mood.

"All good here. We completed the funding agreements for the research projects and the money has been transferred as of this morning," Ashley reports. We received a large anonymous donation covering the funding I was so desperately missing.

A part of me suspects the source is Dominic. It makes me feel all sorts of things, starting with resentment that he's trying to hijack all the spheres of my life even after he left. Or is that an apology? Screw him.

But there is another unfortunate outcome of his gesture—hope. Hope that it was him. Hope that it means he's reconsidering his decision. Hope that he wants to come back. Hope. Hope. Hope.

"That's good. Ashley, can you take over the oversight of the legal clinic? Pass some of the admin tasks to a volunteer if you need to free up the time, but I need to focus on other things."

Like avoiding anything that reminds me of Dominic. A fucking behemoth task since we used to share a hallway, and I can't not think about him every time I enter my building and see Cesare.

Yes, I know his name. I even chat with him occasionally because I'm that pathetic. Somehow, it makes me connected to Dominic. Oh my God, I'll have to move.

"Of course. I'll get in touch with Patagonia and take care of things on this side. Before I forget, there is a potential donor who would like to meet in person. Can I set it up?"

Oh, I really don't have the energy to meet with people, to schmooze, to even pretend interest, but I can't pass on opportunities like this. "Okay, set it up, my calendar is pretty much open."

"It's in Denver. Would you mind if I tag along?"

She hasn't tried to participate in fundraiser meetings before, but I guess even Ashley sees how incapable I currently am. "Denver? Really? Who is it? Why our foundation? You better look into them, Ashley, so we don't waste our time. And yes, if it's a highly probable target, let's go together."

I should walk. The streets are matching my mood anyway, and I'm hoping to clear my head. Of what I'm not sure, because there is no clearing my mind of him. But I can try to move a bit, at least for a few blocks.

For years, I've done my work out of guilt and duty, and while I've always loved it, I found a lot of frustration and anger in it. Dominic changed that. He somehow sucked me into his stupid enthusiasm and relentless drive, and showed me joy in grave situations.

His ideas, his ability to get energized about possibilities. He doesn't see them as another insurmountable mountain that you climb only to discover there is a swamp to pass, an ocean to swim. Another barrier. A new hurdle.

He sees everything as an opportunity or a challenge, and tackles them with winning energy.

At the same time, he enjoys any victory. Even a small one. Where I would get immediately sucked into *there is more to do*, he celebrates the milestone by hitting the road running toward the next one.

I don't know if it's a healthy way of doing things, but what little of his enthusiasm has rubbed off on me has made me happier than I've been in years. And prouder of my accomplishments.

I can't discount the fact that the foundation achieves more with that attitude. I can throw all the money in the world at the problem, but it's my mindset that makes the difference.

I have Dominic to thank for that. Even though right now it's hard to find that mindset. Also something I have him to thank for. And for the mind-blowing orgasms. And what was it all good for? He left me anyway.

He chose his shady client and stormed out. Over the past few weeks, I've considered a life where he'd do what he does and I'd just look the other way. On multiple occasions, late at night, unable to sleep and staring at the ceiling, miserable and lonely, I picked up the phone to call him. Almost.

I wasn't seeking a relationship and somehow I found myself in one, but as much as I miss the annoying bastard, I can't compromise my morals. I often teased him about purgatory, but if we stayed together... if I ignored what he does, I'd feel my work was tainted.

My feet are soaked and chilled to the bone. I've been walking for over an hour. I don't want to go home. Dad and Bianca are gone, and my apartment is emptier than ever before.

It's as if they took its energy and vibe away when they left. But they didn't. It left with the man who didn't care to stay. Or to argue with me on my point.

I call Sydney, but I get her voicemail. Paris is gone, so I sigh and dial Gio.

"I'm not talking to you about my love life," he growls instead of a greeting.

"So there is a love life to talk about?" I can't help but laugh. He certainly shocked us last week.

"What do you want, Lo?"

The hum in the background sounds familiar. "Are you at the club? Can I come have a coffee with you? I'm about ten minutes away."

"Why?"

"Jesus, Gio, I don't want to be alone. No love life talk, I promise. Can—"

"Okay." He hangs up. What is it with the Cassinettis and their phone manners? Bianca does the same thing.

I arrive to find him at his usual table by the glass wall overlooking the city skyline. Right now, the view is sheathed in fog, or whatever this wintery condensation is that makes everyone miserable. Even more than we already are.

"Jesus, Lo, what's with your shoes?" He looks around, apparently embarrassed by me.

My suede boots are soaked, practically destroyed. He's probably not too pleased with my jeans and sweatshirt. They are nice, but definitely not good enough for this stuck-up place. Well, he could be happy I'm wearing jeans. It's been leggings for the past few days. Today's outfit is an upgrade.

As I sit down, I have to admit his bespoke suit screams in contrast to my casual, carelessly put together attire. "Sorry, I didn't plan on coming."

"Is this how you normally dress?" His scrunched-up face looks like he's just discovered I have an infectious disease.

"Yeah, bro, discovering life now that you're actually looking around?"

The server interrupts our *friendly* siblings' spat and we both order wine.

"So your boyfriend is coming back soon?"

Seriously? I came to forget the whole thing. To get reasonably distracted and force the time to pass faster without the constant droning of my mind over the part of my brain that stored all the memories of Dominic and then swelled like a tumor.

Gio doesn't know we broke up, so I guess I can't blame him. In fact, how does he know Dominic has been gone?

"What do you mean?" *And can we talk about something else?* I don't say that because it would only make him think there is something to talk about.

"He dropped his client. It's made the headlines. Not a front-page story, but it's juicy enough news."

His words reverberate inside my body, my heart racing like a herd of galloping horses. My head throbs as though they thundered through my temples.

Forgoing all my intentions not to discuss this, I blurt, "He dropped the Napoli murder case?" It must be that. Unless Dominic has already picked up other high-profile cases.

"You didn't know? I thought it was a mutual decision. The official quote is *personal reasons.*"

I want to stand up and run to Chicago. Or to Dominic's apartment here. Or at least to a private corner where I can call him. But I don't move. I don't blink. I don't allow hope to direct my actions. Or reactions.

"What's going on? Frankly, I've met Napoli once, and the fucker is bad news. It wouldn't look good for your foundation to be associated with someone like him."

The server brings our order and I swallow the whole drink down without thought, then return the empty glass to the table.

Gio immediately gestures for a refill. "You're acting strange, Lo. You know I don't like drama. I don't know how to deal with that. Shall I call Syd, or someone who is not me?"

I chuckle at that. "Gio, Dominic and I broke up because I asked him not to take that case. I haven't spoken to him since he left three weeks ago."

"Oh." He takes a sip of his wine. "I'm not an expert in that area." He fidgets and looks away. It's funny to see my stern, bossholish brother squirm around an explanation.

"I can't claim I'm a relationship expert either. I didn't even want the relationship." I don't think I've been this confused in a long time.

What does it mean? Why did he drop Napoli? It's been three weeks since he left. Did he find out Napoli was guilty after all? Or did Dominic's decision have nothing to do with the case?

"You looked happy with him. He got you, and you're not the warmest person in the room, but somehow he reveled in your frost and thawed it a bit.

Mind you, I didn't really know him aside from that Christmas lunch."

"Yes, but he left. He left to defend a criminal." Finally, my other glass of wine arrives. This time I only take a sip.

"Okay, one mistake. And it looks like he corrected it. When I look at taking over a business, I assess if we can pivot and change."

"Even if his decision has anything to do with me, there is still the fact he left. He chose his work over me. Over my principles. He stormed away because I challenged him. Again, I have no experience, but if my dad stormed out and left for three weeks every time Bianca challenged him, our family would be together only three months of every year."

"Come on, your dad is a softie. It would have been at least six months each year." Gio's lips quirk up.

"Yeah, but the point is, neither of them ran. I can't be abandoned like that every time things get complicated."

"What's the name of your assistant? Avery?" He makes a gesture with his hand, wading through the air as if he could snatch the answer there. And why are we changing the subject?

"Ashley." I huff. Where is he going with this?

"Okay, Ashley is important to you, isn't she?" He plays with his cufflinks.

What the fuck? I nod, scowling.

"Has she ever made a mistake?"

"Of course she has. What are—"

"Did you forgive her?"

"Of course. People make mistakes—"

"But her value outweighed the issue."

"Are you analyzing my relationship like it's a business decision?"

"Do you get the point?" he quips.

I chew on my bottom lip, the thin stem of my glass smooth under my fingertips as I run them up and down. One mistake. If Dominic indeed dropped Napoli because of me, am I willing to look past that? But there is a bigger question.

"If he dropped him only because of me, I don't want to bear such responsibility. It would mean he made a radical change to be with me. Not because it was the better choice, but because I asked. People say relationships require compromises. Perhaps on the smaller, day-to-day stuff they do. But this is a life-changing decision."

If Dominic made that decision because he felt half as shitty as me about our breakup, if he dropped the murder case to get me back, I don't think I can live with that. I don't want him to defend criminals, but at the same I can't be the sole reason for such a change in his life.

"Relationships are messy. Takeovers, spreadsheets and project management tools are less volatile." Gio raises his glass.

"But not everything is a fiscal transaction. Are you staying here for dinner?" I gather my purse and stand up. "I'm going home now. Something tells me I have another sleepless night to look forward to."

Initially, I had planned to stay as long as possible, to escape the void in my place and my heart. But now I'm drawn to my home, because what if... That's stupid. Still, I hope Dominic might be there, across the hallway, waiting for me.

Cesare is not working tonight, and I'm disappointed because his face would give me a hint. I know I'm being unreasonably optimistic about the development.

I told Gio I wouldn't accept if Dominic dropped Napoli just for me, but who am I kidding? My body is practically vibrating with need. And my heart? My poor heart needs a win. Badly.

I march out of the elevator, half expecting the wall to be lined with boxes. There are no boxes anywhere, of course. I hesitate for a moment, and then I knock at his door.

The answer is silence.

I knock again.

I check my phone. Perhaps I should call him?

A part of me wants to, but Dominic decided to leave. He needs to decide to come back.

And my heart needs to stop hoping.

I stare at the unyielding door for I don't know how long before I collect myself, leaving my hope scattered on Dominic's welcome home mat.

Chapter 24

London

People teem around the departure hall. The announcements ring in my ears. I used to love airports. The exhilaration of new destinations, new adventure, new experiences. I'd get the thrill even when picking someone up.

Right now, I hate airports. Though arguably there isn't much I like lately.

I pick up a tea and stand at the side of the coffee shop. Ashley is late. She also didn't send me my boarding pass or flight information, other than the terminal and departure time. And she forgot to share the file on our new potential donor.

Frankly, her performance in the past two days has been chaotic, elusive and weird. She is stressed about her first big donor meeting. I should be more supportive and make things easier on her. I have been anything but that.

In fact, I've been missing in action. This morning I called Ashley to cancel or go without me, but her near-breakdown propelled me to action. I showered. First time in three days. I pulled out a dress. First one in four weeks. I put on lipstick.

I still look like shit. Because I feel like shit. A call for a flight to Aruba echoes through the hall, and a tiny jolt of thrill sweeps through me. I should take my annual trip. That would get me out of this funk.

After I realized Dominic was not coming back and his reasons for dropping Napoli have probably nothing to do with me—and yes, somewhere between him entering my life and exiting it swiftly, I started to form opinions based on assumptions, not facts—I tried to reach Paris to join her in Europe, but I couldn't get her. Maybe a solo trip to Aruba, or Thailand...

"I'm sorry I'm late." Ashley interrupts my daydreaming.

"Good morning. It's okay. You're here now. Let's go." I start toward security.

Ashley has our boarding passes and we get through reasonably swiftly.

"You told me our flight is at eleven, but there is no eleven o'clock to Denver."

"It's because our flight leaves in twenty minutes, so

we better hurry." She bolts, and I startle for a moment before I pursue her.

"What the hell, Ashley?" I pant as we reach the gate.

"Ladies, you need to go to your seats now." The attendant rushes us through, lifting the rope. We're the last ones to board.

"We don't have seats together. You're here." Ashley points to a seat in business class. "We're going to Chicago."

She doesn't necessarily step back, but kind of leans away from me, as if she's expecting me to slap her. Since when have I used physical violence?

I don't understand what is happening. Why would she pretend we're going to Denver? Regardless of her motivations, my heart starts a stampede at the mere mention of the city.

"I'm sorry," Ashley squeaks. "I was worried you wouldn't want to go because you know who lives there."

"So you tricked me?" I snort, shaking my head. I'd have canceled the trip if I knew. "Ashley, I'm not stupid. The chances we would run into Dominic are non-existent."

"Excuse me, you absolutely need to take your seats now," the flight attendant urges, and Ashley is too eager to disappear into the rear of the plane.

I sit down and look back after my assistant. I regret boarding this plane. I was doing just fine sulking at home. Not only does my close coworker think I'm completely unreasonable—and in this case she would have been right—but an uncomfortable anxiety squeezes at my chest.

All because I'm Dominic bound. I mean Chicago bound.

It's only once we start taxiing that I realize she didn't leave me any information about the meeting. I had planned to prepare during the flight, but I guess I'll have to improvise.

In the cab, Ashley finally gives me a topline bio of the donor—an heir to a chain of candy shops I've never heard of—and I feel utterly unprepared for the meeting.

Instead of googling my prospect, I search the other cars, hoping for a glimpse of him. It's irrational, improbable, and frankly embarrassing, and it pisses me off.

Perhaps it's good we came here, so I can attack my stupid feelings head on, on his territory, and somehow get over myself. Over him.

The car pulls to a stop on a charming residential street with large brownstones and impressive oaks, with thick tree trunks lining both sides. It's a peaceful neighborhood with no signs of life.

"Are we meeting him at his home?" I ask Ashley as we get out of the car.

"Looks like it." She points to a house with white shutters and large windows.

"Okay, Ashley, you'll have to lead the meeting since you made sure I'm unprepared. Are you ready?" We ascend the steps.

"Mm-hmm." She rings the bell. She doesn't sound or look ready. In fact, she looks like she might throw up. For fuck's sake, I'll just have to wing it.

Winging it becomes a distant memory when the door opens, and now I feel like I'm going to throw up.

"I'll see you later," I hear Ashley's words and footsteps retreating.

He is even more handsome than I remember. His face is laced with dark signs of exhaustion. His hair is slightly longer, falling over his forehead. It gives him a boyish, ragged look. And while his jaw is clenched, his eyes are soft. I almost wish he was smirking, because I miss that perpetually cocky expression.

"Chils," Dominic rasps.

I missed you. It's so nice to see you. My life has derailed without you, and I can't remember how I lived before.

"You got Ashley to lie to me?" is what I end up saying, because old habits die hard.

A shadow passes over his face. "I was desperate.

Would you come in, please?"

I look down at the threshold, picturing quicksand and hot coals in one. Two days ago, I thought I'd run to him, relieved that we could get past our differences.

In the two days of lying in my bed, I cried myself out of those feelings and hardened myself to survive.

The newly-forged walls feel like shackles. I'm scared to trust. Though my heart screams to tear down the walls at the sight of him.

"Chils, please." Hurt and regret lace his voice, and there are so many feelings in those two words that my legs finally move forward and I step inside the house.

I halt even before he closes the door behind us, because if I thought Dominic at the door was the big surprise of the day, I can't even describe the level of shock ramming through me right now.

I'm standing in the middle of a very familiar reception area. It's not identical to the one in New York, but it's similar in its design, feel and peacefulness.

"What is this?" I don't look at him, because those dark eyes crack my defenses at the best of times.

"A new hospice, the start of your Chicago expansion." He is only a foot away, his scent wrapping me in a pleasant embrace.

"How did you get this done in such a short time?" A voice in my head laughs at my question, but I can't help but avoid the elephant in the room.

All I want is to throw myself at him, but... There are no ground rules. Right now, the only painfully obvious thing is the potential for more heartbreak.

"A lot of bribes," he tries to joke, but when I whip my head round and glare, he raises his arms in surrender. "Too soon."

I step away from him, needing to breathe air that isn't infused with the appeal of Dominic Cressard. "Who owns the building?"

"Me. I used to live here till about three weeks ago, when I tore apart the interior and, well, you see the result." He puts his hands in his pockets. "Do you want to see the rest of it?"

I don't know what I want. I want him to tell me what this all means, but I'm afraid because there is a whole lot of hope attached to such a conversation, and I don't think I can survive having any more of my hopes crushed.

"Later. Where will you live?" I hear the distant hum of life outside, but here I only hear my heart thumping with a hesitant thrill, and my mind rebelling against everything, trying to protect me.

"I was hoping with you." He raises his eyebrows and cocks his head, pulling a slow, alluring, though shy, smile.

I gasp and step back. Not forward, I step back. What's wrong with me?

"Chils, you once told me that not all good intentions are for the other person's benefit. I think the opposite applies too. Not all bad decisions are meant to hurt. I made such a decision, and I hurt us both." He lifts his foot, but then changes his mind and doesn't step forward, just shifts his weight.

"You dropped Napoli." I seek that one final confirmation I need. "Why?"

"That kind of work doesn't fulfill me anymore."

Relief rushes through me in a sound that is somewhere between a gasp and a whimper. He didn't want to appease me, to make a gesture. He decided to change. For himself firstly. And by extension for us. If there still is an us.

"I only wish I'd realized that sooner." He looks at me through hooded eyes, and oh, what that does to me. Clearly my body is already on board with reconciliation. My heart has never accepted the break-up. It's my mind that requires more evidence.

Dominic continues, "I wish I understood your *ultimatum* for what it was, a plea for me to realize what's best for me. And before you ask... No, I'm not trying to find a better spot in purgatory. I'm just trying to find a better spot in this life. Chils, you're engraved on my mind, in my heart—" he steps closer, only mere inches between us now, "—and probably even in my soul, because let me tell you, my moral score has improved doing all this selfless shit." He gestures around us, and I try to stifle a sob.

Dominic rubs my arms with his huge hands. "Rocco teased me yesterday that I'm doing it for a woman, but there isn't a doubt in my mind that I'm not. I'm doing this because you showed me how many people benefit from small acts of kindness. But if I get my woman in the process, that would be great."

"These are not small acts of kindness." I sniffle, tears rolling down my cheeks.

"I was kind of hoping you would focus on the latter part of that statement." Dominic cups my cheeks. "Chils, I used to take things for granted and they lost their value. The loss in your life taught you not to take anything for granted, and I think we can find the middle ground together."

Our eyes lock and we still, frozen in a tender moment of finding harmony. With his thumb, he wipes away my tears. The sense of calm descends on me, and suddenly I see this relationship as any other adventure I've ever experienced.

Grasping at the thrill, living to its fullest, staying here and now. Grounded while spreading our wings.

I don't have to fear the commitment, because while no one can guarantee he won't leave me, building memories with Dominic during the time we might be given together is priceless.

It's worth the risk. He is a force of nature who digs to unearth my joy reservoir, regardless of how deeply I try to bury it. I need this man in my life, because my life is better when he makes me laugh, annoys me, teases me... loves me.

His eyes drop to my mouth, but he doesn't close the distance. Every fiber in my body screams with recognition, with burning desire and peaceful contentment.

"I missed you." I want to say the other three words, but I can't yet. And I think he understands.

Dominic crashes his lips against mine, and it hits all the marks and more. Our kiss is exploratory, as if it was our first, but also familiar, like returning home after a long time. It's desperate with our combined longing, relief and adoration.

My face is lost in his hands as he angles me for a deeper connection, and for a brief moment I regret not having my long hair anymore. I miss those fingers in my strands, fisting and pulling.

He pulls away. "I have something for you." Reaching into his pocket, he looks at my cleavage and frowns. "This might be pushing my luck, but I bought you this."

He takes my hand and drops something into my palm. A chili-shaped golden pendant.

I chuckle.

"I was hoping you'd wear it on your chain, but...

Where is it?"

I touch my cleavage, even though I know there is nothing there. "I took it off. Kyle will always be a memory to cherish, to ground me, to remember, but it's time to move on."

He seizes my mouth and I wrap my arms around his broad shoulders and whimper against his lips, satisfied and crazed for more at the same time.

I squeeze the pendant in my hand. He didn't get me a necklace, only a pendant to add to the one I've been wearing. Not trying to replace my important memory, but simply add to it. I'm so overwhelmed by this consideration that I cling to him, unsure how to show my gratitude.

We can't stop kissing, trying to make up for the lost time that we were apart. The kiss is sensual, but it's not just foreplay, it's so much more. It's a seal. A confirmation of our commitment.

When we pull away for air, Dominic keeps his hands on my face, holding onto me like I could disappear.

"There are beds upstairs. Would that be inappropriate?" He grinds his hips against me, the evidence of his need bulging against my pelvis.

I bite my lip. "I don't know. We can always burn the mattress."

"Ralph would be proud of us." Dominic winks, but

his face falls when he sees my expression.

"Ralph—" I choke out his name, unable to continue.

"I'm sorry, Chils." He wraps his arms around me, pulling me closer to that space of safety, owning me, but also liberating me.

"I watched porn with him the night before." I sob.

Dominic lifts my chin with his finger. "So, I have corrupted you after all."

I laugh through the tears. "Take me upstairs, Cressard."

I yelp as he scoops me up and carries me while I can't stop grinning at him. In the first bedroom, Dominic drops me on the bed and covers me with his body, devouring my mouth again.

I'm trapped under him, unable to even get undressed, but I don't mind. We have all the time in the world. And as though our minds have synced already, Dominic rises slightly, his eyes fierce on me.

"I told you before, Chils, that I can't promise you forever. I was wrong. I want forever with you. Regardless of how long we have in this life, I don't want to spend another minute without you. So let me correct myself. I can't promise how long forever lasts, but I promise to cherish every minute. With you. For you. Beside you. In you." He gives me that cocky grin. "Until my last breath. I love you, London."

Epilogue

Dominic

One month later

"I'm leaving. Could you type these up?" I drop a folder on the desk, not even realizing which volunteer is getting stuck with the task of deciphering my handwriting.

"Leaving already?" Nia teases me from her desk. I've been here all day, and it never seems enough.

"Some of us have a real life out there. Besides, I have you to slave away," I deadpan. We've grown close, but it doesn't hurt to remind her who the boss is. Nia has become my New York version of T.

T stuck with me when my firm split up. My partners couldn't get past my reluctance to continue with some of our clients. As a result, my firm is a smaller shop, but we have a roster of clients we can trust.

"Ha, you keep forgetting we don't work for you, Dom." She clicks her pen, amusement all over her face. "Do you have exciting evening plans?"

"None of your business," I quip. "Finish what you can and get out of here at a decent hour." I turn to everyone else before I exit. "Like before midnight." I chuckle.

Nia wasn't wrong. I do have exciting evening plans. I'm taking Chils out for dinner. We haven't been on a proper date in the longest time, and I don't want our partnership to become about work only. We need to make more effort.

The past month has been packed with activity. The hospice in Chicago is already reaching its capacity. Both legal clinics are packed with clients. Between the two cities, my pilot has been busier than ever.

We have our home base in Chils's apartment here in New York. When in Chicago we've been staying at a hotel, but we're closing on a new small place there as well.

Of course, Chils fought me on that because she doesn't want to own anything, but I ignored her objections, and in the end, we co-signed the offer. It wouldn't really matter because I could have just bought the place myself, but I need this commitment from her.

We talked about marriage down the line, but we agreed it has never been on our radar, and we don't need a piece of paper to make our relationship real. It's been real since it was fake.

I know Chils is a hundred percent in. She proves it daily. Though she hasn't said the L word yet. Funny how I'd never uttered it myself before, and now I crave hearing it. Not that I'd ever admit that to anyone.

When I arrive, the apartment is empty. I take a shower, shave and put on a suit. We have a reservation at Chils's brother's restaurant Casa Cassi, but we're going to miss it at this rate. I text her.

Me: Where are you?

Chils: On my way.

Chils went to see her father this afternoon. Micah has been doing reasonably well, mostly coping with the side effects of his treatment, but recovering.

Me: ETA???

Chils: One to ten minutes.

Before I can snarl at her over the text, the key turns in the door.

"You're lucky it ended up being one minute. Why ten? Were you planning to crawl up the stairs?"

I help her out of her coat and kiss her, lingering

over her lips and reveling in the heat and scent of her. I'm kind of addicted.

"Well, it always takes longer because Cesare's stories are so riveting." The two of them are practically friends now. "He wasn't working tonight, so I'm here faster."

"Thank God. I'm starving. Get changed quickly."

She takes off her boots, her eyes lingering on me. "You'd like me to crawl to you, wouldn't you?" She throws my comment back at me with a delicious darkness in her voice, and my cock welcomes the innuendo.

I seize her lips again. "We're going to be late."

"Massi will keep our table, or find us a new one." She drags her nails down my back, her breath melting me into this change of plans. Almost.

"Go get ready, Chils," I growl, and she laughs and saunters to the bedroom.

Ten minutes later, the shower stops running. I check my watch. Another ten minutes pass and she doesn't come out, nor do I hear sounds coming from the bedroom.

I march in there, determined to drag her out even half-dressed. The woman really can't—

I stop in the doorway, and all thoughts come to a screeching halt, my blood rushing south. Chils stands by the wall of windows, her back to me. She is wearing some sort of red and black, lace and silk lingerie and shiny red heels. Nothing else.

In the dim lights of the room and lit up by the city below, I admire her silhouette. The perfectly shaped skull, the long neck, her slender shoulders, slim waist, and that beautiful curvy ass. In the stilettos, her legs seem longer.

She is a vision as she slowly turns around. My cock strains against my zipper. I'm ready to pounce, and at the same time mesmerized by the sensual picture in front of me.

"That crawling comment got me sidetracked." She sounds innocent, almost apologetic, knowing very well such a subdued demeanor would awaken the beast in me.

I loosen my tie and yank it off. "Maybe I need to punish you." Her eyes flicker with excitement, but she looks down quickly to hide it. "Don't move," I growl.

I take my time unbuttoning my shirt, sliding it off my shoulders, while drinking in the beauty of my woman. I shed my pants and boxers next, my erection jutting out, almost painful.

Chils watches me. The only movement is her heaving chest.

"On your knees," I order, and she drops. "Good girl. Now you can crawl to me."

She licks her lips and swallows. I have to fist my

cock, to ease the strain. Chils lowers her palms, touching the carpet with grace and delicacy.

When she moves, I almost stumble against the wall behind me. The swaying of her hips reverberates every fiber in my body, shaking me to the core. How did I get this lucky?

She reaches my feet and pushes up. Kneeling in front of me, she eyes my cock first and then she looks up, as if asking for permission. But I have other plans for her.

"Raise your arms above your head."

A flash of defiance flares through her eyes, and I swear a blush covers her face. It's the sexiest sight on Earth.

She lifts her arms up, and I use my tie to bind her wrists together. She is frowning at me now, a war behind her eyes.

I pull her up to standing roughly and she gasps, still holding her arms up, unsure. I cup her between the legs and I chuckle, feeling her juices in my palm even through the soft layer of her underwear. "Ready for me as always."

I rip off her panties, shredding it to pieces, and Chils whimpers. I grab her ass, probably bruising her, but I can't wait a moment longer.

This woman is everything. My partner at work.

My girlfriend. My soulmate—one that discovered I had a soul left in me. My lover.

I hoist her up and pin her against the wall. She wraps her legs around my waist and loops her tied hands around my neck. I enter her smoothly and then we both still, staring at each other for a moment, relishing the connection.

My knees buckle under the spell of the feel of her around me. I lean into the wall with both hands, pressing her tighter between me and the cold surface, just to make sure we don't collapse.

The sheer influx of feelings floors me. I almost have to look away from those scorching, beautiful eyes that are staring at me with breathtaking, gut-wrenching intimacy.

And then she delivers the last blow that turns this game into a frantic chase for release.

"I love you, Dominic."

Gio

A few months earlier at the gala

I hate these events. I have nothing against supporting a good cause. But why people need to small talk, eat a five-course meal and dance to donate money is beyond me. I'm happy to write a check from the comfort of my office.

Gina's voice drills into my brain, yapping about something inconsequential. I pull my phone out of my pocket. It's my go-to avoidance mechanism, but it doesn't always work with my family.

They expect human interactions from me—annoying, and so unnecessary. Whoever invented small talk was deranged. It's a waste of time.

"...Mila saved the day." Gina takes a sip of water.

The name pulls me back into the conversation, and I meet my sister-in-law's eyes, frowning.

"London's event planner canceled at the last minute and Mila took on the job." Gina interprets my frown as the need for more information.

I don't care about Mila Ward. The woman hates me. Who knows why? The few times I've seen her at my brother's restaurant, she glared at me and treated me like I vomited all over her clothes.

Not that I care.

Well.

Okay.

I cared for a brief moment. She grabbed my attention the first time I laid eyes on her. In the middle of a major crisis at Casa Cassi, she held her head high and commanded the situation with a calm professionalism.

Cool, collected, beautiful. Full of grace. I don't

remember the last time watching a person riveted me, but she held my attention without even knowing it.

A queen.

From afar.

My fascination died when I heard her giggling and blabbering. Jesus.

"Excuse me." I nod to Gina and amble away to check the markets.

Boring my eyes into the screen, I hope no one will approach me with another attempt at talk. My eyes scroll through the blinking numbers, but my attention drifts away. I look up, and my eyes land on her.

Mila Ward—all the magnetic sunshine of her—stands across the room. As soon as my gaze finds her, she looks in my direction and her eyes widen for a split second.

Unlike most of the women here, she's not made-up and dolled-up with tons of products holding her together.

Her blue eyes pull me as if she's the only woman in the room. I lick my lips, suddenly regretting I have a phone and not a drink in my hand. I ignore—and fail—the weird feeling in my stomach. London must have sourced bad catering.

I swallow, and in the rhythm of the music

humming in the background, I lose my usual restraint and let my eyes travel down Mila's curves.

Jesus. What is she wearing? That dress is practically pushing most of her out on display. I ball my fists, and my stomach rolls in disgust. That outfit has its purpose, and my bet is on a husband-hunting mission.

Unfortunately, I've met my share of gold-diggers in my life, and the way she looks right now confirms her intentions tonight.

Why do I care? Or feel irritated by that? Mildly irritated.

Someone approaches me and I look away. Several of the longest minutes of my life later, when my ears are practically begging for silence, I make my way to the bar. This whole socializing gig requires liquid rein-forcement.

To my dismay, aside from looking for a drink, I also scan the room to check on the event planner.

I spot her stumbling toward the exit. Fuck. Is she drunk? I doubt she would jeopardize her work that way. She leans her arm against the door frame and lowers her head, before she pushes the door open and slips out.

Before I evaluate my actions, my legs move to follow her.

Oh, oh, the chemistry between Mila and Gio. While you're waiting for their story, Reckless Deal, enjoy Violet (she interrupted London and Dom's intimate moment after the disastrous theatre performance) and Art (whose dominant presence didn't escape Dom) in Chosen By the Billionaire.

In this enemies to lovers romance, the socially awkward hacker brings trouble to Vi's steps, but their love story is **"an excellent read from beginning to the end"**, according to a reader's review.

London and Dominic go on a wild adventure together and Dom surprises her with two proposals (none of them what you may expect). Read all about it in the bonus scene here: www.maxinehenri.com/dare or scan:

Also by Maxine Henri

Untamed Billionaires Series

Tempted by the Billionaire (A Fake Relationship Romance)

Chosen by The Billionaire (An Enemies to Lovers Romance)

Chased by the Billionaire (An Age gap/Innocent Heroine Romance)

Stolen by the Billionaire (A Forbidden Love Romance)

Reckless Billionaires Series

Reckless Fate (A Second Chance Billionaire Romance)

Reckless Desire (A Single Dad Billionaire Romance)

Reckless Dare (A Fake Relationship Romance)

Reckless Deal (A Grumpy/Sunshine Bosshole Billionaire Romance)

If you loved this book, please spread the word and leave a review here. One sentence is enough to help other readers and make me very happy.

Acknowledgments

After Reckless Desire came out, so many reviews mentioned they couldn't wait for London's story that I froze. I mean, I was thrilled that people were excited about my next book, but the pressure was real.

At one point I sent a frantic message to my editor that I'm worried London in her own book is not living up to the hype she stirred in Sydney's book.

You know what the amazing editor Jess wrote back? "LOL. She is cool in her own book too!"

I hope you agree with her, dear reader. But guessing by the fact you're reading this, you got far enough to find Lo and Dom cool.

And while I can't wait for you to read about the rest of this large, complicated family (Gio is next), I'm also sad London's story is finished. Dealing with a sensitive subject of death isn't easy in the genre like romance. While I write angsty books, I want to bring joy and hope to you. Hopefully, I tackled the heavy subject with the dignity I aimed for.

This book brought me so much joy while writing it

and there are people who I need to thank for joining me on my writing journey.

Here they are in no particular order:

- The already mentioned fabulous editor Jess
- Dan who finds mistakes where there are none anymore
- My author gals who kick me when I need it and inspire me daily (Kat Bammer, Mila Kane, Sienna Judd, D.E. Haggerty, Gabrielle Sands)
- Many amazing indie bestselling authors who share their knowledge generously (TL Swan, Craig Martelle, Melanie Harlow, Zoe York, Mark Dawson, Skye Warren, Nick Erik, to name a few)
- Martin, Max and Henry, thank you for eating pizza and waiting patiently until I emerge from my writing cave

But the most honorable mention goes to you, darling reader. It's you who inspires me to write. It's you I think of when I want to give up. It's you who makes this passion of mine the best gig in the world. Thank you!

About the Author

Maxine Henri is a contemporary romance author who infuses her stories with steamy passion and complex characters. When she's not crafting stories that will have you swooning, she can usually be found sipping on a cup of black tea while reading a good book. Or traveling to new destinations.

Maxine believes that stories matter. They facilitate emotional journeys, inspire and entertain. And when it comes to books and fiction, stories are a great escape and probably the most beneficial addiction on this planet.

Her billionaire romances are the perfect escape, offering a taste of luxury and adventure. Maxine introduces heroes who may have a dark past, but are always balanced by a lighter side. And her leading ladies? They're strong, independent women who may be a little broken, but always find their way in life.

You can connect with her on any of these platforms: